DAYZEE DAZZLE

AND THE

ON-SET ONSLAUGHT

Other Books by Edward Allen Karr

SERIES: Thrills N Kills in the Hills
(Racy, Comical Horror in Beverly Hills)
Dayzee Dazzle and the Kildare Killers – Book One
Dayzee Dazzle and her Manic Mansion – Book Two
Dayzee Dazzle and the Cadaver Collectors – Book Four
*　*　*　*　*

SERIES: Socrates Lewis Stories
(Psychological/Religious Fiction)
Crosswinds – Book One
Crossovers – Book Two
*　*　*　*　*

SERIES: Fringes Of Infinity
(Contemporary Fantasy Fiction)
Lin Finity and her Mayhem Rising – Book One
Lin Finity in Holding On – A Novella
Lin Finity and the Words Unspoken – Book Two
Lin Finity and the Islands of Time – Book Three
Lin Finity and the Flights to Forever – Book Four
Tayo Tersoo and the Hunter of Souls – Book Five
*　*　*　*　*

SERIES: A World So Close
(Middle-grade Fantasy Adventure & Coming of Age)
Jayden Blue and the Gift to Imagine – A Prequel
Jayden Blue and the Sword in his Shadow – Book One
Jayden Blue and the Call of the Wings – Book Two
Jayden Blue and the Lair of the Iron Lions – Book Three
Jayden Blue and the Journey to Val ka'Yoom – Book Four
Jayden Blue and the Forest of Night Fallen – Book Five
Jayden Blue and the Wait of the Sun – Book Six

*　*　*　*　*

DAYZEE DAZZLE
AND THE
ON-SET ONSLAUGHT

Thrills N Kills in the Hills
Book Three

Edward Allen Karr

Lakeside Letters, LLC
30628 Detroit Road, #247
Westlake, OH 44145

Dayzee Dazzle and the On-Set Onslaught
Thrills N Kills in the Hills Book Three

First Edition, 2022
www.LakesideLetters.com

Cover design by JD Smith Design

ISBN-13: 978-1-950886-26-5

"Alright, well, there's a bunch of them. We've dealt with dead guys before. Bruno, can you . . . I don't know . . . clean up the mess, somehow?"

"Sure, Dayzee. But that isn't all. I think the last driver to come in left the gate open, and—"

"Wasn't the dead cowboy in charge of the gates?" said Dayzee. "Damn, you just can't get reliable dead Colombian cowboy help these days."

"Oh, Dayzee, he was blind, too, remember?" said Marilyn.

"Hard to see without a head," Sophia said with a smirk.

"Really, he lost his head too?"

From Chapter 14 – Also without a Head

Table of Contents

Chapter 1 – Here We Go Again

"Oh my, this can't be what humans mean by getting some tail!" Dayzee said as she stared at the ceiling of their favorite hangout, the Prism, with a big grin.

She looked down only long enough to find her cocktail, then she gazed back up at the ceiling with a deep sigh. On the barstool to her left sat Sophia, and two seats to her right sat Marilyn. Behind the bar, Kenzie and Mack stared at the display while ignoring every other patron, all of whom were oblivious to the spectacle.

Just to Dayzee's right sat the current anatomical arrangement of their one-time protector, Bruno, a man who only recently had his full height restored. But his human form had vanished as the Guild's experimentation on him had launched him into a surprise transformation. His long, thick, purple snake body coiled around his barstool, while his head, complete with a lit cigarette and a ball cap, gyrated and bounced in time with the jukebox's beat.

"I'm next," said Sophia, Marilyn's twin sister and one half of the Kildare Killers.

"Oh no, Sissy," said Marilyn. "You've already had so much fun with Kenzie when Kenzie was still Kenzie and not Kozy. I want to go next."

"I'd argue with you, but I like when you say funny things like that."

"There you two go again," said Kenzie. "Someone called Kozy?"

"It's a joke," Dayzee said in barely above a whisper. "There's no one called Kozy."

"Not right now anyway," Sophia said with a smirk.

Only the rattling of Bruno's tail competed with the low classic rock. His amorous tail could have been louder if he hadn't slithered it up and around Dayzee's leg, between her thighs, and lodged it somewhere under her skirt that gave her a non-stop grin.

"I think I've seen enough," said Kenzie. "I mean, that whole scene in your attic, Dayzee, was insane. And now, this?"

She finished putting fresh drinks in front of all of them, and Sophia said, "Hey, you have to admit, it's kind of exciting, right?"

"Yeah, no doubt. Freaky, though."

"What about you, Mack?" said Marilyn. "You don't mind serving beer to a snake, do you?"

"Nah. I'm starting to get what Dayzee always says about how anything can happen in Beverly Hills."

"West Hollywood," Bruno said while his tongue flicked in and out.

"You just never quit, do you?" Dayzee said between rapid breaths.

Bruno grinned at her, turned to Mack, and said, "Barkeep, you know I can't pick up that bottle. Give a snake a break, alright?"

"Sure, why the hell not?"

Mack held the bottle up, Bruno tipped his head back but not enough to lose his cap, and Mack poured while Bruno mostly hissed and gargled it around before it bubbled its way into him somewhere.

Kenzie and Mack both left to carry on their bar duties, and Dayzee said, "I do believe I could do this for—"

"Ugh," said Bruno as he snapped his snake head to each side several times, flinging his cigarette onto the floor and his cap onto the bar.

"Oh, that's terrible timing," said Dayzee. "I'm really going to miss that tail of his."

Bruno started stretching his head toward the ceiling and snapping it back down, bunching up his shiny purple snake skin like a spring.

"What's next for Bruno?" said Marilyn. "Nobody knows!"

With his head almost touching the lights and beer signs above them, Bruno began belching, and most of the beer he'd swilled gurgled up and out and spilled all over the floor.

"Sheesh," Sophia said with another smirk before snapping her fingers for another round.

Seconds later, a naked, human-looking Bruno lay twisted around the base of his barstool, smiling and shaking his head.

"Oh, I still need a minute to cool down from that," said Dayzee. "Bruno, I'm putting in a request for the next time you change: be a snake. An even bigger snake. With a faster rattle."

"I never got my turn," said Marilyn. "I'm even more itchy now."

"You're always itchy, Sis," said her sister. "I promise you: we'll both get what we need real soon."

Dayzee looked down and said, "Well, big guy, you should at least get dressed."

"Oh, right, Dayzee. I just need a minute too. Somehow, that felt as good to me as it did to you."

"Still, get some clothes on. Probably nobody cares—people get naked in here all the time—but nobody wants that bare ass on a barstool."

A minute later, they all had fresh drinks, including a fully dressed Bruno, who wore jeans, black boots, a black t-shirt, and a ball cap that said "Surprise Surprise" on the front.

"Sophia!" said a loud voice from near the entrance.

All four turned to look, and Sophia said, "Oh, it's that wannabe producer guy that stopped us on the sidewalk the other day. Remember him, Sis?"

"I sure do, Sissy. I think he's stalking you."

"Or maybe you? I mean, who wouldn't stalk you? I do all the time."

He closed the distance and stood between Sophia and Dayzee. He wore a thin black jacket and a bright blue shirt, and his smile showed rows of perfect, gleaming teeth.

"I remember you," said Sophia. "Did our agent ever get in touch?"

"No, she sure as hell didn't. Some nerve, if you ask me. Fine. She's out of the deal. Just sign this NDA, and I'll give you the script, and you and your gorgeous sister—"

"Her name's Marilyn," Sophia said with a glance toward her sister. "Not 'that' Marilyn. Just way better."

"She sure is. Just sign, and we can get going on this. I just know you'll love it. Here's a pen, scribble your names here where—"

"Hey, hold up," said Dayzee. "What kind of pathetic joke are you? We're stars. You don't just push papers at us and—"

"You're just jealous because you don't have our offer yet. Soon, though. For now, stay out of the way, Dayzee Dazzle."

Bruno stood, his head practically scraping the rafters lost in shadows, and looked down on the man.

"Well, who the hell are you?" said the producer. "Hey, if we ever cast for Frankenstein, you'll be at the top of the list."

Bruno looked at Dayzee and said, "Is that funny? I didn't get the Earth Humor and Witticisms download."

"I did, and trust me, it's not funny," said Sophia. "He's just a jerk."

"Sissy is right," said Marilyn. "Bruno, you're still our protector, right?"

"Oh, yes, Miss Marilyn. I sure am."

"How about getting busy with some protecting, then?" said Sophia.

"Right away, Lady Sophia."

"What are you all talking about? Stop playing games and—"

Bruno reached a massive hand around the man's throat, rendering him silent. With his other hand, he pinched the jacket between his shoulders and lifted him up. His shiny loafers dangled and kicked, and he waved around papers in one hand and a pen in the other.

"Bravo, Bruno!" Marilyn said as she snatched the script from him.

"Time to take out the trash," said Dayzee.

"His voice sure got annoying fast," said Sophia.

"Be right back, ladies."

Bruno toted the quieted man to the back door. The jukebox continued to play, and not a single Prism patron paid any attention.

*   *   *

"I kind of like having him around," Dayzee said before finishing her drink.

"Even when he was only this high," said Sophia, holding her hand at the stool's level. "What a perfect pool boy that was. Just the right size."

"Can he still breathe underwater?" said Marilyn. "If so, we can get naked again, put him in the pool, get him busy, and tell him not to come back up until—"

"Dayzee?" Bruno said while leaning into the bar through the doorway to the Prism's backyard.

"Problem taken care of?"

"Oh, um, yeah . . . you could say that."

"Something's wrong," Marilyn said with a gentle shake of her head. "I know that look."

"Just spill it," said Sophia. "What happened? He ran home crying?"

"Uh . . . no, he won't be crying. I, uh, I couldn't help it. I turned back into that snake. Only for a second or two, but—"

"Oh, don't tell me you used that amazing tail on him. Actually, that would be quite a sight. Maybe we could get Jiff out here with his camera, and you could—"

"No, Dayzee. Nothing like that. I, um . . . I mean, the snake, um, he—"

"Just say it," said Sophia. "Your beer's getting warm."

"Alright. Here it is: I . . . I mean, the snake . . . well, he bit the guy's head clean off."

Dayzee stared at him, but the twins leaned forward to look at each other, Sophia grinning and shaking her head and Marilyn giggling with a hand trying to hide it.

"You what?"

"I'm sorry, Dayzee. Blame it on the sorsciencery?"

Marilyn said to her sister, "Oh my God, Sissy, another headless body. Here we go again!"

Sophia said, "We just can't get away from them, Sis."

"Bruno," said Dayzee, "you—I mean, the snake you—ate that guy's head?"

Bruno shook his head and chuckled.

"No, Sweetie, I—"

"It's Dayzee."

"Right. Dayzee. No, Dayzee, I spit it out. Even as a snake, I wasn't about to eat that thing. Who knows where's it's been?"

Marilyn giggled more and said, "I have a few guesses."

Sophia smirked and downed her drink.

"Where is he now? What did you do with him?"

"His body or his head?" said Bruno.

"Both," she said with a grin. "They still kind of go together, don't they?"

"Oh, he's just sitting at the picnic table back there."

"And his head?"

"It's sitting there too."

"Well, we can't just leave them there. Can you at least grab the body to take with us?"

"Sure," said Bruno, "but what about the head?"

"Leave it. Halloween decoration," said Sophia.

"Uh-oh," said Marilyn. "He's going to be looking for head, just like all the rest."

"No, Mare," said Dayzee. "There's no assassin from the Guild bringing him back to life. He's just dead. End of story. Lights out."

"Um . . ."

"What now, Bruno?"

"Dayzee, I'm not completely sure about that. I'm full of that sorcery junk, remember? When I bit him, maybe some of that, that stuff, maybe it got—"

"Oh, fine," said Dayzee. "We're used to headless guys walking around. Why don't you grab him and his head, and we'll take them—"

"She said 'them!'" said Marilyn. "Is it one guy or two?"

Sophia chuckled and said, "Approximately one, Sis."

"For now, let's just say that there are two, Mare, and we'll take *them* with us. God, only in Beverly Hills."

"Dayzee, we're actually in West Holly—"

"Just grab the body parts, Bruno!"

Chapter 2 – Telepathic Pheromones

The Prism's heavy wooden door shook from a loud thump near the top, and the ice in Dayzee's cocktail rattled and sloshed around. Another thump, closer to the level of the sidewalk outside, pried her steel blue eyes open even wider, and she looked to one side at Marilyn, then to the other side at Sophia, then up at Bruno, looking down at her, a headless body draped over one shoulder and a severed head in his hand.

"Dayzee," said Marilyn, "whoever's out there probably just wants a drink. Why don't we just go?"

"Sis is right," said Sophia. "Just open the door, and we can—"

"No, girls. Wait. Listen a second. That's not somebody knocking."

She shook her head slowly as she glanced toward the bar and saw that Mack and Kenzie were busy with bar patrons and not paying any attention to them. A look around showed that no one else cared either.

Another heavy thump, closer to her behind, which was wrapped in a tight skirt that she was pressing back against the door, prompted her to chuckle once and finish her drink.

"Alright, listen, girls. And Bruno. Remember everything we've been through? Do you really think there's just some normal people out there that are—"

"Who said 'normal?'" Sophia said with a grin. "Remember where we are?"

"Oh, Sissy makes a good point. It might be another headless guy, not a normal guy, although both are probably looking for the same thing."

"And it isn't a drink," said Sophia, and she and Marilyn clinked their glasses with big grins.

"You know," said Dayzee, "maybe it's that sniper that's been taking shots at me?"

Sophia shook her head and said, "Hey, maybe it's a headless sniper. That has to happen eventually."

"How would he aim, Sissy?"

"Girls. Well, if it is just another headless guy, sniper or not, we should still—"

"Wait," said Bruno. "I didn't tell you everything. I think I know what's out there."

Sounds like three more puffy boxing gloves pounding on the door followed, and Dayzee fumbled without looking, trying to find a way to bolt the door.

"Just wonderful, Bruno. What didn't you tell us?"

"Those are birds. I'm sure of it. Big ones too. They're trying to—"

"Kill us, I know," said Dayzee, and she looked to the bar for a refill. "Another assassin must have been sent after us, and it took control of birds this time, and like an old Earth horror movie, they're going to—"

"No. Not even close. Those are all girl birds. They can sense what I'm about to transform into, and they all want a piece of me. Really, I'm starting to want a piece of each of them too. I wonder just how many birds I can—"

"Wait a minute," said Marilyn. "How do you know those are birds? And why would they want anything to do with you?"

"Ditto that," said Sophia. "You just changed back from being a giant purple snake. No sane lady bird would ever—"

"That's what I need to explain. When the Guild injected all that sorcery garbage into me, I turned into some kind of wolf or something. After that, I—"

"We remember," said Dayzee. "You killed everyone, then you turned into a bunny, right?"

"Yeah, but here's the thing: when I opened the door to get out of the lab, after I'd ripped them all apart, guess what was waiting for me?"

"Aw," said Marilyn, "a bunch of sweet little girl bunnies?"

"Not exactly, Miss Marilyn—horny little girl bunnies. A whole flock of them."

"But you didn't have time for them, did you?" said Dayzee. "You wanted to get through the portal back to us, so you—"

"Oh no, Dayzee. I found time. Whew, that was something. Talk about getting some tail. Cute, fluffy tail too. My, oh my. Now, Easter on this planet will always—"

"Oh, I get it," said Sophia. "You can tell you're about to turn into some kind of bird. Is that it?"

"Yes, Lady Sophia. You nailed it."

"And when you're a bird, you're going to nail all of them?" Dayzee said and hooked her thumb toward the door.

Ten more heavy thumps shook the door, and Bruno said, "Well, not those—they're killing themselves to get at me. There will be more, though. Count on it."

Kenzie came over with fresh drinks for all of them.

"I thought you were all leaving."

She looked at what Bruno was carrying, frowned, and forced a smile for Dayzee and the twins.

"We were, Kenzie," said Dayzee, "until the scary movie started out there."

"In here too," Sophia said with a laugh, pointing at the head, which only looked back at her quietly.

"No, it isn't like that," said Bruno. "They'll ignore the rest of you. Me too until I change. I just don't know when that'll be."

"Alright, then," said Dayzee, and she tipped her drink all the way back and finished it. So did the twins. Kenzie handed Bruno his beer, and he swilled it all down.

"Wonderful," said Dayzee. "Just another day in Beverly Hills."

"West Hollywood," Bruno said with a grin.

"Whatever. We're on Sunset—that's all that matters."

"You're coming with us, aren't you?" Sophia said while smiling at Kenzie.

"Ooh, I knew it, Sissy."

"Stop, Sis. I'm just asking."

"Yeah, I'd love to get back to Dayzee's mansion. Do we still have that limo?"

"Nope. They towed it," said Dayzee.

"I'll find us something," said Kenzie. "Wait inside until—"

Seven more thumps rattled the door and got Dayzee's eyes to bug out again.

"—until I yell for you all to come outside."

"You're a car thief?"

"No, Marilyn, I'm an actress, remember?"

Dayzee glanced at Marilyn, who shrugged and shook her head. A look at Sophia showed that she was grinning and nodding.

"Well, what the hell. Alright, Kenzie, set us up. Hey, I haven't heard any birds beating on the door for a while. You alright, Bruno?"

"I don't feel like I'll be a bird anymore. The sorcery's taking a break, I think. I just feel like Bruno now."

"How do the birds know anyway?" said Sophia.

"It's like pheromones probably. Maybe telepathic pheromones?"

"Makes as much sense as anything else. I say we get going, Dayzee."

"Okay, Fia. I'm opening the door. Kenzie, make a run for it."

"In heels that high?" Marilyn said with a giggle.

"I'd like to see that," said her sister.

"I bet you would, Sissy. Me too!"

*　*　*

"A hearse? Kenzie, what the hell are you—"

"Relax, Dayzee. It was the closest thing I could find that could carry us all back to your mansion."

They'd all stepped over and around the small pile of woodpeckers, owls, and doves lying around dead and dying near the door.

"I also got the Indigenous Life Forms download," said Bruno, "and that,"—he pointed to a bird at the top of the heap—"is a sapsucker."

"That's funny, Sissy," said Marilyn. "I've known more than a few saps."

"Oh, I could really put together some jokes on that," said her sister with a grin. "Remind me later."

Dayzee brushed back her thick, wild blond hair and crossed her arms. She stood on the clean concrete sidewalk in front of the Prism Bar and Grill in West Hollywood, her glossy black high-heeled boots reflecting the Southern California sunshine. She showed off her film star figure in black fishnet stockings, a short black skirt, and a mostly unbuttoned white blouse.

"A hearse sounds about right to me," said Sophia. "Sis and I are the Kildare Killers, after all. Something that's made to haul dead bodies makes perfect sense."

She flicked back her silky, long black hair and popped another button of her tight red blouse before adding, "And you just know there are going to be more dead bodies." She stood grinning in her short black skirt and pointy black heels.

"Sissy's right about that. Hey, we already have one too!" said Marilyn, Sophia's twin sister, as she tried to pull down her very short white dress. Her stunning, wavy blond hair cascaded down over her shoulders, and her blue eyes shined as she studied their new ride with her high white heels bright against the concrete.

"Remember all those guys walking around, looking for head, Dayzee?"

"Yeah, Mare, of course, I remember. You miss them?"

"I know I do," said Sophia. "I'm kind of glad we have at least this one."

"Why, Fia?"

"I admire the honesty of it. For one thing, a guy without *that* head can't try to convince us he just wants to be friends. It's obvious what he's looking for. He can't even hide it."

"No, he sure can't," said Marilyn. "Even though he's only thinking with the other one, he's still—"

"Mare, we don't have time to analyze all the dead guys we've known. We need to—"

"Just how many has it been?"

"I lost count, Fia. Anyway, we need to get back to my house. Remember Cliff? The reality show he insists on starting today?"

"Oh, of course, I remember," said Marilyn. "Sissy told him we'd slither right over there. That's funny because Bruno had just turned into—"

"A purple snake," said Bruno. "Yeah, and Dayzee, you liked me being a snake."

"Oh yeah, a rattlesnake too," said Dayzee. "Oh my, the things you did with that tail of yours."

The Guild had injected into him sorciencery mixtures, an uncontrollable and unpredictable blend of science and sorcery, before he'd escaped through the portal to Earth. No one knew how long he'd continue to morph into random life forms, some real and maybe some only imaginary. He'd reclaimed his ball cap that said "Surprise Surprise" across the front, and a fresh cigarette dangled from his mouth.

"You liked that tail of mine, huh?"

"Oh my God, Bruno, it was like—"

"I never did get my turn," Marilyn said with a big pout. "I'm getting so itchy I can't even stand it."

"Sis isn't the only one," said Sophia. "You know what I need? I need another fountain of youth. The first chance I get, I'm going to—"

"Girls, just stop. It's too soon for another fountain—you'll both be way out of control if you do that. We need to focus. Kenzie," she said and turned to grin at the Prism's barmaid, whose long brown hair fell softly over her shoulders, drawing attention to her tight t-shirt, which stretched over her breasts and fell short of her even tighter jeans, leaving a strip of smooth skin to be viewed, "you really shouldn't have stolen that—"

"Oh, Dayzee, I didn't steal anything. I'm not a thief. I'm really just an actress. Well, a barmaid sometimes too."

Sophia looked away and grinned, Marilyn looked down and sighed, and Dayzee nodded and smiled.

"Yes, of course, you are. Everyone is. Well, not the guys, maybe. Sometimes, I suppose, depending on the storyline, but we don't have time for that now. What do you mean, you didn't steal it?"

"Listen, we have our own driver. The hearse dude!"

"What the hell is a hearse dude, and why would he want to drive us around? What's in it for him?"

"Have you seen my sister?" Sophia said with a grin.

"That goes doubly for my Sissy," said Marilyn. "Oh, and you, too, Dayzee. That earthman will be doing more than just driving us around."

"Girls, shouldn't you wait until you can check him out before making all those plans?"

"I don't even care right now," said Marilyn. "I'm about to strut back into the Prism—"

"No one struts like my Sis."

"—and drag that cutie Mack down behind the bar. Or maybe on the pool table!"

"You call that itchy?" said Sophia. "I'm ready to test out Bruno right here on the sidewalk."

"In broad daylight?" said Marilyn. "What will people think?"

Dayzee shook her head and grinned at Sophia.

"Such a sweet kid. She still doesn't get it."

She turned to Marilyn and said, "Mare, it's Beverly Hills, remember? People are too caught up in their own lives to care about anything else. Now, let's get a peek at our new driver before we head for home."

Kenzie turned around, waved her hand in circles above her head, and whistled so loudly that Dayzee and the twins covered their ears.

"My God," said Dayzee. "Where did you learn that?"

"Oh, I grew up on a ranch in Wyoming. We did that all day long."

"Sounds fun," said Sophia. "You do look damn cute doing that, though."

"I agree, Sissy," said Marilyn.

"But, Kenzie," said Dayzee, "that's how you call him?"

"With him? Sure. He came all the way from Colombia to be a cowboy."

"Well, what the heck is he doing in the Hills?"

"Driving us around in a hearse," Kenzie said with a grin.

"Oh. Sure. Of course."

The driver's door opened, and a man with nearly black skin, wearing baggy black jeans and a white tank top, stepped out. His lean, pumped-up muscles carried a sheen from the growing heat, and he wore a wide-brimmed white western hat and mirrored sunglasses. He slammed the door, stood at attention, and grinned, showing a single twinkling diamond in one of his front teeth.

"Ladies, meet The Kid."

"Oh, I think I will," Sophia said while scanning him up and down.

"Me too, Sissy. I'm ready for a rodeo."

"Is he our driver or what?" said Kenzie.

"That's his uniform?" said Dayzee.

"Eh—maybe *he* stole the hearse," said Kenzie. "Yeah, that might be it."

Dayzee grabbed a hand of each of the twins flanking her and said, "Girls, we sure are in for some bizarre thrills this time . . ."

Chapter 3 – Look at that Hat

With The Kid behind the wheel and Dayzee up front with him, the twins had Kenzie squeezed between them in the backseat, and Bruno had laid himself down in back after saying, "Hey, there's a dead human in this long box back here."

"Does he still have his head?" Marilyn said with a giggle.

"Sadly, yes," Bruno said with a grin. "Would you like me to remove it, Miss Marilyn?"

"You'd do that for me? How sweet."

"That sure sounds fun," said Dayzee, "but we already have a headless guy on the other side of that box. You two cozy back there, Bruno?"

"Well, I don't know about cozy. We'll make it to your mansion, though. How about if I toss him and his head in the box, and we can—"

"He said, 'him and his head,'" said Marilyn. "That's just silly."

"Sure, why not?" said Dayzee. "Let's hope that neither one of them will be walking around looking for anything. Maybe the one that the snake Bruno bit but not the other one. We're done with that assassin, remember?"

"I'm starting to kind of miss all that," said Sophia. "I hope our new headless guy starts walking."

"Or dancing," said Marilyn.

"Sis, none of them were ever—"

"Alright, girls."

"We can't be sure about there being no more assassins either, Dayzee," said Bruno. "I have no idea what might have tagged along with me before they destroyed the portal back inside the Prism by that big statue guy."

"Seriously?" said Kenzie. "You'd all want another assassin so you could go through that attic scene again?"

"What attic scene?" said Bruno. "Yeah, you should all do it again . . . for me. I want to see it. Whatever it was."

"That's kind of funny, Bruno," said Marilyn. "I'm in. How about you, Sissy?"

"Sure . . . maybe. It sure scared your photographer friend away," said Sophia. "Jiff was his name, right?"

"Oh, he's not running scared," said Dayzee. "With any luck, he's out buying a new camera. I still can't believe how that sniper shot his camera to pieces, and that guy—"

"She said 'guy' again!" said Marilyn. "It was just a closet door!"

"That's funny, Sis. It sure did grow something like a horny guy would, didn't he?"

"Sissy, you called him 'he!'"

"I did, didn't I? Anyway, Kenzie, about The Kid—he doesn't say much," said Sophia. "Is he shy or something?"

"I don't know," said Kenzie, "but I get the impression he's self-conscious about his English not being so good."

"Well, that's not a big deal," said Dayzee, "because we—"

"Oh, and I think he's mostly blind too."

A long moment of silence captured the idling hearse. Bruno lifted his head up and stared, and Dayzee turned around to look at Kenzie.

"And he's our driver?"

Kenzie shrugged and said, "Well, let's hope for the best."

Sophia gave Kenzie's thigh a squeeze and said, "I always do. This is just perfect. He's our guy."

Dayzee twisted farther around to see Marilyn, and she shrugged and said, "He is pretty hot, Dayzee. And the Flats is right around the corner, easy for even a blind driver to find."

Dayzee looked past the twins and Kenzie in the backseat toward Bruno, and he said, "I might be too tall to drive this thing anyway."

Dayzee sighed and said, "Fine. Home, James."

"The Kid," said The Kid, in a slow, deep voice that poured like spicy molasses.

"Not you too. Alright, whatever. I bet you're not going to last long anyway. Not with those Killers in the backseat. Home, The Kid."

"That sounds silly too," said Marilyn.

"Kid. Just Kid," he said with a sparkling grin.

"Nope, I'm staying silly. Home, The Kid."

"Hey, just for fun, let's ride east on Sunset first, and if The Kid can put on this thing's flashing lights, maybe we can get a line of cars to follow us."

"Why would we do that, Fia?" said Dayzee.

"Why not? It's the Hills, right?"

"You're making a lot of sense."

"I like the idea," said Marilyn. "They won't be dead guys driving, though."

"Not right away," said Sophia. "You know that we seem to attract a lot of dead guys, though."

"Girls, you create them. Then, you burn them down to nothing. You're the Kildare Killers."

"Well," said Marilyn, "we just can't help ourselves."

"The Kid," said Dayzee, "show us what you got. We want a screaming U-turn, spinning tires taking us east, then another careless U-turn to bring us back home. Think you can handle that?"

"Si."

Marilyn giggled and whispered to Kenzie, "Uh-uh, he really can't."

"He's still a good driver," said Kenzie. "I mean, look at that hat."

"What does that have to do with anything?" said Dayzee.

"I have no idea," said Kenzie. "I'm pretty sure I lost most of my mind up in your attic when . . . well, whatever that was."

Sophia gave her thigh another squeeze and said, "That's alright. You're still hot. That's mostly what matters."

"Now that we have all that sorted out," said Dayzee, "drive, The Kid."

The Kid turned the wheel to the left, never looked with his nearly-useless eyes, floored the gas, and screeched the hearse around to face east. With the engine redlining, the tires spun, and they all rocketed a mile down the road before he whipped the car around and put it in park.

"I lost my cap out the back window," said Bruno. "Hell of a ride, though."

"Why does that window even open?" said Sophia. "So the dead human can change his mind and climb out?"

"That's funny, Sissy. Yes, but only if he still has a head."

"Well, one of them back there still does."

"We'll pick your hat up on the way back," said Dayzee. "You know what to do, The Kid," said Dayzee.

"Si. Light. I like lite beer too."

"Um, how about just the hearse lights for now," Dayzee said before she turned to smile at the twins and Kenzie. "If you survive long enough, I'll set you up at the house. So glad you know the important words."

The Kid flipped a switch near the visor, and the car's flashing beacon came to life.

Marilyn turned and pointed through the rear window and said, "We caught one already. This is easy."

Sophia and Kenzie both turned, paused to share a smile before looking out the back, and Sophia said, "And another one. How many do we want?"

"Oh, I don't know," said Dayzee. "I don't even know why we're doing this."

"Isn't it some kind of law around here that everyone needs to do crazy stuff?" said Sophia.

"Seems like it," Bruno said from the back.

"Two is good enough to start the parade," said Sophia. "Let's go slow and see how many more we can drag with us."

"Better yet," said Marilyn, "let's go fast and see if they can keep up."

"Oh, great idea, Sis," said her sister. "Drive, The Kid, drive!"

She reached forward and tipped his hat over his eyes.

"Si!"

"No, he sure as hell won't!" said Dayzee.

*   *   *

The Kid locked the brakes, and the hearse fishtailed to an abrupt stop outside the closed entrance gate to Dayzee's mansion in the Flats. Six cars behind them crunched together at the unexpected stop, but none of them hit the hearse.

Looking out the back window, Sophia said, "Well, that's a shame. No one told them to follow us, though. That's on them."

"You're so right, Sissy. So, what's next? What do we do with them?"

"I have no idea, Sis. I didn't think that far ahead. It just sounded like fun."

"It sure was," said Kenzie. "I think I'm starting to understand all of you. I mean, the kills are kind of sad, but the thrills are . . . well, thrilling."

"Now, you're catching on," said Sophia. "Don't forget: they're just earthmen anyway."

"Well, yeah, because what else could they be?"

Sophia leaned forward to say to her sister, also leaning, "She's kind of a sweet kid, huh?"

"You would know better than anyone," said Marilyn. "I haven't forgotten all of the times you two were in a bed upstairs and your clothes were—"

"Hey," said Sophia, "never mind that. Dayzee, what's the plan?"

Dayzee turned to look at the back seat, and The Kid held the wheel with both hands and stared out through the windshield.

"Well, let's see. We have two itchy Kildare Killers, a renegade actress slash barmaid from the Prism, a very tall former snake named Bruno, and—"

"And a blind driver that can't speak English," Sophia said with a scoff.

"I bet you're pretty itchy, too, Dayzee," said Marilyn.

"God yeah, I sure am. Yeah, all of that. And—"

"Two dead guys. One missing a head."

"No, Sissy," said Marilyn, "he still has his head. Sort of. It's close, at least."

"Right," said Dayzee, "we have two dead bodies, and we're just getting started. And take a look through the gate. Cliff is there with his crew to start filming 'Kildare in the Hills.' Check it out: they already set up some kind of lighting post thing in the yard.

"Oh, and I forgot about that moving guys' truck. And the carpenter's truck too. They're dead and gone, but we need to get rid of those trucks."

"I still think burying them in the backyard would work," said Marilyn. "Remember how we planned to make that headless, one-legged dead guy dig the hole?"

"Sis, we never planned that. That was a bad idea from the start. How could he—"

"Girls, it's too late to hide the trucks anyway. Cliff already saw them. We just need to drive them out of there."

"A good job for a blind guy," Sophia said with a grin.

"Oh, Sissy is sure right about that."

"Alright, that'll work. I'll open the gate, The Kid will drive in, and before all those funeral groupies can follow us, I'll close the gate."

"I like this plan," said Marilyn. "But why would they follow us in?"

"Looking for a party, Sis?"

"Oh, that makes sense. There's free food when humans expire."

"Hey," said Sophia, "is it possible that all those people know the dead human in the box?"

"Oh my God, wouldn't that be funny?" said Marilyn. "How could we find out?"

"We give him back," said Bruno. "I'll just drop him on one of the cars. They can sort it out."

"Alright, but we can't let Cliff and his crew see any of that," said Dayzee. "Bruno, you stay with The Kid while we distract Cliff. Then, can you toss our dead earthman over the fence?"

"The headless one or the headed one?"

"Let's keep the headless one. Just the headed one for now."

Bruno glanced at the high fence, grinned, and said, "Oh, hell yeah."

Dayzee found her phone, tapped a few numbers, and the entrance gate to her mansion in the Beverly Hills Flats swung in. The Kid gunned the engine and raced the hearse inside, and Dayzee locked it up before their funeral train could follow.

"Well, that was easy enough," said Dayzee. "I thought they'd—"

"Oh, hang on," said Bruno.

Everyone except The Kid turned to see Bruno on his hands and knees, looking from one to the other with his head twitching up and down and side to side.

"Uh-oh," said Marilyn.

"Can you still talk?" said Dayzee. "Try to at least give us a clue."

Bruno growled, turned his head up toward the ceiling, and let out a gentle roar as if he was only practicing.

"I think he's done talking," said Sophia.

"No, Lady Sophia. I just had to get that out. I can still talk."

"Alright, then," said Dayzee. "What's going on with you? That growl didn't sound like a bird."

"No, Dayzee. No birds this time. I feel a mountain lion coming on."

"Wonderful. Are you going to kill us?"

Bruno erupted in a mix of roaring and laughing and managed to say, "Hell no. Remember how I treated you when I was a snake?"

"Well, good, but don't get any romantic ideas, Mr. Lion."

She turned to The Kid.

"The Kid, find a button to open up this thing's back door. Lion boy needs to run."

"Hey, can we just feed the dead guys to the mountain lion?" said Marilyn.

"Sis, that's crazy. Bruno would never—"

"Wait a sec, Fia. Mare might be onto something. Bruno, how about it?"

"I would, but I can imagine the nasty jokes I'd never hear the end of."

"He's right," said Sophia with a snicker. "Oh, I sure would give him hell."

"See, Dayzee? No, I'm not eating any heads."

"Fine. We'll figure something out."

Chapter 4 – Dazzle Me, Sissy

Sutcliffe Gutsquid broke out a wide, shiny white grin at seeing Dayzee, the twins, and Kenzie approaching, their heels clicking on the driveway paving stones.

"My, Dayzee, you sure know how to make an entrance. As do you, Marilyn, and you, Sophia. I won't even ask why you're all tooling around in a hearse, but I love it. I will ask, however, who *you* might be?"

"I'm Kenzie."

"A pleasure to meet you, Kenzie. I'm Cliff. You sure remind me of someone. Oh, I know—that Kozy fellow. Should I assume he's arriving—"

"See? There's that name again," said Kenzie. "Just who the heck is Kozy anyway?"

"Oh, Kenzie," said Dayzee, "there's no one real named Kozy. I told you, that was just a funny Halloween joke, and we—"

"He was no joke, Dayzee," said Cliff. "A specimen like him could never—"

"Could never be real. That's right," said Sophia.

"Sissy's right," said Marilyn. "Hey, Cliff, do you have a favorite bedroom in this gigantic mansion of Dayzee's?"

"Huh?" He looked up at the long line of windows on the second floor. "Well, yeah, but—"

"I bet I know why it's your favorite," Sophia said with a grin.

"Oh, I sure know why too," Cliff said with his own grin, "but he, Kozy was—"

"Not real. We know," said Dayzee. "Hey, we're just about ready to start the reality show. What do you think of the place?"

Cliff looked from Dayzee to Sophia, then to Marilyn. He met Kenzie's staring gaze and shrugged, and she only shook her head. He turned back to Dayzee.

"We're almost ready. We got that light tower set up for when that gorgeous Beverly Hills sun goes down. We also have some loose scripts, which are mostly just ideas for conversation topics."

He rose up onto his toes and looked past the four girls.

"What was . . . I just saw a big cat or something running along the fence behind those bushes."

He pointed and scanned the area. Only Kenzie turned to look.

"That's just Bruno," Marilyn said while shaking her head.

Cliff looked at her until Sophia said, "He just needed to run, we think."

He kept staring at Sophia until Dayzee said, "The neighbor's cat, Cliff. That's all."

"It looked kind of big."

Marilyn giggled and said, "Hmm . . . that reminds me of something Sissy and I found in that favorite bedroom of yours."

Cliff laughed and said, "Alright, so there's a cat. Big deal. Are there big cats in Kildare, girls?"

They nodded and smiled.

"Then, let the show commence!"

*   *   *

"The first thing we should do is to—"

"Have a drink, Cliff? I agree. The bar is always fully stocked."

"Yes, that's good, but I meant clearing out the driveway. You've got a delivery truck, a pickup, and now a hearse. When your new cars get here, I'd like to film their arrival. How about if we move some of these others out?"

The twins looked at each other, then at Dayzee.

"Um, sure, Cliff. Let me go give some instructions to our driver. He'll—"

"It's Kozy, isn't it? I knew he was—"

"There he goes again!" said Kenzie. "Who the hell is Kozy?"

Cliff took a good look at Kenzie and said, "Why, he could almost be you. He looks a lot like you."

"Nonsense," said Dayzee. "Kenzie, he's just being funny. What he's really trying to say is that he wants you in on this reality show too. What do you say?"

She stared at Kenzie and waited for an answer.

"You want me to be in your reality show? Really?"

"Yes, we all do. You're an actress, right?"

Sophia grinned at her sister, who only raised her eyebrows and stared.

"Yes, I sure am. Okay! Yeah, I'd love to be in your show!"

"Good. And now,"—she turned toward Cliff—"let's not have any more crazy talk about someone that you think was named Kozy."

Cliff stared at her for a few seconds, then let out a deep breath.

"Fine. I just want to get started. Kenzie, great to have you on board."

"First," said Dayzee, "I do need to talk to our driver. He likes to be called The Kid."

"Maybe we could find a part for him to—"

"No, Cliff," said Dayzee. "I don't think he's going to be around long enough."

Marilyn giggled and got elbowed by her sister.

"Why don't all of you go get started on a few drinks, and I'll chat with The Kid. Alright?"

"Sure, whatever you want, Dayzee. You're a star!"

*　*　*

"The Kid, we have all kinds of favors to ask of you. Do you understand enough English?"

"Si, hear good English. Speak? Eh . . ."

"Good enough. First, we need to get rid of those bodies."

"Head?"

Dayzee stared at him and said, "I barely know you, and you're already . . . oh, *that* head. Yes, the head too. Let's go take a look in the human box."

They walked around to the hearse's back door, and The Kid swung it open. A soft pounding sound came from inside the casket.

Dayzee shook her head and said, "And there's our assassin. Wonderful. Damn Guild. Can you move that with both bodies inside?"

"The Kid is strong."

"I hope so. Fireproof, too, would be good."

"Que?"

"Nothing. Alright, drag the box close to the gate, I'll pop it open, and you push the whole mess out onto the sidewalk. Sound good?"

"Si."

The Kid tugged on the casket, pulling it out from the vehicle, and he lost his grip and let it drop. The top sprung up and locked open, Dayzee screamed softly and glanced toward the house, and the headless guy began climbing out.

"Oh, just wonderful. The Kid, you need to protect me because that dead guy, he's going to . . . he's . . . wait a second . . . he doesn't even care about me!"

The dead guy left in the opposite direction as mountain lion Bruno, walking along the fence and disappearing behind the line of tall shrubs.

"Now, head?"

Dayzee stared at him again and began to grin. She pointed at him and said, "Oh, I think you understand English better than you let on. Let's take care of business first, alright?"

"Si," he said with a gleaming grin.

"As for *that* head,"—she pointed at the blinking and scowling head in the casket—"just toss it back there behind the bushes too. Who knows, maybe Bruno the lion will decide to gnaw on it anyway?"

The Kid picked up the head and faced the long, dense wall of landscaping, with only a narrow path between it and the tall wrought iron fence. He held the head up like a bowling ball, ignored its snapping and snarling, then executed a perfect four-step approach, sending the head tumbling far along the gloomy path.

"The Kid, you're a bowler?"

"Si. The Kid uses big balls."

Dayzee snickered and said, "Well, maybe we'll see about that."

"Si," he said with one tooth glinting in the sunlight.

"Well, alright. That's progress. Now, this body that really is still dead, can you leave it on the sidewalk, then push the box back inside?"

"Si, The Kid can."

He grabbed both ankles, Dayzee hit some numbers on her phone, and he dragged the corpse out to the walk. Then, he pushed the casket inside the hearse and slammed the rear door while Dayzee sealed up the gate.

"Well, that was easy. Except for the headless dead guy walking around somewhere. Now, the hearse. Oh, you know what? We should get rid of the funeral party people out there. How about you light this thing up again and lead them somewhere? Maybe a ride back down Sunset?"

"Then?"

"It doesn't matter. Jam them all up in a parking lot maybe."

"Si, I do that."

"You're alright, The Kid. Carry on."

She gave him a crisp salute, which he returned, his diamond catching a bit of the Southern California sunlight, and he fired up the hearse as Dayzee reopened the gate.

With The Kid leading the procession back toward the Prism, Dayzee closed the gate and began a determined strut toward the house.

*   *   *

"See, girls," said Cliff, "when the cars arrive, we'll—oh, wait. Kenzie, you'll need a car too. I'll make a call and set it up."

"That's not necessary, Cliff. I'll just grab a ride with Sophia if I need it."

Marilyn elbowed her sister and giggled.

"Sure," said Sophia, "that sounds good. How much driving are we really going to be doing anyway?"

"Parking, I bet," Marilyn said before her sister poked her again with an elbow.

"Well, okay, then. About the cars. They should be showing up soon, all driven by men in snazzy uniforms. They'll line up . . . oh, Dayzee's back. We were just discussing how sharp young men in stylish uniforms will be bringing—"

"Oh my God," said Dayzee. "Uniforms. That reminds me: I need a whole new yard crew."

"What happened to the old crew?"

"Well, nothing, Cliff. They sort of aren't in that business anymore."

"Or any other business," Sophia said as she looked away with a grin.

"It doesn't matter," said Dayzee. "We'll interview a new company the first chance we get, won't we, girls?"

"Oh, I'll do some interviewing," said Marilyn. "We'll need at least one that's good at digging holes too."

Everyone stopped and stared at her.

"Mare? You really think we'll—"

"Sis is right, Dayzee," said Sophia. "Plan on it."

Dayzee shrugged and looked at Cliff.

"These gorgeous twins think of everything."

"I have no idea why you'll need holes dug except maybe for planting new trees. Remember that part of the show? Transforming this place to be more like an estate in Ireland?"

"That's exactly right, Cliff," Dayzee said with a deep sigh. "That's what Mare meant."

"Trees are good and I guess cats too. Look, my lighting guy, Julian, is going over to that shrub line to find the cat. He's a cat lover, that one."

"I'm still not sure whether that's Bruno's type or not," said Dayzee.

"Well," said Sophia, "right now, no human is probably—"

"A bigger cat lover than Julian!" said Marilyn.

"Yep, that's what I meant. Good old Julian, he—"

A loud roar and a silenced scream rang out over the estate, and everyone turned to look. The last known location of Julian showed only a couple of branches waving lazily before they came to a rest.

Dayzee turned back to Cliff and said, "Um, we don't really need a lighting guy while it's daylight, do we?"

"Uh, no, I guess not. Maybe I should go—"

"Nonsense," said Sophia, and she hooked his right arm. "Let him play with the kitty."

"Well, I don't—"

"About that drink," said Marilyn, and she took his other arm.

"Sure. A drink sounds like a fantastic idea. But we still need to clear out this driveway. The hearse is gone, which is good, but that moving truck really needs to go."

"I'll do it," said Marilyn. "That sounds kind of fun."

"I'm with Sis. We'll move it out of here but only because we can't bury it."

Marilyn giggled.

"You girls. Dayzee, these twins are phenomenal. That kind of dialog is priceless!"

"Aren't they, though? Maybe I can move the pickup, then."

"Common labor? Not for my three stars. Oh, Kenzie, you'll be a star too. I'll get some of the crew to move them."

He took out a small satellite phone and barked some orders, and three young men ran out of the house, two to the delivery van and one to the pickup.

"You sure know how to boss men around," said Dayzee. "I'm a little jealous."

"Well, I do pay them."

Dayzee held her hands up and said, "I've tried that, and still . . ."

The large, boxy truck started with a loud backfire and began rolling toward the exit gate. Marilyn leaned behind Cliff and whispered her sister's name. Sophia leaned back too.

"Sissy, I can't take it anymore. I'm too itchy."

"I know, Sis. Me too."

"Let's catch that truck."

"You think? Really?"

"What are you girls whispering about?" said Cliff.

"Oh, Cliff," said Dayzee, "I don't think you want to know."

Both girls turned toward Dayzee, smiling and nodding their heads.

"Girls, don't. Just don't. You know that that's going to be trouble."

"Oh, Dayzee," Marilyn said with a pleasant smile, "I'd rather do it and be hated for what I am than loved for something I'm not."

"Well said, Sis," said Sophia. "And Dayzee, all that talk about a girl's mind, her talents, her creativity . . . nonsense. This is the fountain I want."

"Best one yet, Sissy. I bet that other Sophia never knew about our kind of fountains."

"Girls, can you at least wait until they drive that truck out of here?"

Marilyn smiled, shook her head, and said, "Dayzee, that's just silly. You know better than that."

"Do NOT open that gate, Dayzee."

"Fia? Really?"

"What's going on back there?" Cliff said over his shoulder as the twins released him and hurried toward the idling truck.

"I, uh, I think they have a crush on your crew, that's all," Dayzee said as they watched the girls cut across the lawn, stopping several times to pry their heels loose from the turf.

"They are rather impetuous, aren't they? My God, in that upstairs bedroom the other day, when you were having elevator problems."

"I know. I heard all about it. They really can't help themselves sometimes."

"Should I be chasing after that pickup?" said Kenzie. "I mean, if it's for the show, I suppose I could—"

"There will be plenty of time for that later," said Cliff.

"Yeah, save it for when the cameras are rolling," Dayzee said with a chuckle.

*　　*　　*

"I mixed the potions, but I don't have any drinks to put them in," Marilyn said as they approached the truck.

"That's fine," said her sister. "We'll just pour them down their throats. Not like they can say no."

"I really do love Earth sometimes, Sissy."

She handed Sophia a small vial and circled around to the passenger side. Sophia looked up at the driver.

"Hey, we need that gate open to drive this thing out of here," said the young man behind the wheel.

Sophia didn't answer. She only smiled at him and began unbuttoning her tight red blouse, revealing a lacy black bra that barely covered her breasts, almost showing two very important details. He lost sight of her big blue eyes and focused a bit lower.

"That's better. Stay right where you are,"—she finished the buttons, dropped the shirt behind her, and unhooked the clasp stretched tight between her breasts—"I'm coming up."

*　　*　　*

"Do I look good in a white dress?" Marilyn said to her guy.

"Uh, yeah. Hell yeah. But we were supposed to—"

"Oh, look how easy it is to move it aside," she said as she worked the tight dress up over her hips, twisting it from side to side and tugging it up until it wrapped around her waist. He stared at her white panties with his mouth hanging wide open.

"Mm . . . Earth."

"Huh?"

32

"Just keep watching," she said as she shimmied out of her underwear and kicked it to one side.

She stepped up onto the running board and opened the door.

"No place for me to sit? Wait, I see the perfect place."

She climbed up, swung her right leg over both of his, and straddled him.

Her twin sister had done the same with her hypnotized earthman, and since she was wedged between him and the steering wheel, her bare breasts were pressed into his smiling face.

"Keep going, Sis," Sophia said as she held his head with both hands.

"Oh, of course!"

Marilyn slipped each thin strap down over her shoulders, showing the mesmerized man that she wore no bra. She turned to her sister with a smile.

"It's almost too easy, Sissy."

"Well, you're spectacular, Sis," she said, looking down with a grin.

"So are yours, Sissy. We're twins. Show me!"

Her sister rotated away from the driver to show off her pair, then rubbed her way back to facing him.

"There, that's better. Good earthman."

She could see only his eyes looking up at her.

"God, I'm so itchy, Sissy. Let's really fire these guys up."

"No. No burning, Sis. These guys are for our show, remember?"

"Barbs, then? Just a little?"

"Oh, I'd sure love to, but no, we better not with these guys. Let's promise ourselves that we'll do it all soon, alright?"

"Oh, okay, Sissy. As long as you promise."

"I do."

Sophia turned to her guy, held up the bottle, and said, "Here's your first treat. Come on. Open up."

She wiggled until he could turn his chin up between her breasts, and she poured it all in. She held his mouth closed and said, "Swallow it all."

"They say that a lot on this planet, Sissy."

"They sure do," she said as she smothered him again. "Good boy."

Marilyn did the same with her guy, with the truck in park, ready to leave Dayzee's estate but not going anywhere at all. Both girls lowered themselves down on their exposed, helpless earthmen and began bouncing in time with each other.

The Kildare Killers quickly picked up the pace, eager for what they knew would give them their next fountains of youth, that miracle process that would keep them young forever.

*   *   *

"Well, they're certainly not going anywhere," said Cliff. "I must admit that I am a bit jealous."

"Oh, Cliff," Dayzee said, "maybe you and I can plan a little something for later? You can show me just exactly what happened up there with you and those gorgeous twins. How does that sound?"

He grinned and nodded and said, "Yes, I'd like that."

"Hey, what about me?" said Kenzie. "I think I will go see that pickup guy, whether the cameras are going or not. I know what Marilyn means about getting itchy all the time."

She turned toward the idling truck and froze.

"Dayzee, look!"

Dayzee and Cliff turned to see ten or more mountain lions, all female, pawing at each closed gate. Some were howling, some were growling, and a few were jumping as high as they could to try to get inside.

"Neighborhood cats, huh, Dayzee?"

"Oh, I don't think so, Cliff. Those are—"

She saw lion Bruno break through the line of shrubbery between the gates and begin trotting toward them. A second later, the entrance gate began to swing in.

"Oh, shit! I left my phone in the hearse. Damn that The Kid!"

"That really does sound silly," said Kenzie.

The lone mountain lion locked up in his tracks and looked behind him. With a loud yip and his tail between his legs, he began running through the grass until he'd reached the light tower that Cliff's crew had set up. He managed to claw and scrape his way up to the tiny platform high above the ground just as twenty or more cackling lions circled the base and stared up at him.

"Should we run or something?" said Cliff.

"Nah, they want our boy up there. We're safe."

"Um . . . Dayzee," said Kenzie, and she gestured with her eyes for Dayzee to look.

She looked past Cliff and saw the dead snakebit guy walking slowly toward them. At the sound of brakes squealing, she snapped her head around to see The Kid skidding to a stop on her driveway.

"At least he didn't close the gate, so maybe we can somehow herd them back out," she said, "God, this is getting—"

The Kid closed the gate.

*　　*　　*

"Oh, Sissy, mine's just about ready."

"Mine too, Sis. Remember, let's try not to kill them, alright?"

"Next time, then?"

"Sure. Yep, we deserve it. Maybe with that new lawn crew?"

"Oh, for sure, Sissy. We'll make sure Dayzee hires a few extras."

Both men's faces were buried in the Kildare Killers' breasts while they rode on their laps, both smiling. The girls reached across to hold each other's hand.

"Same time, Sis?"

"Mm-hmm, Sissy. Let's look at each other too."

"Alright. That really is a breathtaking sight."

"Dazzle me, Sissy."

With deep groans, both men fulfilled their part of the bargain, processing the potion in whatever way an earthman does and giving each twin the unexplainable magic of a fountain of youth.

Just as each girl felt them deliver, Marilyn squealed, Sophia grinned and shook her head, and each saw the intense starburst of light streaming from her sister's eyes.

Chapter 5 – Circus on her Lawn

The Kid saw the lions, let loose a loud "Whoa!" and dove back into the hearse, where he quickly powered up all of the windows.

"You know, maybe we *should* go inside, Cliff," said Dayzee. "This sure is some crazy commotion out here."

"I think you're right, Dayzee. We really should—wait, what the hell is that?"

He pointed to the moving van, which had a cab lit up like kids were playing with flashlights inside.

"What in the universe *is* that?"

"Universe, Cliff?"

"Yeah. Could those be flares?"

"Big trouble is what I'd call that," Dayzee said with a chuckle. "This is going to be fun. You thought they were riled up before."

Cliff turned to hurry toward the house but stopped for another look at the tower and the lone mountain lion at the top.

"He better not wreck anything up there."

"He won't, Cliff. That lion will be really—"

"Damn lions," said Kenzie.

Dayzee jerked Cliff to a stop and turned toward Kenzie.

"What did you say?"

"I said, 'damn lions.' Why did I say that, Dayzee?"

"Oh my God. Anything else on your mind, Kenzie?"

Kenzie bit her lip and looked at the driveway.

"Come on. Spit it out. We don't have all day."

"Okay. I don't know why, but I feel like wearing that hat you put on me for the Halloween party. Remember that?"

"Oh my God again! Yes, I sure do remember it. Let's get inside. This is going to be so fun!"

"Should I understand any of this?"

"It'd be scary if you did, Cliff."

"Weird happenings like these are exactly why 'Kildare in the Hills' will be an instant, planet-wide hit!"

Dayzee squinted at Cliff for a second, then she took another peek at the headless guy drawing near, not seeming to be in any particular hurry.

"Still, let's get that drink. Oh, and a hat for Ko—um, for Kenzie."

*   *   *

"Oh, Sissy, I feel better already."

"Dayzee should have told us about this years ago. Still, better late than never. How do I look?"

"Even more gorgeous than before. How about me?"

"Sis, you're a knockout. You know, every time we do this, it just makes Earth even easier for us."

They both looked down at the film crew guys, each with eyes closed and faces mostly buried between their breasts.

"Yes, it certainly does. Well, we're done with these two. Sure you don't want to burn them up?"

"I want to, but we need them for the show. I'm trying so hard to remember that there's no need."

"Except that it feels so good. And I have so much energy now. I really want to burn someone up."

"You sure are right about that. Me too. But let's let these earthmen live. They're here to work on our new series, remember?"

"I don't even care. But okay, Sissy. Hey, won't they wonder what just happened?"

"Dayzee told me that they won't even remember. It's a perfect system."

"I kind of wish we *had* to finish them off. Just like all those yard guys."

"Well, with them, we really did have to. They saw that headless dead guy dancing around, and—"

"I knew he was dancing!"

"—and now, Dayzee has to find a new crew. We shouldn't make Cliff hire all new guys, should we?"

"I don't suppose so," said Marilyn. "Okay, let's go have that drink."

"I think I'll get undressed while I'm drinking just because I want to."

"No, let me do it. I'll undress anybody right now!"

*   *   *

"I hope you don't mind, Dayzee," said Cliff, "but I had one of my guys nail a piece of plywood over that front door to your mansion. What happened to it? It looked like some insane animals attacked!"

"That's wonderful. Thanks, Cliff. We'll get a carpenter to fix things up properly soon."

"So, you won't satisfy my curiosity about what tore it apart like that?"

Dayzee shrugged and said, "It's the Hills, Cliff. Things happen, that's all."

He stared at her for a few seconds, then looked at Kenzie, who only shrugged.

"Well, okay, then."

After Cliff had walked past the patched-up door and into her foyer, Kenzie followed, and Dayzee paused to look one more time at the circus on her lawn.

She muttered under her breath, "Oh, you're a bit of a coward, huh, The Kid?" as she watched him reopen the gate and back the hearse to the road.

A glance at the top of the tower showed her a tall, naked man curled up and hanging on for his life. She scoffed and almost yelled to him, but instead, she scanned the ground. She saw all of the girl lions quiet and with their heads hanging low, filing across the lawn toward the open gate, some growling their disappointment.

One last look revealed that the headless guy had turned around and was stumbling back toward the larger of the two guesthouses at the rear of the property.

"You won't get any head back there," she said aloud and chuckled.

"What's that, Dayzee?"

"Oh, nothing, Cliff. It's just amazing how sometimes impossible problems just kind of fix themselves. I really do like Earth sometimes too."

"Trust me," he said, "there are worse places."

He held Dayzee's gaze and grinned. She shook her head and pointed at him.

"There you go again, pretending to be from some other planet."

"No, I already made it clear that I wasn't from a different planet. But wherever I'm from, I bet it's happy hour there. How about that drink?"

*   *   *

While walking across the yard, Sophia smoothed down her skirt and Marilyn tugged on her dress to get it back in place. They got themselves covered on top, too, before they'd reached the base of the lighting tower.

"It would have been more fun if we'd dressed each other instead," said Marilyn.

"You're right, Sis. Hey, whatever happened to that photographer, Jiff? If he was here, I'd definitely be the one undressing and then, maybe, dressing you again. Maybe not the dressing."

"Same here, Sissy. Oh, look at that: that's Bruno way up there."

"Hey, Bruno," said Sophia. "Welcome back."

"God, Lady Sophia, it's good to be back."

"You're naked," said Marilyn.

"Do lions wear clothes, Miss Marilyn?"

Marilyn only giggled.

"Can you get my clothes from over by the gate?"

"Let's make a deal," said Sophia.

"Yes, Sissy, let's make him earn his clothes back."

"What would you like, Lady Sophia?"

"Pool time!"

"Yep, like Sis said. After that, then you can get dressed. So, get your naked ass down here."

"Yes, Lady Sophia."

They watched from a revealing angle as their very large protector shimmied down one of the support posts and soon stood facing them.

Sophia smirked and said, "Sis and I should check for slivers."

"Everywhere, Sissy."

They saw that Bruno was looking past them, so they turned to see. The headless guy was approaching, his hands reaching blindly in front of him, grasping at anything it could find.

"Uh-oh, Sissy. He's looking for head."

"I saw The Kid bowl that head back behind the bushes."

"That's still funny, Sissy. Here's another guy looking for head, and all the while, it had already found a bush."

"That really is funny, Sis, because—"

"Girls, maybe we should plan for pool time later and maybe run for the house now? I'd rather not wrestle a dead guy all naked like this."

"Oh, fine," said Marilyn. "But I'm still itchy."

"When are you not, Sis?"

"Oh, he's aiming for the guesthouse again. I'll grab my clothes and meet you inside."

*　*　*

"Cliff, pour yourself something, and mix us up whatever you think we might like. I need to take Kenzie upstairs to find that costume hat of hers."

41

"Sure, Dayzee. Don't take too long. Those new cars will be here soon. Hey, can you open that gate so my guys can get those trucks out of here?"

"Oh, I forgot all about those, what with the lions and all."

"Damn lions."

"Yes, Kenzie! That's right! I don't know where The Kid drove off to, Cliff, but I can open the exit gate from in here."

She tapped a code on a small keypad near the intercom.

"Done. Now, Kenzie, about that hat."

She took Kenzie's hand and led her up the stairway from the kitchen.

"You really don't know how big this house is, do you, Dayzee?"

"Someday, Kenzie, we can all go exploring. We should probably draw up a map, too, like Mare said."

*   *   *

"See, Sis? Isn't that easier than digging a big hole in the backyard?"

The twins watched both trucks roll out through the exit gate, take a right, and head toward Sunset Boulevard.

"Well, Sissy, it's not like we were going to dig the hole, remember?"

Sophia shook her head and said, "Nope, and we never will. We don't really do any work except in front of cameras."

"For our own reality show too."

"That's right. Bruno, I'm surprised you were smoking before."

"Oh, that. I think it's just when I'm a snake. I didn't even think of it when I was a lion."

"How was that? What did you think about?"

"Oh, Lady Sophia, all I wanted was all those hot lady lions."

"They were hot? They just looked like lions to me."

"Yes, Miss Marilyn. To me, too, now. But when I was a lion? Oh my!"

"But why did you run from them? You looked scared."

"They weren't just looking for sex—they were hungry too. I would have been shredded alive. I wanted them one at a time to climb that pole, and—"

"And climb your pole?" Marilyn said with a giggle.

"Yes, exactly, Miss Marilyn."

"I just can't imagine what's next for you. Unless maybe you're done playing around like that?"

"I still feel kind of funny, Lady Sophia. I think there's still a bunch of sorcery crap brewing inside me just waiting to blow up again."

*　　*　　*

"I left the entire costume in this room, Kenzie."

Dayzee led her into the bedroom from which she and Kozy had watched the Kildare Killers finishing off the last of the yard crew workers near the pool.

"Oh, I like this room. I don't know why, but it's kind of exciting. Why is that, Dayzee?"

"Maybe it's the view?"

She grabbed the hat that Kozy had worn, a black one with a short brim and a badge on the front, placed it on Kenzie's head, and led her toward the window.

"Take a look. Quite a sight, huh?"

"Yeah, you do have a beautiful yard."

"Here, stand behind me and look over my shoulder. Yeah, like that. Anything?"

"Well, it's still a nice backyard. I need to get in that pool sometime too."

"Just for fun, hold my waist and peek over my shoulder."

"What good will that do?"

"Who knows? You know this house is weird, right? Give it a try."

Kenzie placed a hand on each side of Dayzee's waist, touching some of her skin between the top of her skirt and the bottom of her blouse.

"This is freaky. It's like some kind of deja vu or something."

"Like . . . it's making you want more?"

"Yeah. Like that. Like I'm almost remembering something too."

*   *   *

"Where's Dayzee and Kenzie?" said Sophia.

"Oh, they went upstairs," said Cliff, "for some kind of hat for Kenzie."

"She wanted to wear her hat?" Sophia said with a big grin.

"Yeah, she kind of insisted. Why?"

Sophia didn't answer. She grabbed her sister's hand and ran with her up the stairs as well as they could in their tight wardrobe and high heels.

Cliff looked at Bruno, who only shrugged, then he handed him a beer.

*   *   *

"What happens next in that deja vu of yours?" said Dayzee.

"Oh, I'm embarrassed to say."

"Remember what happened in the attic? It can't be any stranger than that."

"Oh, for sure. Okay, I don't know why, but I feel like grabbing you. Undressing you."

"Oh, well, we sure are alone up here. Just for the hell of it, why don't you—"

The door swung in, and Sophia said, "There you both are. Hey, what exactly is going on up here?"

Kenzie took a step back from Dayzee and said, "Just getting this hat. You like it?"

"Oh yeah, I really do. That's hot."

Marilyn elbowed her and giggled, but Sophia ignored her.

"We were just enjoying the view, girls," said Dayzee. "For some reason, Kenzie felt like wearing that hat. Isn't that something?"

"It sure is," Sophia said just before her sister whispered in her ear.

"Tell her to get into the rest of the uniform, Sissy."

"No, Sis, I can't ask her to—"

"I bet she wants to."

"Fine."

Marilyn continued. "And you're all fired up from the fountain, aren't you?"

"Like you can't imagine, Sis."

"Well, then . . ."

While Kenzie was admiring her hat in the dresser mirror, Sophia said, "Hey, just for kicks, why not put on the whole costume?"

Kenzie began smiling before looking toward Sophia.

"I want to, but I thought you'd all think I was crazy."

"Those boots probably won't fit," said Dayzee, "but I have some that are even better."

She saw Marilyn tipping her head and darting her eyes toward the door, and she added, "Get started on the rest, Kenzie, and Mare and I will find those boots. Fia can help."

"Wait," said Sophia, "I should probably—"

"Nonsense, Fia. Help Kenzie out. Your sister and I will be back. Soon. Sort of."

Before Sophia could protest any further, a smiling Dayzee and a giggling Marilyn had left the room and pulled the door shut after them.

Chapter 6 – Quite a Feast

"You really should always listen to your sister, Fifi."

Sophia looked into Kenzie's big brown eyes and smiled back at her.

"I'm pretty sure you don't need any help changing into that costume, Kenzie."

"Hmm . . . I'll tell you what I need when we have more time. They could be back anytime, so for now, there's only time for a wardrobe change."

"Oh . . . for the reality show. Right. That's good—that'll be your costume for the show."

"You can start with the hat."

"You mean, you can't even—"

"No, I sure can't. I'm too tired from everything that's happened."

"Now, you're just being goofy."

"I know."

She gave Sophia a big grin, and Sophia took a few steps to stand in front of her. While grinning back at her, she reached up with both hands, picked the hat off of her head and without looking, spun it toward the bed.

"Good start, Fifi. Now, the t-shirt."

Kenzie raised her arms straight up and waited, giving Sophia a big smile. Sophia let out a deep breath, stepped closer, and got a grip on the shirt's bottom hem.

*　　*　　*

"Mare, why do you do these things to your sister?"

"It's fun. Besides, she's at least as itchy as me. It's all I can do to not run in there myself. After that fountain, I'm sure I'd drag you in there too."

"Oh, Mare, you wouldn't have to drag me. I told you it was too soon for another fountain. You and Fia never listen, though."

"Aren't you due for another one?"

"Soon, yeah. I need to locate an earthman for that."

"Oh, that's right. Hey, what about Cliff?"

"You know, Mare, I'm not completely sure that he is an earthman."

"You don't think he's that thing that Kozy was talking about, do you? That parasite thing from some insane asteroid?"

"The way things are going, nothing would surprise me. How long should we give your sister in there with Kenzie?"

"I know Sissy is itchy, but we have cameras ready to roll downstairs. Oh, and our cars should be here soon too."

"Tell you what: we'll find some way to stick them in a room when there's more time. How about that?"

"Yes, let's do that. We'll find out one way or another if Sissy was really only acting all this time."

*　*　*

"Oh, that feels better," Kenzie said after Sophia had lifted her t-shirt up and off and threw it toward the bed.

"I always feel better without clothes too," Sophia said while gazing at Kenzie's bared breasts. "Alright, time for that jacket."

"What, no shirt? Fifi, you don't want me to wear even a shirt?"

"Well, no, because Kozy never—"

"Stop. Stop right there. Just who the hell is Kozy?" She put her hands on her hips and shrugged, shaking her breasts. "Don't try to tell me it's some kind of joke. Nobody jokes that much."

Sophia looked back up into her eyes.

"Um . . . how about if we discuss that later? We're about due on-set, and we just have enough time for this costume change."

Kenzie shook her head slowly, smiled, and said, "Alright, Fifi. This time. Hey, what about these jeans? Aren't there some kind of costume pants?"

"Well, yeah, those jeans really aren't—"

"I still need help," Kenzie said as she leaned her head and smiled, her hands still on her hips.

Sophia sighed, smiled, and began loosening the belt and pulling down the zipper.

*　　*　　*

"So . . . Bruno, is it?"

"Yeah. Cliff?" he said, pointing.

"Yep. How do you know Dayzee and the twins?"

"I, um, I was kind of like a bodyguard for them."

"Well, you certainly are an imposing figure. I have no doubt you took excellent care of them. Past tense? You're not their bodyguard anymore?"

"Um, not officially, I guess. But yeah, I still watch out for them. Just a while ago, back at the Prism, there was this guy giving them some shit, and I put an end to that in a hurry."

"What did you do?"

"Hell, I just bit . . ."

"Yes?"

"I, um, bit my tongue to keep from cussing him out. Yeah. Then, I got rid of him."

"He could probably tell that you might rip his head clean off, huh?"

Bruno swallowed the rest of his drink, looked to the stairway, and said, "Yeah, exactly. Where are those girls anyway?"

*　　*　　*

"These are the boots, Mare. Cute, huh?"

She held up a pair of short black velvet boots with high narrow heels and thick platforms.

"Oh my, those are sexy as hell. Do you think Kenzie will wear them?"

"Only until Kozy comes back."

"What? What are you talking about?"

"Mare, I think the hat is just the start. You know what else happened while you were fountainizing those film crew Earth guys? Kenzie said, 'Damn lions.' Out of nowhere. That's what Kozy started saying before he had to leave. He was getting to be quite the comic."

"Dayzee, are you saying that Kenzie will be Kozy again? With all the One-Eighty muscles and everything else?"

"I have no idea. I don't think anyone does. We'll have to ask Bruno about it—maybe he knows something. In the meantime, we should get back in there."

"Yes, and let's forget about knocking. Let's just charge right in there and see if either one still has clothes on. Every other time, somehow, someway, they both always seemed to lose their clothes. I bet they're not even standing up anymore!"

*　　*　　*

"Did you see all those mountain lions before?"

"Yeah, that was something."

"Where were you?" Cliff said while rubbing his chin. "I didn't see you with the girls when they got here. Just that driver of theirs."

"Oh, I, um, I was in the back of the hearse. I fell asleep back there. I did see those cute lions, though."

"They were cute?"

Bruno coughed.

"Well, if you're into zoos and stuff like that. Actually, they just looked like lions. Ordinary lions."

Cliff stared.

"Just your average lions."

Cliff frowned a few seconds while gazing at Bruno, then he finished his drink.

* * *

"Sure you want me to put that jacket on, Fifi?"

"Yep, it's part of the costume. Here."

She held the jacket behind Kenzie, and when she put her hands in the sleeves, Sophia pulled it all the way up, then brushed her long brown hair out from under it.

"Now, button it for me, Fifi."

Sophia groaned softly while letting out a deep breath.

"Oh, that damn fountain. I can barely—"

"I didn't see any fountains out there. Dayzee has everything else, though. Come on. Button up my jacket."

Sophia stepped in closer and reached around, both facing toward the door. Her hands fumbled around, trying to find any buttons that she could.

"Hey, this thing doesn't even have any buttons."

Kenzie laughed and said, "I know, Fifi. Keep trying, though."

Sophia ran her fingers along the edge, her fingertips inside and dragging along Kenzie's skin, not finding a single button.

"Ooh, that cloth is just the right kind of rough."

Sophia chuckled once, then pinched the fabric and rubbed each side up and down a few times, causing a deep sigh.

"Maybe the buttons are on the inside, Fifi. You should check."

Sophia had just started pulling open the jacket's lapels, saying, "Oh, I sure will—" and the door was flung wide open.

"Oh, that sure looks fun," said Marilyn. "That thing barely covers your boobs. Maybe we should all dress like that."

Sophia let go and stepped to one side.

"Hey, just helping out. That jacket doesn't have any buttons, though."

"Who's complaining?" Dayzee said with a grin. "Kenzie, you're absolutely stunning."

"I think the jacket is just too big," said Marilyn. "Hey, I know—let's get the jacket off of that headless sap from the Prism. He's still out there somewhere, isn't he?"

"Yeah, Sis. Dancing around, I bet."

"Yes, he is."

"Well, why the hell not?" said Dayzee. "We need to do something about him anyway."

She glanced out the window and said, "Perfect. The Kid just rolled through the gate. That's his next job: steal a jacket from a headless dead guy."

"If he stops dancing long enough," Marilyn said with a big smile.

"He'll still be looking for head, though," Sophia said with a smirk.

"When you're right, you're right. Okay, we need to—"

"Let's teach him to bowl with his own head."

"Oh, not you too, Kenzie. That sounds especially mean."

"I think I'm losing my mind. It's this house, isn't it?"

"It's a crazy old mansion, Kenzie. Yeah. Alright, I'm going to give some orders to The Kid. Mare, you're with me. Fia,"—she handed a black skirt and the pair of boots to her—"finish dressing up Kenzie, and we'll meet you downstairs with the dead guy's jacket."

"She can probably dress herself, Dayzee."

"Yeah, Fia, but what fun is that?"

Marilyn shrugged at her sister, and she and Dayzee left the room.

*   *   *

"How much do you weigh?" said Cliff.

"On this planet, you mean?"

"That's funny. Yeah, let's talk about this planet."

"About six-hundred pounds. Earth pounds."

"That's quite a feast. It would take a while to—"

"Huh? What are you talking about? How could I be a feast?"

51

"Oh, um . . . I mean, like if those lions had caught you. Yeah, if the lions were eating you."

"Not a pleasant thought, Cliff. Not at all. How about another drink?"

"Are you hungry? Maybe we should find you something to eat? You should eat."

Bruno tilted his head and stared with a frown.

*   *   *

"Alone again. I probably could put that skirt on myself."

"Yep, but I bet you won't."

"No, I sure won't."

"Alright, but then, we're going down for—"

"Ooh, Fifi. Yes. Let's."

"Down *stairs* to get the show started. Here, step into the skirt. Good."

Sophia leaned over, holding the skirt, and Kenzie held onto her shoulders as she put each leg through. Sophia began pulling it up.

"It sure is tight," Kenzie said. "Might take some effort."

With Sophia yanking at it, and Kenzie shifting her hips around, they'd managed to slide it along her thighs until the top band was snug around her waist. While looking in her eyes, Sophia tried to give the bottom hem a tug.

"Short too," Kenzie said with a smile.

"It looks good, Kenzie. Step into those boots, and we're good to go."

*   *   *

"Dayzee and Marilyn," said Cliff. "Glad you could join us. Where are the other two?"

They turned and grinned at each other before Dayzee said, "They'll be along any minute now. Wardrobe changes can take a while, you know."

"Yes, I do know," said Cliff. "I just got a text about the car delivery. They said about ten minutes."

"Just enough time," Dayzee said and began walking toward the front door.

"Time for what?" said Bruno.

"To find a new jacket for Kenzie," Marilyn said with a wink. "From that guy, you know? The one from the Prism when you—"

"Oh, that guy. Dayzee's going to get it from him?"

"No, silly. The Kid will have to do it."

"Isn't he mostly blind?"

"Yes, Bruno, but he'll just have to figure it out. He won't be around long anyway."

"Why not?"

Marilyn only shook her head slowly and smiled.

"You're silly, Bruno."

*   *   *

"Hey, The Kid—I have a job for you."

"Si," said The Kid as he leaned against the fender of the hearse. He'd left the exit gate open, and he handed the phone back to Dayzee.

"Remember that head you bowled into the bushes?"

"Si. Head."

"Oh, you have a one-track mind. Forget the head. It's about the body that's roaming around somewhere. We need you to get its jacket. Can you do that?"

"Si, but no head?"

Dayzee stared at him for a few seconds, then said, "God, you're a stubborn one, aren't you? Get the jacket, and we'll see. Alright?"

"Si, The Kid get the jacket."

He waited with a big smile, staring at her breasts, his diamond twinkling.

"Yes! Go!"

*   *   *

Dayzee walked back into the kitchen just as Sophia and Kenzie reached the bottom of the stairs. Kenzie wore the tight skirt, short boots, a baggy suit jacket without buttons, no shirt, and her hat.

"Well, that's quite a sight," said Cliff. "Ladies, I see a star in the making."

"Stars are really big and contain far too much mass," Kenzie said before stopping and turning toward Sophia.

"Why did I say that?"

"Eh. Don't worry about it. We're finally all ready to get started."

"No, not exactly," Dayzee said as she shook her head. "The Kid is out looking for that spare jacket for Kenzie."

"Oh, that's right," said Sophia. "Good job for a cowboy."

"Who's a cowboy?" Cliff said as he looked from face to face.

Dayzee said, "The Kid wants to be one. That's why he's here from Colombia."

"And to drive for us," said Kenzie.

"We could probably squeeze in some story angle involving a cowboy," said Cliff. "Let's talk to him about—"

"No, Cliff," said Dayzee. "I keep telling you: he probably won't be around long enough."

"He's planning on leaving?"

"Well, maybe not planning, exactly. Bruno, what's wrong?"

Bruno had set his empty beer bottle on the bar, took two steps back, and raised his arms straight out to the sides.

"I . . . I think . . ."

"Uh-oh," said Marilyn. "Is he trying to fly?"

He lowered his arms, then raised them again.

"I . . . I don't think so, Miss . . . Miss Marilyn."

"It's just one thing after another with this guy," Dayzee said, chuckled, and picked up her drink.

"Bruno, are you okay?" said Cliff.

"He'll be fine," Sophia said with a smirk. "The big guy is just full of surprises. See the hat?"

When Bruno began to vibrate from his boots to his ball cap, Dayzee said, "You know, Cliff, maybe we should give him some privacy. I need to check on The Kid anyway. Care to join me?"

"Shouldn't we . . . I mean, he—"

"Nah. Come on. Let's go."

She grabbed his arm and pulled him toward the back door.

"Girls, it's up to you. You can come with us, or you can stick around for however the hell this all ends up."

"I'd like to stick around and make sure he—"

"No! Come on, Cliff. Get moving!"

She shoved him toward the door, and her heels clacked on the hardwood floor as she kept pushing him along.

"I'll keep an eye on him," said Sophia. "Someone will have to put his hat back on his head."

"I don't think—"

"Move, Cliff! Hey, maybe our cars are here? Let's go look."

Marilyn took Kenzie's hand and pulled her after Dayzee and Cliff.

"I'll take good care of Kenzie for you, Sissy."

"Yep, I bet you will."

Just as Dayzee opened the door, they heard a loud roar and then a scream.

"Uh-oh," said Marilyn. "I bet that was The Kid."

"He can roar like that?" said Cliff. "Even a real cowboy couldn't—"

"No," Dayzee said as she pointed toward the front of the house. "The Kid must have left the gate open. We have at least one lousy lion looking for trouble."

"Damn lions."

"Oh my God!" said Marilyn. "Is that who I think it is?"

"Not yet, Mare," said Dayzee. "Maybe soon, though? In the meantime, Kenzie, I could just kiss you!"

Chapter 7 – Keep Talking Sexy

"No, no, no!"

Dayzee stopped Cliff with a tight grip on his arm, and Marilyn and Kenzie bumped into them both from behind when The Kid's screaming rang out again.

"Oh, that can't be good. Cliff, we'll check on the driver, but you . . .you should wait in the guesthouse."

He looked at the pair of houses far across the lawn on the other side of the pool. Two of his crew were carrying equipment into the larger of them, and a third was checking things with a tape measure.

"Dayzee, this is just too exciting. How about if I get a camera over here real quick, and whatever's going on with that cowboy, we can—"

"He's not a cowboy. A pretty good bowler," she said with a chuckle, "but no kind of a cowboy. Look, we'll catch up with you in a sec. Run along, Cliff!"

He stared for a moment, then turned and walked across the lawn, waving to his crew.

"Things do get complicated, Mare. Kenzie, we can bring you the coat—you don't have to get involved in this nonsense."

"No, Dayzee, this looks like fun. Let's go."

"It looks more like danger to me," said Marilyn, and she held her breath and waited, studying Kenzie closely.

Without smiling, Kenzie said, "There is certainly an abundance of danger in our vicinity."

Marilyn clapped her hands together, laughed, and said, "Soon, Dayzee! I just know it!"

"Well, we can't wait for that. We need to get that jacket for Kenzie or whoever. Oh, we should probably help The Kid too."

Another loud scream emanated from behind the line of shrubs, followed by a roar close by, then the sounds of running and snapping of dry twigs.

"Yes, to the danger we go!"

"Oh, Mare . . ."

*   *   *

Sophia blinked her eyes, and where Bruno had stood, mumbling and shaking, now sat his clothes in a crumpled heap. His cap sat off to the side. She stooped down, prodded the black t-shirt, and jumped up quickly when a voice similar to Bruno's, but much higher pitched, came from somewhere in the pile.

"Lady Sophia. I'm in here. A little help, please?"

"Sure, Bruno."

She started dragging the t-shirt to one side, and Bruno said, "No, in here."

She tipped over the cap, and a tiny mouse sat up on its haunches, twitching its nose and whiskers and blinking rapidly.

"This is the worst."

"Worse than being a snake?"

"Or a lion. I can't protect you and Miss Marilyn like this. Or Dayzee. Or Kenzie. I suppose she's one of your gang now. I remember her looking pretty good in that costume you put on her."

"You like her, Bruno?"

"Not anymore. I want a teenie girlie mousie. Maybe more than one. Yeah, yeah, yeah, a whole squirming pile of them."

"Well, I'm not sure you'll—hey, all the lady mountain lions came after you, but how come no snakes?"

"Are there those kinds of snakes in the Hills, Lady Sophia?"

"Maybe a few but mostly the kind that walk on two legs. Besides, that was West Hollywood."

Bruno tipped his mouse head back and chattered like a squeaky whistle.

"Good one, Lady Sophia. Yes, that was—"

"Wait, Bruno. Did you hear that?"

They both listened to the scratching at the base of the front door. Then the back door.

"Oh, boy. There's all those ladies you're itching for."

"Help a mouse out, Lady Sophia. I can't open the door. Not with these."

He held up his two small hands, wiggling his even smaller fingers.

"No, you sure can't, and I'm not about to."

"I bet I could chew through it, but that would take too long. Who knows what I might be by then?"

"A giraffe, maybe?"

He pointed his furry snout toward the ceiling and chattered, then he shook his mouse head.

"Oh, I guess this is pretty amusing. We are in Beverly Hills, right?"

"Yes, go ahead and say it. You've earned it."

He chirped, "Only in Beverly Hills!" and squeaked at the ceiling, his tiny paws holding his chubby belly.

*   *   *

"There they go! Run!"

Dayzee led them along the line of bushes, and where they could squeeze through to the shady path along the fence, they all rushed in.

"My God," said Dayzee, "you really are a cowboy!"

"Si!"

The Kid stood with his arms crossed and his diamond barely twinkling in the darkness behind the shrubs. At his feet lay the lady mountain lion, on her side, with vines wrapped around all four legs.

"It's a Beverly Hills rodeo!" said Marilyn.

"Si!"

"Lions have never been used for such western North American extravaganzas," said Kenzie. "Typically, domesticated livestock varieties of animals have—oh my God, what am I saying?"

"Keep talking sexy like that," said Marilyn. "We're still in a whole lot of danger."

"Mare's right. Hey, The Kid, this is the lowest part of the fence. Can you loosen your lasso—"

"She said 'lasso!'"

"—and give our lady friend the old heave ho?"

"Si. Lady go bye bye."

"Aw, that's kind of cute the way he said that."

"Isn't that so, Mare? He's quite the romantic cowboy."

The Kid loosened the bindings, snatched up the kicking and clawing animal, and tossed it backward over his head. He turned to watch with the girls as it twisted in the air, the lashings fell aside, and she landed on all four paws.

While she sprinted away, Marilyn said, "We're still in so much danger, Dayzee. You too, Kenzie."

"We really are, Mare. Don't forget that Bruno told us he couldn't be sure that another assassin didn't tail him to Earth through the portal."

"I kind of miss that assassin. No one really got hurt, and it was non-stop danger. That's what we need, Dayzee: more danger."

"Why, Mare? Oh, you're hoping that Kenzie will—"

"Yes, I sure am. Watch. Hey, Kenzie, pick a number between one and ten."

Kenzie stared at Marilyn without blinking. She didn't hesitate.

"One-eighty."

"Oh my God," said Dayzee. "Mare, this is unbelievable! You're right—we need a lot more danger."

The Kid started snarling.

Dayzee said, "Easy, Tex. Trying to scare us doesn't count."

His snarling continued. His mouth stretched open to each side, leaving an opening just tall enough to show his diamond tooth.

"Um, Dayzee, I don't think he—"

He threw his sunglasses over the fence and lunged at Kenzie, reaching for her throat with both hands.

"No, don't you dare!" said Marilyn. "Sissy would kill us!"

Instantly, her right hand began to glow white-hot, and she slapped it onto The Kid's heart. A cloud of fast-cooking Colombian cowboy smoke filled the dim alley behind the bushes as Marilyn scorched her way through.

* * *

"I want cheese too. Mostly, though, I want all those lady mouses. Let them in, Lady Sophia. Let them in!"

"Already, that squeaky voice of yours is getting annoying. No, Bruno, we can't fill Dayzee's house with mice."

"Cheese, then?"

"Sure, let's check the fridge. Want a ride?"

"I do, I do, I do!"

"Geez, I hope this phase doesn't last too long."

She scooped him up and placed him on her shoulder, and he clapped his bitty hands together as they left for the kitchen.

* * *

The Kid's hands dropped to his sides, and his singed body slumped quietly onto the thick mat of pine needles.

"Mare, help me get him over the fence."

"Wait a second, Dayzee. Kenzie, how do you feel?"

"I feel good! That was weird, but I must have blacked out for most of it. I like my hat!"

"Oh, boy. Alright, Mare, let's feed him to the lions."

"There are still a bunch of lions out there?"

"They probably didn't go too far. And when was the last time they had a cooked meal?"

"Yes, you're right. You were sure right about him not being around very long too."

"Yep. Easy come, easy go. Dinner time."

The three of them managed to push the still-smoking body over the fence, and seconds after hitting the sidewalk, three mountain lions pounced on it. Together, they began dragging it down the sidewalk and out of sight.

"Seriously, Mare. Where else?"

*   *   *

"How could you eat so much? You're just a tiny little thing."

Bruno sat in the middle of a placemat on Dayzee's kitchen table. He held a chunk of cheese, nibbling in between making comments.

"Lady Sophia, I'm hungry like I still weigh six-hundred pounds."

"You will again if you keep up like that," she said with a grin.

"Hey," he said before pausing to kick a back leg blindingly fast, scratching his chin, "what's with that Cliff guy? He seemed like he was eyeing me up for his next meal."

"Cliff is a cannibal? Oh, I don't think so, Bruno."

"He was joking around about different planets and how I'd make a nice feast . . . just weird stuff like that."

"Are you sure? We better talk to Dayzee about that. Maybe he really is from somewhere else."

"Okay, okay, okay. Open the door now. Open the door."

"No, Bruno. No lady mice for you."

"Outside, then. Outside, then."

"You've had enough cheese?"

"Yeah, yeah, yeah! Outside! Lady mouses!"

*   *   *

"I had plans for him," said Dayzee. "We were about to have our own private little rodeo."

"Aw, you're itchy, too, aren't you, Dayzee?"

"All the time, Mare. Alright, Kenzie, there's the jacket from that guy at the Prism, hanging there on that branch."

"I really don't get to wear a shirt?"

Dayzee turned to Marilyn with a grin and said, "She's such a sweet kid."

"And you're going to both watch me change?"

"Yes, we sure are," said Marilyn. "Why should Sissy have all the fun?"

"Mare's right. Look, if it'll make you more comfortable, I'll take my shirt off too."

"Me too!" said Marilyn, and they both began to strip.

"Things are different around this house, aren't they? Not just up in that attic?"

"Oh, Kenzie, how much time do we have?"

Dayzee had pulled her blouse open all the way, and Marilyn had dropped her straps down over her shoulders. They stood waiting and smiling with fully exposed breasts.

"Well, that sure is a sight," said Kenzie. "Okay, off with the jacket."

She tossed the over-sized jacket into the shrubs and stood topless too. When she reached for the smaller jacket, Dayzee grabbed her wrist.

"Maybe not so fast with the jacket? Tell you what: you lose that skirt, and Mare and I will lose some more clothes too."

Kenzie turned to look at the street through the fence and said, "I'd love to. But what will people think?"

Dayzee scoffed and grinned at Marilyn.

"She really is sweet. She'll catch on."

To Kenzie, she said, "They've seen so much through the fence that they don't even look anymore. Alright, you obviously need some help getting out of that skirt."

Kenzie grinned and put her arms out to each side.

"Mare, let's help her with—"

"Dayzee, is that you behind the bushes?"

"Oh, Cliff! Yeah, we were just checking on The Kid."

"How is he?"

Dayzee fought a laugh and said, "He left. He was feeling like a take-out dinner."

"He was even hotter than we first thought," Marilyn said with a laugh. "He was smoking hot."

"Mare, that's funny."

Cliff parted the branches and saw all three standing mostly naked from the waist up, Dayzee and Marilyn holding the top of Kenzie's skirt.

"My, oh my. I don't know what's going on back here, but I love it. I just love it!"

"Oh, Cliff, we were just going to . . . um, we thought we'd—"

"Pine needles," said Marilyn. "We were chasing after The Kid, and we all got these itchy needles all over us."

"We sure are itchy," said Dayzee.

"I think we finally got them all picked out of our clothes."

"Maybe you should all check again," he said with a big grin, looking from pair to pair.

"Don't we have some cars showing up soon?"

"Huh?"

He looked up at Dayzee's eyes.

"Oh yeah, they'll be here any second. I got the boys setting up along the driveway."

"I hope we have time to change," Dayzee said as she slipped back on her blouse.

"I'm waiting for Kenzie to change," Marilyn said with a big smile.

"That's coming, Mare. I think you're right about that."

"One-eighty? Why did I say that?"

With Dayzee nudging Cliff along, back through the wall of shrubs, all three fully-clothed girls followed. They began the walk back to the mansion's back door.

"That's a shame about that driver of yours," said Cliff. "Good help is hard to find. Maybe he'll come back soon."

"Oh, that reminds me: I need to hire another yard crew."

"What happened to the last one?"

"I, um, I guess you could say I fired them."

"Ha!" said Marilyn. "She said 'fire!'"

Cliff glanced at Marilyn, who only shook her head and grinned back at him.

When they'd gotten close to the door, Cliff said, "My God, what's with the rats?"

"Uh-oh," said Marilyn. "Dayzee, you don't think—"

"I'm sure it's fine, Mare. Cliff, this always happens when we burn through the yard help. All kinds of things start to—"

"'Burn through,'" Marilyn whispered while giggling softly.

"Anyway, we'll get that cleaned up soon," she said before pounding on the door.

They all heard Sophia yell, "Don't come in here!"

Chapter 8 – Four Varieties of Danger

Through the back door, Dayzee said, "What's wrong now?"

"Oh, we're going to need a minute, alright, Dayzee?"

"Sure, Fia. Is everything, um, good with Bruno?"

"There is one small problem. A very small problem. Just hang on a second."

Sophia dropped the napkin that was hiding Bruno the mouse after Dayzee quit knocking.

"What the heck are we going to do with you?"

"Out the front door! Lady mice!"

"No, Bruno, we'll just have more mice running around here, all looking like you. Why don't you just hide somewhere until I can chase Dayzee and the rest of them back out of the house?"

"Oh, okay, Lady Sophia. First, I want to stuff my cheeks with cheese."

"Not surprised. I probably would too."

She held a chunk near him, and he nibbled away at it until his cheeks had stretched into two small balloons.

"You look ridiculous."

"Only because you're not a lady mouse."

She scoffed, scooped him up in one hand, and set him on the floor.

"Go burrow in somewhere . . . whatever mice do."

"Okay," he squeaked, "just don't set any traps!"

He looked at the ceiling, chattered for a second, then ran and wiggled his body bloated with cheese under a closet door, his twitching tail the last part to disappear.

*   *   *

Sophia opened the door and said, "So glad you didn't just walk in."

"There were too many mice," said Dayzee. "They were all—"

"Lady mice. I know."

"How would you know that, Fia?"

"Um . . . probably the lipstick?"

Dayzee only squinted and stared at her until Cliff spoke up.

"I have no clue what's going on around this mansion of yours, Dayzee, but I like it. We're going to need cameras rolling 24/7. I don't want to miss a second of it!"

"How did you scare them all away?" said Sophia.

"I didn't. They ran around the house somewhere. Maybe to another door?"

"Good. Those horny little—"

"They're horny, Sophia?" said Cliff. "Horny lady mice?"

"Well, they must be," said Marilyn. "Look how big their families are. That's all Sissy meant."

"Yeah, Sis. That's right. Anyway, come on in, everyone."

Dayzee walked far enough through the kitchen to view the foyer, and she pointed at the mangled trim around the entryway to the living room.

"Oh God, we still have to get that fixed. I hired a carpenter, but he never finished."

"Slacker," Sophia said with a smirk.

"At least he took a stab at it," Marilyn said with a giggle.

"Good one, Sis. Two stabs."

After Dayzee had rejoined the group, Cliff looked around and said, "What happened to that big beefy guy? Bruno, was it?"

Behind his back, Sophia whispered to her sister, "Beefy?"

When he turned to see what she was doing, she said, "Oh, he, um, he kind of scurried off somewhere. He'll be back, though."

Cliff walked to the table and said, "Even this will make the show interesting. Who leaves a block of cheese out with all kinds of tiny bite marks in it? Really, who does that?"

"Reality stars from Kildare?" Marilyn said with a pleasant smile.

Cliff pointed at her and said, "Exactly. Now, all four of you should do whatever you need to get ready for your first shoot."

He looked at his watch and said, "Those cars should be here in about fifteen minutes. They'll be on the driveway, and all of you, the brightest, most radiant reality stars in the world, will be on-set!"

* * *

Bruno sat up in the dark closet space and twisted his head from side to side, sniffing. He stooped down to peek under the door and fought to not squeal when he saw high heels, belonging to whom, he didn't know, walking toward him.

A quick snap of his head to search for a hiding spot left him frozen in place at the mysterious sight. Far back in one corner, across the clean wood floor, a tiny light showed itself, visible only from his level.

He sat up again and sniffed all around. That didn't help, so he plopped down, reminded himself to feed off of the cheese in his cheeks, and followed an erratic, random path toward the curious light.

Spying into the narrow opening, he saw the usual lumber and drywall of the wall construction, and on the other side, a similar slit—with a dim light beyond.

At the sound of heels clicking close by, he tucked his ears back, poked his head through the opening, and began squeezing his body through.

Shouldn't have eaten so much cheese! he told himself.

He jabbed his head through to the wall's far side and saw a poorly-lit circular room. A glance up showed him a dusty skylight far above in the roof covering the third floor.

In the center of the room, he saw a rusty railing built in a circle and the beginning of a winding staircase made of old stones coated with moss.

The second wall opening was tight, and he wiggled and wedged until he'd pried his body through. He sat up for a moment to groom, rubbing his paws over his deflated cheeks over and over.

Then, with an excited squeak, he scurried for the stairs.

*　*　*

"This closet is gigantic!" Kenzie said with a big smile. "Look at all the clothes!"

"See that door?" Dayzee said while pointing toward the back of the large room lined with shelves, cabinets, and racks.

"No, don't tell me."

"Yep, even the closet has a closet."

"What's in that one?" said Marilyn. "Stuff you don't wear anymore?"

"No, that's for costumes I wore in films and series and things."

"I thought you kept those up in the attic?" said Sophia. "Remember when we dressed up Ko—"

"As koalas for that zoo film?" said Marilyn.

"Yep, that's right, Sis. Koalas. We never did find the right costumes, though. Dayzee, you have more than that?"

"Girls, there's just too many for the attic. How about if we save the costumes for some other time, though? We just need basic stuff for when our cars show up. Fia, what's wrong?"

Sophia was glaring from face to face, and in a slow, controlled voice, she said, "Who cares about clothes? I just want to rip mine off already. Yours, too, Dayzee. Sorry, Sis—you too. Kenzie, you are so going to be first. I'm going to—"

"Stop, Fia!" said Dayzee. "I told you not to take another fountain. It was way too soon!"

"Sissy's right, though, Dayzee," said Marilyn. "I can barely concentrate. Yes, I want us all to get naked up here in your humongous closet, but mostly, I can't stop thinking about . . . you know . . . what's his name."

"No, I don't know," Kenzie said before coughing once and standing up straight and tall. "But for some reason, I've become keenly aware that we are all subject to unrelenting dangers of increasing magnitude."

She shook her head and blinked a few times.

"Yes, that's right!" said Marilyn. "Keep thinking about how that blind cowboy driver guy got possessed. Oh, and there's still a headless body walking around out there somewhere. Lots of danger!"

"That's not all," said Sophia. "I was talking with Bruno, before he turned into a mouse, and he—"

"He what?" said Dayzee.

"He's a mouse, he ate a lot of cheese, and he's hiding in the closet by your kitchen. That's not the point. The thing is that—"

"No, I think that's a pretty damn important point," said Dayzee. "That's who was eating the cheese?"

"God, Dayzee, just take your clothes off already!" said Sophia. "We can talk and undress at the same time, for God's sake!"

Marilyn grinned while pulling her straps off of her shoulders, and she shimmied out of her dress to stand there in panties and heels.

"You too, Mare? Girls, it was just too soon to—Fia, let me go! Fine, I can undress myself."

"God, I wish Bruno wasn't a mouse," said Marilyn. "I'd give that big guy a ride."

"Oh, that's another thing," said Sophia while unbuttoning her blouse. "It sounds like Cliff is a bit of a cannibal. He was talking about Bruno being like a large part of a cow."

She turned to look at Kenzie, who'd slipped the headless guy's jacket back off of her shoulders, and said, "But damn, you sure look good. You really do work out."

"I knew it, Sissy. Dayzee and I won't tell."

Kenzie grinned and said, "Neither will I, Fifi. Why are you standing so far away?"

"Why indeed?"

She took a step closer but stopped when Kenzie extended a palm in her direction.

"Stop. There are four varieties of danger simultaneously threatening our bodily integrity and on-set appearances."

Marilyn clapped her hands and let out a small giggle.

"One: there is at least one headless intruder on the grounds that is, or likely soon will be, possessed by another assassin that accompanied Bruno through the portal at the Prism."

Kenzie's thighs began to swell with new muscle.

"Oh, here we go," said Dayzee with a grin. "This should be fun."

"Two: the dead, incinerated Colombian cowboy neglected to close the gate. There could be numerous hungry Earth felines lurking behind the shrubs, waiting to pounce."

"Oops. Didn't think of that one," Dayzee said while nodding.

Kenzie's shoulders and arms puffed up, while her breasts began changing to packed muscle."

"Yay!"

"I'm with you on this one!" said Dayzee.

"Eh," said Sophia, "I miss those. They were perfect."

"Three: Bruno is progressively losing more of himself to whatever animal he becomes. Note the cheese cravings."

"Well, what's so bad about that?"

Kenzie's voice became deeper, and a facial stubble developed.

"His next form might be a savage, sex-crazed, womanizing, bipedal animal only distantly recognizable as humanoid."

"Keep talking dirty!" said Marilyn.

"Oh, Mare . . ."

"Try to tell me you won't want some of that, Dayzee!"

Sophia took another step, and the strong hand that used to be Kenzie's rested on her forehead.

"You said four," Sophia said with a smile. "What else?"

Marilyn giggled and said to Dayzee, "You know what's next, Dayzee. So much danger!"

"Four: the preponderance of circumstantial evidence suggests that Sutcliffe Gutsquid is, in fact, harboring the aforementioned parasitic life form from a remote asteroid."

Kozy stood before them in all of his danger-induced glory, and the other three all stared down at his horizontal and most prominent feature.

"Oh, I'm not waiting this time," said Marilyn.

"No one's asking you to, Mare. Get while the gettin' is good!"

"I kind of miss Kenzie but not all that much," said Sophia. "I'm calling seconds."

"Kenzie will be back eventually," said Dayzee. "I guess I'm batting third."

"Even if Kenzie's back?"

"Oh yeah, Fia. Either way!"

*　　*　　*

Down the steep staircase Bruno hopped, turning in so many circles that he lost count. When at last he'd jumped to the dusty floor, he took another look straight up, seeing the skylight so far away it could have been a small square star.

Stone walls merged with the shadows, forming a sullen ring around the tiny mouse as he sniffed and looked in every direction. He stopped when he saw an ancient wooden door, rounded at the top, and built of weathered vertical planks drawn together by thick metal straps bolted across them.

He squealed with delight when he noticed a trace of light through a crack where a splinter in one of the boards had long ago fallen away. A quick gallop on all four paws brought him to where he could peek through.

The mouse blinked over and over while feeling like he was staring at a dark circle with a pinpoint of light in the very middle. After his eyes had adjusted, he realized that he was gazing along a dark tunnel that offered some sort of curious lit-up goings-on at its end.

He couldn't resist. He wiggled his chubby body into the narrow, ragged slit, risking a sliver and thinking that if he'd known the adventures that had awaited him, he might not have been so ravenous with the cheese. Or maybe he still would have.

After clawing with his front paws repeatedly, scraping up old dust, trying to drag the rest of his mouse body through, he finally got free, squeaked with glee, and raced down the center of a tunnel farther beneath Dayzee's yard than he could guess.

* * *

"Oh, Mare, you've been waiting a long time for a seat like that!"

"You're not kidding, Dayzee. Kozy is amazing—way better than the average earthman."

"I am especially happy to have returned, Marilyn. Please, have a seat."

"Now, that's funny," said Dayzee. "Such a gentleman."

Kozy stared up with a silly grin from on his back on the soft carpeting of Dayzee's closet while Marilyn knelt with a knee on each side of his waist.

She smiled once at her sister before looking down and running her fingertips along every defined muscle of Kozy's abdomen.

"Oh, that's a sight, Sis."

"Mm-hmm, Sissy."

She held his lean waist with both hands and began shifting around, and Dayzee said, "It's good that no one ever told him it's impolite to point, huh?"

"I am ready to protect you all," said Kozy.

"We all need some of that protecting," said Sophia.

Marilyn hummed softly and took her time, still finding the exact position she'd wanted.

"Oh, Kozy, there we go. I feel so much safer now."

"Huh. I thought Sis would tear into Kozy if he ever came back."

"I think she will, Fia. She's just getting warmed up."

"Mm . . . she's right, Sissy. While you're waiting, why don't you keep me company?" Marilyn said while twisting her tight white dress higher up around her waist and beginning a steady bounce. "Come play with my hair."

"I do like sitting behind you, Sis. How about if I—"

"Hey, something's wrong," said Marilyn. "No! This isn't fair!"

Kozy frowned and said, "It seems that I am . . . I must . . ."

Marilyn rested at the bottom, staring at the changing features and configuration of Kozy beneath her. Dayzee and Sophia stood wide-eyed and shaking their heads as Kozy shifted and morphed back to being Kenzie.

"Marilyn, what's going on? I'm not complaining, but how did I get here?"

"Well, we were just, um, getting dressed, and—"

"And you seemed to get really cold or something," said Sophia. "You started shaking uncontrollably, and Sis, well, she just, she—"

"She had to hold you down so you didn't hurt yourself. That's all," said Dayzee. "But you seem all better now. Mare, I think you can let her up."

"Oh, Dayzee, why would I ever want to—"

"Mare, maybe she'll, I don't know, get cold again later? Maybe?"

"Come on, Sis. Let her up."

"You're just jealous because Kenzie is Kenzie again, Sissy."

"What? No, that's not—"

"What do you mean, I'm Kenzie 'again?'" said Kenzie. "Who did you all think I was?"

Marilyn stood up, and Dayzee said, "Nobody. She's talking nonsense. Hey, Kenzie,"—she looked down at her, still lying naked on the carpet— "pick a number between one and ten."

"Why would I—"

"Just humor her," Sophia said, shaking her head with a grin.

"Seven?"

Marilyn sighed deeply and said, "We might as well get dressed. We're all on-set in a couple of minutes."

"Mare's right. Let's plan to all get naked soon—maybe in the pool next time with Bruno."

"He's a mouse," said Sophia, frowning and shrugging.

"Sure, Fia, but maybe later, he'll be a vicious, sex-starved, womanizing human-ish beast. Like Kozy said."

"Oh, come on already," said Kenzie. "Still with that Kozy thing?"

*   *   *

Bruno had reached the end of the tunnel, and he glanced up for only a second to see a single light bulb hanging on the end of a wire that vanished in the darkness above it.

He looked all around, and when something about one shadowy corner of the space struck him as unusual and deserving a longer study, he jumped straight up and squealed with a tiny paw over his mouth when three young men appeared.

Each wore black jeans tucked into black boots but no shirts. Their muscular arms were highlighted by thick black bands around their wrists and biceps. Each had a jet-black braid rooted on the right side of his head and lying down across his chest. They stood still and stared straight back down the tunnel, never looking down at the mouse in the dust and shadows.

"Hey, who are you guys?" he squeaked.

All three looked down. At the same time, and in unison, they all said, "You are a mouse."

"No, wait. I'm not just a mouse. I'm a—"

All three said, "A talking mouse," and they again looked above him.

"No, listen, you guys. I'm not really a mouse. You just came through a portal, didn't you?"

They all looked down at him again, and when all three again said, "You are a mouse that can—"

"Okay, that's about enough of that. God, you guys got annoying in record time."

They paused and took turns looking at each other before they again stared at the rodent.

Only one spoke, saying, "We are here through the old portal to locate, isolate, and eradicate the renegade Gut Squid."

Bruno made a tiny fist and squeaked, "I *knew* there was something wrong with that guy!" He looked up and said, "Did the Guild send you?"

The man in the middle said, "What is a guild?"

The stranger's nose twitched, and he frowned.

"You smell like cheese."

"I certainly do! Soon, I'll smell like lady mouses!"

Bruno looked up into the darkness and chattered, his tiny fingers tapping on his swollen belly.

Chapter 9 – Of All the Weird Shit

Dayzee pulled in the front door, and Sophia and Marilyn nudged Kenzie out onto the porch. She smiled for the camera, pausing just long enough to display her uniform pants, a jacket with no shirt, and short black velvet boots. Her long brown hair fell softly past her shoulders from beneath her hat, its front badge shining in the Beverly Hills sunlight.

"Kenzie," said Cliff, "the new cars will be here soon. Do you like going fast?"

"Of course, I do! I'm going to make that motor scream!"

She looked toward the driveway, began a brisk walk, and made room on the porch for Sophia.

Standing near the steps in her short black skirt and bright red blouse, unbuttoned low, Sophia looked into the camera with her big blue eyes.

"Sophia, you look ready for just about anything."

"Usually am," she said with a smirk.

"How about a new car for a start?"

"That'll have to do for now, Cliff," she said with a grin.

Her red lips only teased a brief smile before she brushed back her long, silky black hair, looked off-camera, and made sure her heels clicked on the two stone steps and walkway.

Marilyn exited next, her white dress shorter than usual and her white heels higher. Her wavy blond hair lay all over her shoulders, and she smiled, waved, and blew a kiss toward the lens.

"My, oh my, it really is Marilyn. How happy are you to get a new car for the show?"

"A lady never tells. Oh, I could give you a hint, though."

With a short giggle, she spun around quickly, her dress spinning about her high enough to show that she wore white beneath it, and began a slow strut toward the driveway.

"Dayzee Dazzle, don't keep us waiting any longer. We can't stand it!"

Dayzee stepped out onto the porch, wearing her own short black skirt, black fishnets, and short black boots with spike heels. Her white blouse was tight and mostly opened, and she'd mixed thin blue ribbons in with her wild, thick blond hair. She stood with her hands on her hips, gazing toward the camera. She looked each way, then back at the camera, and held her arms out to each side.

"Where else but Beverly Hills?"

"Oh, I don't know," said Cliff. "Maybe Kildare?"

"Starting right now, Kildare *is* in the Hills!"

She dropped her arms, smiled for the camera, and walked off to join the others.

"Okay, cut it," said Cliff.

"Ladies, that was magnificent. Things will only heat up from here!"

*   *   *

"What do you know of the Gut Squid?" all three said as one.

Bruno the mouse stopped his chattering laughter and looked at each of them for a second.

"Hey, here's an idea: pick a spokesperson, alright? You're already making me crazy. Maybe because my brain is so tiny now?"

"Very well," said the man in the middle. "I will orate for all."

"Well, that sounds a bit pompous, but sure. Why not? Now, it should be easier to . . ."

"Yes?"

"To, um . . . oh, I don't feel so good."

"Earth Cheese can do that."

Bruno tried to chatter, but he only held his belly and said, "No, it's not that. It's . . . oh boy . . ."

With a shriek mixing with a laugh and several profanities, Bruno bounced back to his original, human-like stature.

"That's quite a trick," said the man in the middle.

"Getting my clothes," said Bruno. "That's the trick."

He turned to look at the tunnel that had led him to the forgotten room with an abandoned portal.

"Oh. It looked a lot bigger before."

"When you were a mouse?"

"You're kind of a smartass."

The one in the middle looked behind himself, and the other two looked too.

"Oh, come on. That's even more smartassed."

The center man said, "Locate, isolate, eradicate. That is our mission."

"Yeah, I'm with you on that. Hey, how long has that portal been here?"

"It was wormed here long before the planet's inhabitants had mastered walking upright."

"No way. It just happened that Dayzee's house was built over it?"

"Who is Dayzee?"

"Well, you'll just have to meet her. I'm not really sure how we're going to do that, though. I'll never make it through that tunnel now that—"

"You're not a mouse."

Bruno sighed and said, "Yeah. That's right, wise guy."

He looked around and noticed something that brought him a big grin.

"Hey, this isn't so bad. Look, there are rungs built into the wall. You boys can climb, can't you?"

"Yes. We can follow you."

Bruno looked down to remind himself that he was totally naked.

"Oh, I don't think so. I hardly know you guys. After you, gentlemen."

*   *   *

All four girls stood in the brilliant Southern California sunshine, occasionally glancing toward the open entrance gate and making small talk while the camera rolled. Cliff stood behind the camera operator with a big grin.

While Kenzie was saying, "What color car do you want, Marilyn?" and Marilyn was answering, "Oh, it doesn't matter. Maybe white?" Sophia was whispering in Dayzee's ear.

"Dayzee, remember that guy, Julian?"

"Vaguely. He disappeared behind the bushes, right?"

"Well, he's back," Sophia said and gestured with a tip of her head.

Dayzee looked at the mostly unbroken line of shrubs and said, "I don't see anything. Did you?"

"Yeah, he's back. Well, approximately. Oh, look now! Look!"

They both watched beyond Cliff and the camera as a large lady mountain lion walked past a gap in the landscaping with a human head in her mouth.

"Oh, you got to be kidding me!" said Dayzee. "Damn lions! Really!"

"Yep, we have another headless guy roaming around looking for head."

"That's two of them now, right?"

"Yeah, let's try to keep track."

"What are you two whispering about? Making plans about your first test rides?"

"Yeah, I'm *heading* for the exit," Sophia said with a grin.

"With the top off," Dayzee said while grinning and tracing a line across her throat.

"I think you mean 'down,' Dayzee."

She grinned at Sophia and said, "Such a sweet guy."

80

*   *   *

"That is likely the means of reentering the atmosphere," said the lead guy, holding onto the top rung with one hand and pointing at a square metal plate above him. I will—"

"No, wait. You hear that?"

They all listened to the sounds of thousands of scratches on the top surface of the plate. When they'd all quieted down, Bruno said, "Okay, now give it a push."

He turned a handle and rotated the rusty hatch up, letting sunlight inside the deep silo. After he'd climbed up and out, his two partners followed, and Bruno joined them.

"That's odd behavior for Earth mice, isn't it?"

Bruno grinned and waved at the legions of mice surrounding the four of them. Most sat up and twitched their noses, all eyes on Bruno, before they dropped to all fours and scurried in every direction.

"They dig me," said Bruno. "Well, not anymore."

"You seem pleased. You wish to attempt a copulation with one or more of them?"

"Hell, guys. No, not now."

All three of the strangers stared at him.

"Well, maybe a little. It's kind of like a hangover, still. Hey, we're in Dayzee's backyard, in the middle of some landscaping. Let's get back to the house. If you're going to capture that—"

"We do not capture. We locate, isolate, and eradicate."

"Yeah, I get it. I really do. Okay, if you're going to do all that to Squid Guts, then—"

"It is a Gut Squid."

"Will you just let me finish? Damn, you guys. Alright, let's get inside and see what's happening. We have to be slick about this. Dayzee's got some important stuff going on."

"More important than locating, isolating, and—"

"Yes! God, the three of you are—"

"It's only I that speaks."

"Whatever. You're kind of all the same. Alright, let's go."

*   *   *

"The cars are late," said Cliff, "so let's all take a break."

He pointed to the camera and said, "Benny, keep rolling, but mute it. Get a lot of shots of their legs too."

"You don't have to tell me, Boss. I will."

"Ladies, I'm heading in for—"

"He said 'heading,'" Sophia said while grinning and shaking her head.

"Yeah, Sophia, that's right. I need a drink. Hang tight, and—"

"You would sure need a head to do that," Dayzee said with a quick laugh.

Cliff stared at her a second, squinting, then said, "Yeah, well, those cars will be here soon."

He turned and left for the mansion, and the filming rolled on.

"What's all this talk about heads?" said Marilyn. "Oh, it's that one that the cooked Colombian bowled, right?"

"Cooked Colombian. Good one, Sis."

"Yeah," said Dayzee, "that one is still roaming around, but now—"

"How is it roaming?" said Sophia. "God, can't severed heads just sit still until one of those cats can gobble it up?"

"It was just a figure of speech, Fia. Anyway, Mare, yes, that head is still somewhere, but now there's another one too. Remember that crew guy, Julian?"

"Uh-oh. He's dead, isn't he?"

"Well, Sis, when an earthman loses his head, that usually means—"

"That he'll be dancing around looking for head, Sissy?"

Marilyn waited with a big smile.

"Yeah, Sis. That's exactly right," Sophia said and smiled back at her sister.

"Only if the assassin makes him do the jitterbug."

"That's funny, Dayzee," Marilyn said with a giggle.

"Are things ever normal around here?" said Kenzie.

"Nope. Never," said Marilyn. "There's always so much danger. It really never ends."

"Sis is right. That much danger can change a person too."

"Good one, Sissy."

"I never know what you two are talking about."

"I do," said Dayzee. "And they're not wrong."

*　　*　　*

"Good, it's open. I won't have to break it down."

Bruno swung in the back door to Dayzee's mansion, and they all filed in. The three visitors stood in a line and watched him get dressed.

"You would make a substantial meal for the Gut Squid. We're surprised it has not infested you."

"I think it was giving that some thought. It said I looked like a big piece of beef."

"It thinks everything looks like beef."

"That's funny because I'm a vegan."

"As are we."

"So, that's why they hired you for this kind of work?"

"We were created for this. Tree Squids and other plant Squids are of no concern. Only this carnivorous type. We must resume our hunt. Your help is no longer needed."

He tried to lead his two teammates past Bruno, but he put out a meaty paw and stopped him.

"No, you can't just rush out there and take him. Tell you what: let's go upstairs and see from a window what's going on out there. When the time is right, I'll give you the go-ahead. Sound good?"

"Very well. That will help us isolate. Then, we will—"

"Ugh, I can't take much more of you guys. Alright, up the steps."

A fully-clothed Bruno led the way, and after they'd reached the second floor, he turned to the left, into the long hallway, and the three agents followed.

Bruno stopped at the first door on the left and said, "Alright, this should be—"

The leader brushed past him and into the room. He stopped three steps in with his back to the door. The other two continued down the hall, where another did the same in the next room.

Bruno stood and scratched his head with a frown and watched the third hike to the next room and walk in. There was a short pause, and all three doors closed at the same time.

"What the hell?"

He heard the mansion's front door open, and from the top of the stairs, peeking around the corner, he saw Cliff walk through the foyer, on the way to the bar.

At the sounds of three doors opening, he snapped his head around to see all three squid hunters on the march, coming toward him.

"No. Nope. Not yet. Just go—"

The leader had ignored him and tried to walk past, but Bruno snared him with one brawny arm. And when another tried to pass on the other side, a shove from his thick paw sent him stumbling backward. He flung the leader back down the hall too.

"Listen, you guys. I'm all for whatever kind of eliminating you're—"

"Eradicating."

"God. Yeah, that. Just wait, alright? They're kind of in the middle of something with squid boy, and—"

"It is a—"

"I'm about to do some eradicating! Just get back to your windows. I'll let you know when the time is right. Now, go!"

They all walked away, entered their rooms, and closed their doors simultaneously.

"Of all the weird shit . . ."

*　　*　　*

"Girls, let's try to stay on top of things. Now, we know of two—"

"Sis sure was on top of things up in that closet, Dayzee."

84

"Yeah, Fia, she sure was. Alright, there seem to be only two—"

"Too bad we didn't have more time, huh, Fifi?"

"She called you Fifi, Sissy. Hey, the cars are late, so why don't we all run up there and—"

"Girls! You too, Kenzie. We're in the middle of our first shoot, there are headless guys walking—"

"Dancing," Marilyn said with a giggle.

"Fine, they're dancing around, and there are mountain lions in the bushes, and—"

"And the heads are in bushes too," Sophia said with a smirk.

"Oh, you two. And besides that, we think there's something crazy going on with Cliff. Did I miss anything?"

"Yeah," Kenzie said as she pointed toward the mansion. "Bruno isn't a mouse anymore."

They all turned to watch him striding across the lawn toward where they stood on the driveway.

"Hey, cheese boy," said Sophia.

"That's funny, Lady Sophia. I really did like that cheese."

"Did you ever find all those lady mice you wanted so bad?"

"Not until after I'd changed back."

"That's a shame," said Marilyn. "What a cheesy orgy you would have had."

"Funny, Sis. I heard you were going to be a merciless, oversexed, womanizing, monster animal next. Put me on that list, alright, big guy?"

"I'm going to be a what?"

"She's just being silly," said Dayzee. "But if you could somehow choose, then that's what we all want."

"I can't choose. At least, I don't think so. Maybe I should ask them."

He hooked a thumb over his shoulder, and Dayzee, Sophia, Marilyn, and Kenzie all stood with slack jaws as they stared at the three squid hunters, each with a bare chest and a black braid, gazing out of his own second-floor window.

Chapter 10 – From the Inside

"Who the hell are they?" Dayzee said as she pointed at the windows.

The three men, each framed by a window, didn't move.

"Where do I begin?" said Bruno.

"The new guys aren't going anywhere," said Sophia. "How about the beginning?"

"Alright. When I came through the portal at the Prism, I was only about this tall."

He held a hand near his knees.

"I took a beer from some guy, and he—"

"No, no, no. Jump ahead. We don't have all day."

"Sure, Dayzee."

He scratched his chin and looked at the light pole in the yard.

"I really did want all those lady lions. Did you see how they were flicking their tails around for me? Oh, man, if I wasn't afraid they'd tear me apart, I was about to—"

"Bruno," Sophia said with a shaking head and a big grin. "How about starting when you scurried your little mouse ass into that closet?"

"That's funny, Sissy. I can almost imagine how that—"

"Mare, don't you want to know who those guys are?"

Marilyn look down and kicked at the driveway with one white high-heeled shoe.

"Yes, Dayzee." She looked up. "Bruno, tell us about your mouse ass."

She giggled, and her sister elbowed her.

"You two are so cute," said Kenzie. "We need to get back to that closet and pick up where we left off when—"

"Oh, it's all three of you! Mare, Fia, don't ever teach her about the fountain of youth, alright?"

"Would that even work with her?"

"Let's worry about that later. Bruno. The closet."

"Alright, Dayzee. So, I wiggled my mouse ass—"

"Sorry, Bruno," Marilyn said while still giggling. "It's just really funny."

"Yes, Miss Marilyn. It kind of was."

"I mean, you're so big. How could you shrink down to be just a teeny little mouse?"

"It wasn't the science, so it had to be the sorcery. It really is nasty stuff."

"So, you could probably get a lot bigger too?"

"Yes, Lady Sophia, I imagine so. Anyway, I made it through the closet's back wall, where I found this old stairway, and I hopped all the way to the bottom."

"Wait," said Dayzee. "There's some kind of secret room in that mansion? With another set of stairs?"

"Yeah, Dayzee."

"I've been telling people there were more stairways in that big house."

"That's three that I've seen so far," said Sophia.

"Weren't we going to draw a map?" said Marilyn.

"Could there be a fourth floor?" said Kenzie. "An attic above the attic? There could be attics stacked who knows how high! I mean, if there are—"

"Stop! All of you! Bruno, continue."

"Okay. It was more than just another stairway. I got to the bottom, and I found a big door."

"Well, when you're a mouse," Sophia said with an eye roll, "what isn't big?"

"You're exactly right, Lady Sophia. But I think it probably was big. Anyway, I clawed and scraped to drag my mouse ass—"

"Sorry again, Bruno," Marilyn said between giggles.

"It's okay, Miss Marilyn. I got past that door, and there was a tunnel."

"Let me guess," Sophia said with her red lips forming a grin. "A *big* tunnel."

"That's funny, Lady Sophia. Well, it did look big because I was just a mouse, but it really wasn't all that big. I scampered down the tunnel and came to another room."

"A big room!" Marilyn said with a beaming smile and bright blue eyes.

"Yeah, but that's not the weirdest thing."

He turned to look into Dayzee's big, staring, steel blue eyes.

"Dayzee, there's a portal down there. That's where those weirdos came from."

"Get out of here!" She pushed against his chest with both hands but managed only to tip herself backwards. "There's another portal? And it's under my house?"

"Would I make that up?"

"I don't know. Would you?"

Bruno pointed to the second story of her mansion, smiled a big smile, and said, "Am I making them up?"

Dayzee swiveled her head to look at the three strangers motionless in her upstairs windows.

"Who are they? Why are they here?"

"That's funny—I never even thought to ask them their names. I doubt they even have any. But I do know why they're here."

He grinned and waited.

"Well, come on. Tell us."

"Alright. Do you remember when Kozy said—"

"Stop. Whoa, whoa, whoa. Just stop," said Kenzie. "Someone needs to tell me right now who the hell Kozy is. No more bullshit."

"Oh, Kenzie," said Dayzee, "there's really no one that—"

"Look, as much as I like it, I will never go shirtless and wear a hat again. I'm serious."

She winked at Sophia, then glared at Dayzee, who blew out a deep breath and said, "Fine. You are."

She never blinked, but she turned to Sophia, who said, "With a one-eighty kind of twist."

Still staring, she looked at Marilyn, who clapped her hands and said, "When there's lots and lots and lots of danger!"

"I don't understand."

"Well, we barely understand it either. Why don't we plan to have a stiff drink—"

"She said 'stiff!'" Marilyn said with more clapping. "Danger!"

"—back at the Prism, and even though it's hard—"

"Ha!" said Marilyn.

"—to understand, we'll try to explain. Right now, though, we need to hear why those three guys came through the portal. Bruno?"

He turned to Sophia and said, "Remember when I was a mouse, and I told you about Cliff?"

"Yep. He said you were beefy or something."

"Yeah, like a big meal."

"You are one hell of a hunk," Dayzee said as she eyed him up and down. "Cliff isn't blind like that cowboy."

"No, I mean like a real meal. Like digestion. Kozy told us—"

He stopped and pointed at Kenzie, silencing her before she could speak, and she froze with her mouth open.

"—that there was some kind of parasite from some comet or something, and the name Gutsquid reminded him of it. You remember that?"

"Yeah, but so what?"

"These guys said they're here to hunt down something called a Gut Squid."

"Cliff is really a squid?"

"No, he's not a squid, but there's one inside him. And not just any squid, Dayzee. A Gut Squid."

"And just like that, 'Kildare in the Hills' is shot to hell," Sophia said with a scoff.

"Wait a minute, Fia. Maybe not. Why don't we—"

"No more slipping us things all loaded up," Marilyn said with a sigh.

"Like gift cards, Sis?"

"Sure, Sissy. Those too."

"Mare, hang on. Let's talk to these guys and see what's what. Maybe Cliff isn't really—"

"I'm not what, Dayzee?" Cliff said as he handed her a drink. "Sorry, girls, I didn't see a tray to bring out more drinks, and I only have two hands."

"And God knows how many tentacles," Sophia whispered to her sister, who couldn't contain her giggling.

"What's that, Sophia?"

"Maybe flippers, Sissy," Marilyn whispered.

"What, Marilyn?"

"Oh, nothing," said Dayzee. "They'll mix their own. We were heading inside anyway since the cars are late."

Cliff looked at his watch and said, "Well, that's unfortunate. I'll give them a few more minutes then make a call."

"Maybe the delivery guy ate too much and is feeling all bloated," Marilyn said and giggled.

"Good one, Sis."

Cliff smiled and looked from one twin to the other and said, "I love that off-the-wall, spontaneous dialog. This show is going to be such a big hit. The fans are going to just eat it up!"

"Yeah. From the inside," Dayzee said while staring at him with her head tilted.

After they'd started walking toward the front door, she gave a glance up and saw that the three motionless men had moved out of sight.

"This should be fun," she muttered to herself.

*   *   *

Cliff led the way inside, and he stopped at the sight of the three men in black jeans and boots, black braids bouncing on bare, muscular chests, coming down the stairs. They marched in perfect time in a single line, and after they'd reached the bottom, they spread out and hooked their arms together.

"What the—"

"They're weirdos, Dayzee. I told you."

"They're hot," said Sophia. "Kind of like a circus act, though."

"Which room has the trapeze, Dayzee?"

"We'll find it later, Mare."

"We better. I like their hair."

"I do too, Sis," said Sophia. "They sure aren't plain, though, and they're definitely unforgettable."

"That's close enough, Sissy. Good one."

In unison, they took a step toward Cliff, and Bruno hurried to block their path.

"Who are these guys?" said Cliff.

"Oh, them. They, um, they're—"

"They're sure not the new lawn guys," Sophia said with grin, taking turns studying each of them. "They're much too fine for that."

"Sissy is right," Marilyn said as she looked from one to another. "And right from the beginning, they don't have any shirts. That's a plus."

"Yeah," said Cliff, "but who are they? Why are they looking at me like that?"

"Oh, I know," said Kenzie.

She stepped forward to stand with Bruno.

"They're just worried you're going to be mad because they want to be our new drivers. Isn't that right, boys?"

Sophia turned to her sister with a frown, and Marilyn shrugged and shook her head. Dayzee looked at the ceiling and let out a single laugh, then a deep sigh.

The three odd men stared at Kenzie, but they didn't respond.

"Funny guys," said Sophia.

"Well, tell us your names," Kenzie said. "If you're going to be driving us around, we at least have to know your names. You,"—she pointed to the man on the left—"what's your name?"

He glanced to the traveler next to him, then back at Kenzie, and said, "Abbott?"

"Good. And you?"

The man on the right said, "Hardy?"

"Even better. Last one."

She pointed at the man in the middle.

"I guess I'm Moe."

Bruno took a step closer, stood right in front of Moe, and said softly, "You got the Universal Superfluous Cultural Phenomena data dump?"

"Yes, it was mandatory. Regardless, we have work to do."

"Yeah," said Dayzee, "and you will. But the cars aren't here yet, so why don't we all go have a drink?"

The three looked up at Bruno, who towered over them, and he whispered, "An Earth mixture that makes them dumber and leads to trouble."

"The man in the middle, Moe, said, "How will we efficiently locate, and—"

"Isolate, and—" said Abbott.

"Eradicate?" said Hardy.

"Guys, you've already located. Isolating can happen soon—be patient. Then, you can eradicate."

"What on Earth are you all talking about?" said Cliff.

Bruno glanced over his shoulder and said, "That's pretty funny."

He turned back to Abbott, Moe, and Hardy.

"Boys, if anyone ever needed a drink, it's you three."

Moe shook his arms free from Abbott and Hardy and said, "Spread out."

Each took a step to the side.

"Let me guess," said Dayzee. "You're going to start slapping them around too? Maybe clunk their heads together?"

"That wouldn't help us complete our mission."

"This is just silly," said Marilyn. "Come on, Sissy, let's get a drink."

She took her sister's hand and led her toward the bar, Dayzee took the hands of Kenzie and Cliff and followed, and Bruno shrugged at Moe and his partners.

"Okay, boys. Booze first, squid hunting later."

"They are contaminated," said Abbott.

"Huh?" said Bruno.

"Larvae have been deposited," said Hardy.

Bruno shook his head and stared at Moe, who said, "The blonde and brunette have become receptacles for the Gut Squid's offspring."

"Uh-oh. That doesn't sound good."

"It can be remedied," said Moe. "We are trained and have the equipment necessary—"

"And large enough," said Abbott,

"And long enough," said Hardy.

"—to inoculate them as needed," said Moe.

"How? Like, with big needles or something?"

Moe smiled, and his cohorts grinned and nodded.

"Oh, I know that look. Yeah, I don't think they'll mind, especially after a few drinks."

Chapter 11 – Not from Earth

"Okay," said Marilyn, holding her drink close to her lips and ready for another sip, "that's one with a head, and—"

"Which one is that, Sis?"

"Well, that cowboy guy, Sissy. Remember him? He's still around somewhere."

Cliff set his drink down on the bar, looked away from the twins to his left, and said to Dayzee to his right, "Honestly, I have no idea where these conversations come from. But Dayzee, I love it. I absolutely love it!"

"Oh, I think maybe it's just this house, Cliff. It kind of makes strange things happen, I think."

She looked past him as Marilyn continued.

"And then, there are two without . . . you know, and they're dancing around somewhere."

"This is good," said Sophia. "We really should try to keep up with the count."

"Oh, wait," said Kenzie. "Don't forget about the one from the hearse. The one that we got for free."

"Good one, Kenzie," said Dayzee. "Yes, he was a freebie to get us started. Kind of like a free sample."

Cliff turned to study Dayzee for a second. She only shrugged and grinned, then Sophia spoke, and he turned back around.

"So . . . that's approximately four, then."

"Yes, approximately, Sissy. It's impossible to keep an exact count."

"Especially with hungry lions running around?" said Kenzie.

"You are such a big help," said Dayzee. "Yes, the approximate number could be changing all the time, depending on the lions."

"Damn lions."

"Yes, Kenzie!" Marilyn said with a couple of quick claps. "Damn lions!"

Bruno hacked to clear his throat, and all five of them at the bar turned to see him facing them, his thick arms outstretched and holding back Abbott, Moe, and Hardy.

"Oh, Bruno, you and your buddies need a drink too," said Dayzee, and she got up, did a quick strut around the bar, and reached for a few bottles.

"Just a beer for me," said Bruno.

"With extra cheese."

"That's funny, Lady Sophia. Hey, are there such concoctions on Earth?"

"Him too?" said Cliff. "Seriously, this might be too bizarre for the show. Nobody ever talks about mixing a drink with cheese or—"

He set his drink down and held his stomach with both hands.

"Wow. All of a sudden, I'm starving."

"For beef, I bet," said Sophia.

"Probably not for cheese," said Marilyn, shaking her head slowly.

"That is common. The need for intense feeding has a rapid onset," said Moe.

"Ooh," said Marilyn, "I feel kind of nauseous now."

Sophia held her narrow midsection and said, "Sheesh, me too."

Abbott and Hardy grinned, and Moe said, "That is to be expected. It sent a signal to hatch. You are both—"

"Drinking too much," Bruno said while staring at Moe.

Moe stared back and said, "I am only a humble driver, but I recommend that the twins lie down and rest."

"Right now, you mean?" said Cliff. "The cars should be here any minute. The camera guy is set up near the driveway, and he—"

A loud scream erupted from the other side of the front door.

"Approximately five?" said Marilyn.

"Yep, Sis, and they're all dancing."

"Screaming first, though, Sissy."

She grabbed her belly again and said, "Oh, I think I should lie down awhile. Moe, I think you're right about that."

"I recommend that Abbott and Hardy isolate you and your sister to private locations where they can proceed with eradicating—"

"He means where they can rest, that's all. I think his language download might be outdated. Isn't that right, Moe?"

Moe shrugged and said, "Yes, as long as they proceed as directed."

He looked to his right, at Abbott, snapped his fingers, and pointed at Marilyn. He repeated the command with Hardy, directing him to take Sophia.

Marilyn looked at her sister and said, "Before, I was thinking about burning and barbing and—"

"These conversations get more confusing all the time," said Cliff. "We'll need a translator on-staff, or maybe a psychologist, or maybe—"

"Cliff," Dayzee said while shaking her head, "it might be a good idea for us to go investigate that scream, don't you think?"

She hooked his arm and began tugging him toward the foyer.

"Um, sure, Dayzee. I am kind of curious about that."

"Damn lions, I bet," said Kenzie.

Marilyn clapped only once softly and held her belly with a frown and said, "Oh my . . ."

"Me too, Sis," Sophia said while looking at the floor.

"Go with Abbott and Hardy," Moe said. "And I will follow Dayzee and the—"

"Cliff," said Bruno. "His name is Cliff."

"Yeah, I'm Cliff, and I'm curious about that scream. And whatever happened to Julian. Where did he run off to?"

"Oh, I think maybe he danced himself away somewhere, looking for that cat," Sophia said without a trace of a smile.

"Good one, Sissy," said Marilyn, also not smiling. "He's still dancing."

Cliff stopped, causing Dayzee to stop, and he scratched his head while looking from one twin to the other.

"Twins, huh?" said Dayzee. "Come on, Mr. Gutsquid, we need to—"

"I'm still just Cliff, Dayzee."

"Right. Uh-huh. Sure you are."

She yanked on his arm, he took one last look at Marilyn, then Sophia, and he walked with her, Moe falling in close behind.

"We should hurry," said Abbott.

"These things progress quickly," said Hardy.

"Huh?" said Sophia. "What are you two—"

"Just go with them," said Bruno. "They're weird as hell, but I bet you do need their help."

"What about me?" said Kenzie. "I always feel left out of things like I'm expendable or something."

"You're part of the gang," Sophia said with her eyes struggling to stay open.

"Sissy's right," Marilyn said before covering her mouth for a stifled belch.

"How about if I serve you a drink, Kenzie?" said Bruno. "Remember how you used to tend bar before you became a reality show star?"

Kenzie broke out a smile and said, "Well, I'm not a star yet, but I am an actress, so I'm sure ready for it."

Marilyn looked to her sister and could only blink her eyes, and Sophia scoffed so weakly that it was barely noticeable.

"Come with us," said Abbott, and he grabbed Marilyn's arm.

Hardy took Sophia by her arm, and the two odd men wearing only black jeans and no shirts, with long black braids swaying across their muscular chests, led the twins up the staircase from the kitchen.

*   *   *

"Those guys aren't really drivers, are they, Bruno?"

"No, Kenzie, they sure aren't. They're on a mission."

"Yeah? Like what?"

"Just how much do you know about—"

"I know you're not from around here. And I don't mean like The Kid was from Columbia."

Bruno studied her for a few seconds after handing her a fresh cocktail.

"No, I'm sure not from Earth. It's kind of a relief to—"

He noticed that Kenzie was staring with her eyes stretched wide open.

"Uh-oh. You didn't know that?"

Her eyes never changed, but she shook her head slowly.

"Where are you from?"

"Same place as Dayzee."

Her eyes popped open even wider.

"And Lady Sophia and Miss Marilyn."

Her eyes showed so much white that her pupils appeared to be two tiny dots.

"And Cliff. Well, not Cliff, so much, but the squid that's living inside him."

She closed her eyes and started to tip backwards off of her barstool. Bruno reached across the bar, grabbed the buttoned-up, headless dead producer's jacket between her breasts, and held her up.

"It's not just this haunted mansion?"

"Nope. Too much, huh?"

She opened her eyes, didn't speak, and only nodded her head twice.

After glancing down at his thick hand bunching up the fabric and stretching it over her breasts, she looked back up and said, "Well, you've explained just about everything."

Kenzie's face went pale, and she shook her head and stared.

"Hey, I'm just kidding. They're all from Ireland. I'm big, but I'm funny too."

She still stared.

"Um, mostly, I'm just big."

*   *   *

"There are many suitable rooms on this level," said Abbott. "Hardy, take your patient into this room, and I'll—"

"Who are you calling a patient?" said Sophia. "No one calls me . . . I mean, if someone . . ."

She held her belly and began doubling over.

"Sissy, you're starting to look like some kind of patient. Do you feel . . ."

Marilyn leaned back against the wall before continuing.

"Well, we don't feel good, Sissy. They're right about that."

"Hey . . . Abbott," Sophia said with a weak smirk.

"That's kind of funny, Sissy."

Sophia grinned and continued.

"We do everything together. We can rest in the same room."

"Same bed, Sissy."

"Uh-huh. Yep, Sis."

"That can work," Hardy said with a grin toward Abbott. "Abbott and I can synchronize our treatment protocols."

"I have no idea what you're talking about," Sophia said with a loud gurgling from her belly.

"Oh, Sissy, that sounded terrible. I don't even feel like doing all that barbing and burning, or was it burning and barbing?"

"Ugh. It doesn't matter, Sis. But I think it's barbing first, burning later."

"I can't do any of that even if I wanted to. I don't feel so good, Sissy."

The two men partially in black led the twins to the bed, they both lay down, side by side and holding hands, and immediately began to snore while deep rumblings bubbled and ballooned in their bellies.

*   *   *

"Here is good."

"No, Moe," Dayzee said after she brushed back her wild blond mane. "You'll just have to wait."

"What are you two talking about now?"

"Nothing, Cliff. I think Moe just meant that this is a good place for the cars when they get here."

"Oh, sure. Okay. Well, I don't know what that scream was all about, and I sure don't see the camera guy either."

Dayzee looked past him and saw a pair of mountain lions dragging Cliff's employee into the darkness behind the shrubs.

"Yep, we're up to five."

"Huh?"

"Um, I mean, maybe we'll need five cars?"

"Oh, you might be right, Dayzee. That big beefy guy, Bruno, he's—"

"No, I'm kidding. Three is good."

"We're running out of time," said Moe. He looked toward the rear of the property at Dayzee's two guesthouses and said, "Over there is even better."

Cliff followed Moe's eyes, saw the large guesthouse beyond the pool, and said, "You can't be serious. For the cars? How would that work?"

"He won't remember any of this."

"Oh, Moe, that's good. We have a show to shoot, and this is damn inconvenient."

Cliff looked from Dayzee to Moe and said, "More and more, I have no idea what anyone's talking about. I like it, don't get me wrong, but I don't have a clue."

"You said your real name was Dirk?"

Cliff frowned for a second, then he said, "Yeah, and I changed it. I thought it was for the books. Weird books, Dayzee. All about aliens and stuff."

"Well, big fella, your days of writing those stories are coming to a close."

Chapter 12 – Such a Damn Lion

"I'm very glad these two are infected, Hardy."

"That's not really my name. I don't even have a name."

"Understood. We still need to stay in character, though."

"Okay, Abbott. If you say so. Hey, I actually like the blonde better."

"Good. I'd rather inoculate the brunette anyway."

"Earth women are hot."

"They're not from Earth, Abbott. Can't you tell by looking at them?"

"Yeah, it really is obvious. Okay, drag yours closer to the edge of the bed. Like this."

Abbott grabbed Sophia's ankles and pulled her until her behind was at the edge, and he lifted her legs straight up. Hardy did the same with Marilyn, causing her white dress to slump down and reveal her underwear.

"You will need to move that tight garment," Abbott said, and he pulled Sophia's skirt until it stretched tight around her thighs.

"Oh, lucky you," Hardy said with a big grin. "She's ready to inoculate!"

*   *   *

"Yeah, that's not really funny, Bruno. You sure are big, though. That much is true. Do you know what that fountain thing is that they're always talking about?"

"I sure don't, Kenzie. Once, they had a good laugh, talking about how maybe I'd like to try it. Maybe I would? I have no idea, but all three of them say how it only makes them, um, I think the word is 'hornier.'"

"I'm not sure I even need that right now. I'm so excited from finally getting a big role in something like 'Kildare in the Hills.' That's got me really worked up."

"It seems that way, Kutie Kenzie. Hey, can I call you that? I have fun names for the twins, and I really need to get one for Dayzee too."

She caught him taking a quick peek at her breasts.

"Why, sure, big guy. I kind of like that. Hey, why don't you mix me up another drink and bring it around the bar for me?"

Bruno grinned and said, "I'd love to, Kutie Kenzie."

As he was walking around the bar, a cold drink in one hand, Kenzie spun around, and when she leaned back to place her elbows up on the bar, her jacket, which she'd unbuttoned, spread all the way open.

Bruno paused mid-step, smiled, and continued until he stood right in front of her. She smiled, too, and wiggled around until her knees were far enough apart for him to get even closer.

"Kutie Kenzie, that's quite a sight. But Dayzee, and the twins, and the rest of them will probably—"

"Forget them, Beefy Bruno. Anything can happen in this house."

When he stepped back and reached for his belt buckle, Kenzie spun herself around to face the bar, reached for her belt, and stood up just enough to begin sliding her pants partway down her thighs.

Bruno said, "I thought you liked Lady Sophia."

"Oh, you can be sure I do. All this talk about beef, though . . ."

*　*　*

"Just how much will he remember?" Dayzee said with a sly smile.

"Nothing from the first moment he saw me and Abbott and Hardy."

"Well, then," she said, grabbed his crotch, causing him to squeal, and pulled him toward her for a kiss.

"Dayzee, that's ill-advised because—"

102

It was too late, and Dayzee planted her lips on Cliff's.

"—that is a likely route for transmission too."

Dayzee pulled back quickly, dragged the back of her hand across her mouth, and said, "Why didn't you tell me?"

"That was some sweet kiss, Dayzee. How about another?"

"Um, maybe later, alright? You," she said to Moe, after punching his arm, "have some explaining to do."

He scanned slowly down from her eyes, studied her lips a moment, paused at her breasts with a smile, then lingered with a long look at her midsection. He looked back into her eyes.

"What?"

"Luckily, we can fit you into the schedule with either Abbott or Hardy. They should be—"

"I don't get you two, I really don't," said Cliff.

At the sound of engines revving, he snapped his head around to look at the entrance gate to Dayzee's estate, where a line of clean, shiny, expensive cars were idling in.

Dayzee stared only at Moe.

"You mean, he already . . . I mean, that was enough to—"

"Yes."

"Then, I really got shortchanged because from the feel of things, that was a real handful, and it would have been way better to—"

Moe held up a hand, and a long moment passed before Cliff was out of hearing range on his way to the cars.

"The Gut Squid inhabits more than just the digestive tracts of its hosts."

"You mean—"

"Yes. At least one tendril has probably invaded that region of his anatomy too."

"Ew. Fine. Set me up with Abbott. Or Hardy. You know what, let's make it both just to be sure. I haven't gotten a good double inoculation in a while."

*　　*　　*

Marilyn felt her hand in her sister's, and she struggled to open her eyes. She saw that Sophia was sliding up and down along the bedspread at the same rate as her. Her sister opened her eyes, and they gave each other a sleepy smile.

"Sissy, we're being inoculated!" Marilyn said in barely more than a whisper.

Sophia nodded and said, "Mm . . . I like inoculations."

They both turned toward Abbott and Hardy, when one of them, the twins didn't know who was who, said, "The infestation has progressed to a dangerous level. The inoculations must be deep."

"How deep?" said the other.

"Deeper than *you* can go," the first one said with a laugh, and neither slowed down from their steady pace.

The twins looked back at each other, and Marilyn said, "Mine sure is doing a good job, Sissy. How about yours?"

"Better than any earthman ever did, Sis."

"Hey, you know what? I'm already starting to feel better."

"Me too," said Sophia. "You know what else? I didn't realize it until now, but that fountain of youth should have made us a lot crazier than we've been."

"Oh, Sissy, it's because we're infested?"

"Yep, Sis, but not for long. Guess what I'm thinking."

"Sissy, we probably shouldn't."

"You feel that crazy energy coming back, don't you, Sis?"

"Oh, I sure do. Yes, Sissy, I think we should."

"Should we let them finish?"

"Why, of course," said Marilyn. "We don't want any little squid babies dropping out of us, do we?"

"Sheesh, Sis. No, we sure don't."

*   *   *

"Oh my God, Bruno. You are one humongously beefy guy!"

"Ah, Kutie Kenzie . . . just doing my job."

"God, just keep doing what you're doing. I've always wanted to sit at a bar like this," she said while raising herself up off of the stool and angling her bottom back far enough for Bruno to take his best shot. "I feel so cheap and dirty!"

"I'm concerned that you might fall, so I think I better keep you safe."

He pulled her jacket, the one that The Kid had snatched from the dead producer guy, down over her shoulders and left it there. His two big meaty hands reached around and held her breasts as she bounced softly from his strong motions.

"Mm . . . even better. Ooh . . . wow, that's a good angle, Beefy Bruno."

"Hey, I'm still worked up from wanting all those lady lions and lady mouses."

"I can tell. Pretend I'm one of those horny lady lions. Grab my mane and make sure I don't turn around and snap at you."

He gathered up her long brown hair and held it tightly, forcing her to stay faced forward while his other hand continued to enjoy itself.

"I'm . . . such . . . a . . . damn . . . lion," she said, pausing to bounce between each word.

*　　*　　*

Sophia's eyes had closed from the steady rhythm and deep inoculating, and Marilyn gave her a quick kiss on the lips.

"Oh, Sis, what was that for?"

"Mostly because you're hot, Sissy. But I wanted to tell you, too, that I think maybe these guys have done their jobs already. Maybe a while ago, actually."

"Yep, I think you're right. They're just taking advantage of us now."

"I think it's time, don't you?"

"You are so right, Sis."

Marilyn turned toward her inoculator and said, "Hey, there might be a better way."

Sophia said, "You guys are working too hard. Let's get you both on your backs, and my sister and I can help you out. Sound good?"

Abbott and Hardy looked at each other with identical grins, then they turned back to the twins and nodded, each head moving in perfect time with the other.

Sophia whispered, "These guys are weird."

"Barbs, Sissy?"

"Oh yeah, Sis."

"We wish to try your suggestion for continued inoculations," said Abbott.

"We do appear tired," said Hardy.

They both withdrew, took a step back, and let go of the twins' legs, which they'd been holding straight up.

Sophia kept her legs pointed up and said to her sister, "How does that look, Sis?"

"Ooh, with those heels? Hot as can be!"

Sophia dropped her legs to the side, and both girls rolled off of the bed. They each guided their guy down onto the bed, on his back, and stood for a moment to admire the view.

"Yep, they're sure the right guys for a job like this."

"You're right, Sissy, but they haven't seen anything yet. Let's show them."

*　*　*

"Sooner is better than later," Moe said as he and Dayzee watched Cliff talking to one of the guys that had delivered the cars.

"Well, you can't fix him right now. He's busy with—"

"I'm talking about you. If enough time passes, and it is allowed to anchor itself to your spine, you'll—"

"Ew. Change my name to Gutsquid, I know. Fine, let's go find those two guys that look just like you, and—hey, why can't you do it?"

"I'm a manager, and I've been instructed to not perform menial labor such as that."

106

"You're saying you wouldn't want to?"

Dayzee flashed him a smile, held her breasts with both hands and arranged them in her tight blouse, and said, "Just this once?"

"I . . . I, um," he said, staring at her breasts, which she still held, "would like to, but—"

"These skirts are never short enough," she said with a grin, then began lifting the hem, showing more of her thighs.

"I was told . . . um, I mean—"

She spun herself around and said, "Fluff my hair back for me, would you?"

Moe reached up and held her hair with both hands, pulled it all back, and let it drop. She turned enough to look him in the eye.

"What do you say, Moe? Feel like breaking some rules?"

"I . . . I, um, yeah, I sure do. I do need to eradicate the adult Gut Squid first, which is my mission, and then—"

"Oh, I can't wait that long," she said and turned back around. "Fine, let's go find those tag-team buddies of yours."

"Tag team?"

"Watch and learn."

*   *   *

"Sissy, hold his braid like I'm doing."

Sophia grabbed her guy's braid, and each of them pulled tight the thick black hair.

"Oh, here I go, Sissy," Marilyn said as she lowered herself gradually onto Hardy. He smiled up at her while holding her thighs.

"Me too, Sis."

Sophia found her spot, too, and Abbott put his hands behind his head.

"Look at that, Sis. He's a bit too casual."

"Well, these aren't earthmen, Sissy."

"Oh, you're right. You know, I have no idea what might happen when we—"

"Let's find out!"

Marilyn put her arm around Sophia's waist, and Sophia did the same with her sister.

"Do they know what's coming?" said Sophia.

"That's funny, Sissy. You know what I want to do? Let's go all the way all at once, both of us at the same time. Let's do it!"

"Alright, Sis. Are you ready?"

"Now that I've been inoculated, I'm so itchy you couldn't believe it!"

"Me too. Alright. Ready? Go!"

*   *   *

Kenzie tried to turn her head when she heard the two strange men screaming upstairs, but Bruno was still holding her hair too tightly.

"Bruno, what the hell was that? What's going on?"

"Oh, it really is this house, Kutie Kenzie. Strange things are always happening. You just stay right where you are, you gorgeous, nasty lady lion."

"Damn lions."

Bruno stopped himself, then started up again.

"You need to stop saying that."

"I like saying it."

"Just don't, alright?"

"Why? Damn lions. Uh-oh, I feel kind of funny."

Bruno pulled his hand away from her breasts, let go of her hair, and took two quick steps back, fumbling with his zipper.

"Damn lions. Now, I feel even funnier."

"I know what's going on. Hey, do me a favor and pull up your pants. Yeah, like that. All the way. Get that jacket on too. No, no, no, don't get up. Just stay where you are!"

Kozy kept facing the bar and said, "I recognize that there is danger of an unusual sort in Dayzee's mansion, but I also have a strange feeling of unfulfillment. It's like an unfinished meal."

"Yeah, and you're staying unfulfilled, at least as far as I'm concerned. You ain't no lady lion anymore."

"I was a lion? And a female of the species?"

"Yep. Well, sort of. It was like a game. Damn, that was a fun game too."

Bruno finished dressing himself and said, "Alright, you can turn around if you want to, Kozy."

Chapter 13 – Couple of Dead Clones

"They're screaming, but they're smiling, too, Sissy. This is fun."

Abbott and Hardy were grinning and sweating like mad as the twins embedded their barbs to their full depth.

"Oh my God, that feels good," said Sophia. "Look at them smiling, Sis. These guys sure are weird."

"So far, Sissy, this is guilt-free fun."

Both girls continued to do the work for the inoculators beneath them, each with an arm around her sister's waist and bouncing in time. The screams had trailed off, and the men's smiles were gradually twisting into grimaces as sweat beaded up and rolled off of their faces.

"Uh-oh," said Marilyn. "Not so fun for them anymore."

"Still good for us, though. Ooh, barbs are the best."

"Hey, Sissy, let's see if we can get away from them."

"Well, Sis, with the barbs, there's no way because—"

"I know. That's the fun part."

Abbott huffed and puffed and managed to say, "We are trained to show a range of emotions. Are we convincing?"

The twins stared down at him, leaning their heads and squinting, but they never slowed down."

When Hardy spoke, they turned their eyes to him.

"Yes, you could say that we are actors too."

Sophia kept bouncing and said, "What are you talking about?"

"Oh, Sissy," Marilyn said with a big grin. "I think I know!"

*　*　*

Kozy spun his barstool around with his thick arms squeezed into the tight jacket like plump sausages. No part of his brawny chest was covered as the dead producer's jacket stretched far to each side.

"Well, that's not convenient," Bruno said while shaking his head. "Hey, why don't you just find a robe or something?"

"Because . . . I'll be a lady lion again eventually?"

"Yep. Damn lions. You might as well put your hat back on."

Kozy retrieved it from the bar and set it in place.

"Nice. Thanks."

The front door swung open, and Dayzee strutted in, followed closely by Moe, who rubbed at his chin and stared only at what Dayzee was shifting side to side for him in her tight skirt.

"Bruno? Kenzie?"

"We're in here. Well, sort of."

They rounded the corner, and Dayzee's jaw dropped, but she quickly recovered and said, "I knew you'd be back. All that talk about damn lions!"

"Yes," said Kozy, "I've been informed that I was a female lion for a period of time."

Bruno looked at the floor with a grin, and Dayzee said, "Oh, Bruno, what kind of game did you have going on in here?"

Bruno swallowed noticeably and said, "No, it wasn't like that, Dayzee. Kozy wasn't Kozy, but Kenzie was Kutie Kenzie, and we were—"

"Kutie Kenzie, huh? I like that. That fits. Alright, what exactly were you two up to?"

"Oh, Sweetie, I'm not sure I should—"

"It's Dayzee, remember?"

"Right. Dayzee. Um, Kutie—I mean, Kenzie, she—"

"She sure is a Kutie, Bruno, back when she was Kenzie. But now, Kozy is—"

Abbott and Hardy screamed and cackled, and their cries and laughter raced down the stairs and flooded around them at the bar.

"Sophia and Marilyn might be in danger," said Kozy. "I will—"

"Not so fast," Moe said while pointing at Kozy. "At least, I know my team members are not easily injured, even though they cry out."

Dayzee grinned, shook her head, and said, "Really? We'll see . . . "

*   *   *

"What do you mean, Sis?"

Marilyn ignored her sister and pulled Hardy's braid tighter.

"You know that our barbs are supposed to hurt, but you don't really feel that, do you?"

Hardy tipped his head toward Abbott and said, "The infested blonde has—"

"No," Sophia said, shaking her head. "You've already fixed us. We know better."

"They're gorgeous and too smart as well," said Abbott.

They both looked up at the stunning twins, who were still working on taking the full lengths of their unneeded inoculations.

"You are correct on both counts," said Hardy. "Your infestations have been eradicated, and we do not feel any pain."

"Do it, Sissy. I'm going to. Try to pull away from them. Come on, we'll never get another chance like this!"

"Sure, Sis. Ready? Let's do it!"

Both girls raised themselves up to their knees, never retracting their barbs, never letting them go. Abbott and Hardy grimaced as if dying while their torsos were lifted up off of the bed.

"Oh my God . . . that's even better," said Sophia. "I almost hate to burn them."

"Who knew that pulling those barbs could feel so good? You seriously don't want to burn them?"

"No, Sis. I'm going to burn this guy," she said and yanked on his braid.

"Our mission is complete," said Hardy. "Do it. We're just going to get recycled anyway."

"What? What does that mean?" said Marilyn.

"They'll just clone a couple more of us," said Abbott. "Why do you think we all look the same?"

The sisters turned to each other and grinned.

"I think I'm in Heaven, Sissy!"

"Sure, Sis, but let's fire things up. Time to send them to Hell!"

*　*　*

A slow pounding on the front door froze Dayzee before she could predict the fate of the two inoculators upstairs with the twins.

She turned toward the door and said, "Well, it had to happen eventually."

She opened the door to see Cliff standing there while she was already saying, "They got tired of dancing around all by—oh, it's you."

"Huh?" said Cliff. "Who's dancing? There's nothing in the script about any dancing."

She turned to Moe and said, "Are you sure he won't remember anything after you, you know . . . do your thing?"

"It's guaranteed."

"And if you don't do your thing, what then?"

"Complete and total digestion will likely begin soon. Playtime is just about over."

She pointed at him with a grin and said, "Moe, you really do have a sense of humor."

"Want me to make sure that everything out there stays out there, Dayzee?"

"Yeah, I sure do, Bruno." She looked at Cliff while she said, "And don't swat any of those heads into the pool again, alright?"

She waited and watched, but Cliff only stared at her.

"No? Nothing?"

He still stared back at her.

"There are headless dead guys out there, Cliff. Oh, and one of them is that Julian guy . . . the one that liked cats. The cats liked him too. Mostly his head, I bet."

She squinted and paused to study him. He was slow to speak, but he managed to say, "I feel kind of funny. Maybe it's something I ate?"

"Oh, boy. Moe, I think you're up to bat. Bruno, we need to clean up the yard. Kozy? Just pretend you're a mountain lion for a while. We'll get back to you."

*   *   *

Marilyn was the first to get her heat cooking, and she took a deep breath of the aroma of burning whatever the guy was. Sophia wasn't far behind, and they both continued lifting and tugging, raising Abbott and Hardy up off of the blankets while a scent thick like a smoke-filled clone recycling plant filled the bedroom.

"He's still smiling!" Marilyn said and dropped down to rest on Hardy's lap.

"Eh. Not a big deal. Earth guys do that, too, Sis."

Sophia dropped down, too, and both girls continued the inoculation process while dialing up the temperature.

"It feels so good to use the heat, doesn't it?"

"Yep. But look—no other part of him is burning. Just his . . . his—"

"His inoculator!"

"Seriously, you guys can't feel that?"

"Oh, we feel some of it," said Abbott, looking up at Sophia. "It's just better than how we would be recycled. And looking up at you two? What a satisfying way for a discarded clone to go."

"He's a sweet talker, this one," Sophia said with a grin.

"I can't hold it back anymore, Sissy."

"Nope. Let's try to burn them to the ground, Sis."

*   *   *

Bruno began a brisk walk to the front door, and Moe seemed to have a spasm, shrieked, and reached for Cliff. Cliff screamed and took a step back, and in the blink of an eye, Kozy had Moe by the throat and had lifted him high off of the ground.

Bruno laughed once, shaking his head, and exited onto the porch.

"Put him down!" said Dayzee.

"Cliff is important to your career. Moe is not. And since I feel like a mountain lion, and lions, I've been told, like human heads, then I'll take this one for myself."

"Kozy, you've lost your mind!"

While Dayzee screamed, Moe kicked, and Bruno slammed the door shut, Moe's head was removed, and Kozy let his body slump to the floor.

"I'm still hungry," Cliff said while holding his belly.

"Oh, Kozy, that was not good!"

Kozy looked at the head in his hand and the headless body on the floor and said, "I acted without rational thought. I believe it is from anticipation of extremely positive feelings, though I can't define it precisely."

"Hmm . . . something to do with that mountain lion game, I'm thinking," said Dayzee. "Well, we're in real trouble now. We needed that guy. And damn it, I'm losing count."

*   *   *

"I'm loving this, Sissy. But that's as hot as I can go, and I—"

"You really are the hottest thing ever, Sis. That other Marilyn could never do any of that."

"Aw, thanks, Sissy. I'm just saying that even though Hardy is staring at me, and he's—"

"Smiling like a lunatic."

"Yes, he certainly is. Well, I'm certain he's dead."

"Let me guess," said Sophia. "He hasn't quit, yet?"

"Oh no, he's still inoculating."

"Mine too. Not bad for a couple of dead clones, huh?"

"We did think they were a circus act. Remember that, Sissy?

"Clowns. Good one, Sis. The greatest show on . . . where are we again?"

"Earth!"

*   *   *

"Cliff, are you in shock or something?"

"No. Hungry. Eat. Eat. Must—"

"Alright, we got it. So much for 'Kildare in the Hills.' Kozy, toss that body and that head outside for Bruno to bag up with the trash, alright?"

"As you wish."

Kozy tried to straighten out his jacket, but it was wrapped so tightly over his bulging muscles that he couldn't move it. He grabbed an ankle, cradled the grimacing head, and left for the front door.

"See that, Cliff? See how that head was kind of still alive? That's what we've been putting up with around here. Assassins bringing corpses back to life, headless guys dancing everywhere, snipers shooting—hey, I wonder whatever happened to that guy?"

"Feed. Food feed. Eat."

"Tell you what: when that sniper shows up again, you're getting in the way of the next bullet. That's the new plan."

*   *   *

Marilyn sighed, brushed her blond mane behind her on both sides, and said, "Well, now we have two more, Sissy. It's tiring keeping count."

"At least, they still have their heads," Sophia said with a sigh, then she swept back her long, silky black hair.

"Kildare Killers. That's us," Marilyn said with a smile.

"Yep, but we didn't kill all of the dead bodies around Dayzee's mansion. And we didn't pry anyone's head off either."

116

"That's funny, Sissy. We did do some prying, though."

"True, Sis. Either way, these bodies have to go. They came, they—" Marilyn giggled.

"They saw, they inoculated."

"Yes, then they were barbed and burned."

"And they didn't even have the decency to burn down to ashes, which would be a hell of a lot easier to get rid of," Sophia said with a smirk.

"Don't worry. We'll get Bruno to drag them out."

*　　*　　*

Kozy tossed approximately one body out onto the porch and slammed the door shut. He walked back toward Dayzee with a slight frown on his face, a face which looked a lot like Kenzie's.

"Aw, poor Kozy. We need you to get your brain working again. You're more like earthmen than you know—they never know which head to think with either."

"We were at your bar, and I was seated. Bruno was behind me, and my trousers were—"

"Oh, hold up. That's when you were still Kutie Kenzie. Let's recreate that crime scene, but we'll need to switch places. Come on, let's get you all tuned up and ready for whatever the hell might be next."

She took his hand and started to drag him toward the bar in the great room, but she stopped to glance at Cliff, who stood looking at the floor and holding his abdomen.

"We're going to have to feed him—I mean 'it'— soon, but for now, let's go, lion boy."

"Damn lions."

"Yes, and don't you forget it. And there's so much danger, Kozy. Remember the danger!"

"Yes, Dayzee. The screaming upstairs indicates that the twins are in grave danger. I should—"

"No, they'll be fine. They're killers. I mean, no, they're in gigantic trouble. But still, you should take care of me first. That's good—pull my skirt up a little farther. Now, hold my hips and . . ."

Chapter 14 – Also without a Head

Sophia and Marilyn traipsed down the stairway into the kitchen, holding hands and grinning. Marilyn was humming.

"Oh my, Dayzee!" said Marilyn. "And Kozy! Tsk, tsk, tsk!"

Sophia glanced over at Cliff, standing nearby, and said, "And in front of squid boy too?"

Kozy let go of Dayzee and turned to face the twins.

"We were only—I mean, we—Dayzee, she—"

"Never mind, Kozy," said Dayzee. "We'll get back to this later. And don't worry about Cliff—he's more squid than anything else."

"Well, that's quite a sight," Sophia said with a smile and shake of her head. "You wear that danger well, Kozy."

"He'd be helpful in the closet when we're changing, Sissy. There are never enough places to hang up clothes."

"How many hangers do you think we could get on there, Sis?"

"I bet it depends on how much danger is going on."

"Dayzee had him convinced there was tons of danger . . . obviously."

"I still think we need an on and off switch somewhere on him or a secret word, so we could just—"

"Girls!" Dayzee said as she tugged her skirt back down and fluffed back her wild mane. "It finally seems that your fountain of youth energy has caught up with you."

"It did take a while," said Sophia. "It was because of what Cliff infested us with."

"But that's all fixed up," Marilyn said as she finished brushing back her hair. "Those two guys, they—"

"They fixed us," said Sophia. "They sure did enjoy their work too."

"Well, where are they, then?"

"Oh, Dayzee," Marilyn said with pleasant smile, "Sissy and I couldn't help ourselves."

"We sure are the Kildare Killers," said her sister.

"No, you didn't! Tell me you didn't!"

"What's the big deal?" Sophia said. "They cured us, so we're both—"

"I needed them! I'm infected too!"

"Okay," Marilyn said with a shrug, "so, just get that Moe guy to inoculate you. Oh, you'll like the inoculation, too, I bet. Sissy and I got inoculated really well, then we convinced them to lie down, and we—"

"Girls, no! Moe is dead too!"

"How?"

"Oh, Mare, Kozy went crazy and killed him. It seems Kozy can get only so horny before his brain breaks down."

Marilyn clapped her hands and said, "I'll help! I'll help Kozy's brain!"

"It's not his brain you'll be helping, Sis. And you won't be hanging up clothes. You'll be—"

"Teaching him to inoculate me! Yes, I know!"

"Kozy can't really inoculate you, Sis. He—"

"Girls! I swear, you two! Alright, look. Moe is dead and so are his two buddies. What's the count? Do we have any idea?"

Marilyn looked at the floor and shook her head slowly.

"Oh, Dayzee, we're killers, Sissy and I. Not counters."

"Is that with a 'K?' Maybe we could be the Kildare Kounters?"

"Oh, maybe, Sissy. With as many dead bodies as we're piling up."

Dayzee looked from one to the other, and they both smiled back at her.

"Alright, we'll figure that out later. Right now, we have other problems."

"Including that," Sophia said as she pointed at the shrinking spectacle between Kozy's legs. "I guess having a human squid standing there doesn't really count as all that much danger."

"Might as well zip up," Marilyn said with a big sigh.

"Are you still itchy, Sis?"

"I sure am."

"More danger would have helped me out," said Dayzee. "I get itchy too."

"Me too," said Kenzie. "I think I just blacked out or something. What did I miss?"

"And just like that, Kenzie's back," said Dayzee. "Well, Kenzie, you missed a lot. Remember Moe? And his two buddies? They're all dead. Moe even lost his head."

"That doesn't even surprise me anymore. What's his story?" she said while pointing at Cliff.

"Eh. He's just hungry. Oh, wait a sec. Girls, we need to figure something out with Cliff. Moe was going to fix him up, remember?"

Sophia looked around and said, "Whatever happened to him?"

"Bruno took him out to the trash," said Dayzee.

"Is he dancing yet?"

"Who knows, Mare? Maybe. I kind of hope all of them are out there dancing, and we could—"

The front door swung in, Bruno came inside, and he slammed it shut, huffing and puffing with his back against it.

"Dayzee. Things are . . . not good."

*　*　*

"Like how?" said Dayzee.

Bruno grinned at Kenzie and said, "Hey, Kutie Kenzie. Looking good."

Sophia mouthed the words "Kutie Kenzie?" to her sister, who only shrugged.

"I have no idea what happened, Beefy Bruno."

"Beefy Bruno?" Marilyn said silently to Sofia, who only frowned.

"You two can sort that out later," said Dayzee. "Bruno, what's going on out there?"

121

"Well, Dayzee, first of all, you definitely have another assassin getting dead guys to—"

"Dance!"

"Mare, let him finish. Go on, Bruno."

"Sure. Well, they're all over the yard, and they're—"

"Looking for head?"

"Good one, Sissy."

"Girls. Please. Bruno?"

"Dayzee, I don't even know who half of them are! I think two are from Cliff's crew, one is that blind Cowboy driver guy, one—"

"Didn't he get dragged away?"

"I guess he's back, Fia."

"Oh, and the producer from the Prism." said Marilyn. "I remember him."

"And the guy that was already dead in the box, Sis. Remember him?"

"I sure do, Sissy. The free sample."

"And Moe," Dayzee said with a quick head shake. "Also without a head."

"But still dancing," said Marilyn.

"Sis, they were never really—"

"They're dancing now," said Bruno. "Oh, and three cars got delivered, right? That was three drivers, and hell, they're all dead now too."

Dayzee counted for a few seconds on her fingers before giving up.

"Alright, well, there's a bunch of them. We've dealt with dead guys before. Bruno, can you . . . I don't know . . . clean up the mess somehow?"

"Sure, Dayzee. But that isn't all. I think the last driver to come in left the gate open, and—"

"Wasn't the dead cowboy in charge of the gates?" said Dayzee. "Damn, you just can't get reliable dead Colombian cowboy help these days."

"Oh, Dayzee, he was blind, too, remember?" said Marilyn.

"Hard to see without a head," Sophia said with a smirk.

"Really, he lost his head too?"

"Probably, Sis. I bet he's a good dancer now too."

"He was looking for head even before he lost his, if he did lose his," Dayzee said before shaking her head. "Alright, let's get back on track here. Bruno, what else?"

"Mountain lions. The yard is full of them, and they're not so sexy anymore."

"Aw, poor Bruno," said Marilyn. "You really had something sweet going on there for a while."

"Alright, so . . . everyone's dead. We'll just have to—"

"No, Dayzee. Not everyone. There are still three of Cliff's crew alive out there."

"How are they still alive?"

"They climbed up the light pole. Dayzee, they're trapped up there, with headless dead guys and starving mountain lions circling all around them."

"Well, that's not good," said Marilyn.

"They should be happy they have that light pole," Sophia said with a smirk.

"Yeah," said Dayzee, "and they should be glad that sniper isn't—"

A single gunshot ripped out and echoed around Dayzee's estate. A second later, there was a loud thump.

"Sheesh," said Sophia. "I don't know what the count was, but it's plus one now."

*　　*　　*

Bruno began walking through the foyer of Dayzee's mansion and toward the group, saying, "I could sure use a drink."

"We all could," said Dayzee. "We need more than that, though. We need to figure this all out. That means back to the Prism."

"Seriously, Dayzee?" said Kenzie. "With all the dead guys and lions and film guys up on that post?"

"Give it time," said Sophia with a grin. "One already came down."

"Good one, Sissy."

"I wonder if the lions are eating him, Sis?"

"Probably. I would if I was a lion."

"You'd be a really hot lion, Miss Marilyn."

"Aw, thanks, Bruno."

"Even while she's gnawing on someone's head?"

Bruno stared, and Marilyn said, "Even I don't dare to make a joke out of that."

"Alright, listen, all of you. The guys on the pole will have to do the best they can. They can just stay—"

Another gunshot. Everyone stared at each other and waited. A body hit the ground.

"He," said Dayzee. "*He* can just stay up there."

"What about Cliff?" said Sophia. "Should we just feed him to the lions too?"

"I don't know, Fia. Maybe we can figure out some way to cure him of that gut monster thing of his."

"We should try," said Marilyn. "Maybe we can still do 'Kildare in the Hills?'"

"We sure aren't doing Cliff," her sister said with a loud scoff.

"No, Sissy, not with all of his guts turning into squids."

"Sis, I think he just has one big squid in there."

"Squids don't produce reality shows, Sissy."

"Sharks do, Sis."

"Oh, and snakes too!"

"How about—"

"Alright, you two. Look, we need to figure things out. Bruno, you're still too big to drive."

"He was just the right size for some serious driving," Kenzie said with a grin. "Anyway, since The Kid is dead and gone, I can—"

"Dead but not gone," said Sophia.

"Oh, that's right. Dancing. Maybe without his head. Okay, well, I'll drive."

"We have our pick of cars out there," said Dayzee. "Why don't we just—"

A steady pounding began on the front door, then along the walls. Then, bodies were staring in through the front windows.

"Sheesh, even the guys with no heads are watching us."

"That's funny, Sissy."

"Well, they had to come after us eventually. We're used to dead guys chasing after us," said Dayzee. "Let's take a car from the garage."

"What about the squid guy?" said Sophia.

"Let's leave him in the pool, Sissy."

"Squids are saltwater life forms," said Bruno. "He might not—"

"Oh, Bruno, he's not even from this planet. That's just silly," said Marilyn.

*　　*　　*

With Cliff doubled over and both arms wrapped around his waist, and with the twins and Kenzie gazing at the mansion's front windows, where bodies walked past, some looking in, even the ones without heads, and with an occasional roar from a prowling mountain lion, Dayzee brought Bruno with her to the door to her garage.

"Is it safe in the garage?"

"I kind of doubt it, Dayzee. That dead cowboy, he must have hit some wrong buttons and opened your garage too. It's probably full of dead guys and lions."

"Yeah, I bet it's just crawling with all of them. But, Bruno, look at you—your head is practically scraping the ceiling, and you're stronger than any ten earthmen put together. Go clear it out. Clean out my garage."

"You're absolutely right," he said, with his chest expanded for a deep breath. "You know, it's easy to lose track. I've been this high,"—he held a hand low, near his knees—"I've been a snake, then I thought I was about to be a bird . . . remember that?"

"Yeah, I sure—"

"Then, I *did* turn into a mountain lion. A mouse. I've even been a mouse. It's kind of easy to forget that I'm . . . that I . . . um, I—"

"Oh boy, here we go again. If you have any say in this at all, please . . . switch to something powerful enough to slap around lions and dead guys, alright?"

"Oh, Sweetie, you know I—"

"It's still Dayzee. Don't forget it."

"Right. Dayzee. I, um . . . Dayzee, I—"

In a puff of multi-colored feathers, Bruno the parrot flapped and fluttered and landed on Dayzee's left shoulder. When she turned to him, he dug in his claws and leaned away from her, his beak open and one bright eye staring.

"That's just wonderful, Bruno. You're no help at all like that."

"Let me try, let me try, let me try!"

"Like how? You want to buzz around the garage, crapping on them?"

He cackled once and pecked at her ear, then pulled back with his beak almost curling into a grin.

"Hey! That hurt! Alright, fine. Go get 'em, bird boy."

She swung in the door, leaned her shoulder toward the garage, and looked in at two dead guys, one without a head, sitting on the hood of her car, both looking at her, while a single lion stopped in its tracks and tilted its head to study her.

"Why aren't you eating those dead guys?"

The lion still stared.

"Fussy eater, huh? Fine. You'll stop staring at me when Bruno, here, pecks out those big eyes of yours."

She shook her shoulder and said, "Go do your thing, pigeon boy."

Bruno squawked, fluttered his wings, and said, "I'm a parrot, I'm a parrot."

"Whatever. We need that car."

"Oh, Dayzee, I changed my mind. Too dangerous. Too dangerous."

"What happened to pecking at them?"

He squawked loudly, brushed his colorful wing across Dayzee's face, and took off, flying back toward the twins, Kenzie, and Cliff.

Just as the lion began to leap, Dayzee slammed the door and bolted it. She followed the bird, strutting in her high heels toward the giggling and laughter that was welcoming Bruno the parrot.

Chapter 15 – How Many Problems

"Oh, he's so adorable!" said Marilyn. "This is the best one yet. Bravo, Bruno."

"I kind of liked the snake, Sis. I sure wanted my turn too."

Dayzee rounded the corner, her heels still tapping out a sharp tempo, and Kenzie said, "You, um, you have a little something on your shoulder, there, Dayzee."

She stopped, looked down, tried to flick it off, and it gummed up and smeared around on her fingertips.

"Oh, that's just wonderful. Thanks, Bruno, you lousy pigeon."

"I am not a pigeon! Not a pigeon!"

He'd landed on top of Cliff's head, who paid him no attention. He was on his knees near the bar, still holding his intestines.

"That's about all he's good for now," Sophia said with a smirk. "A bird perch. So much for our reality show."

"We might still be able to patch him up, Sissy. How can we kill the squid?"

"What kind of animal hunts squids, Miss Marilyn?" said Bruno. "Maybe I could try to do that next?"

"Can you really control that?" said Sophia.

"No, Lady Sophia. I sure can't."

"I say we pour gallons of alcohol in him," Kenzie said with a laugh. "That's bound to do something."

Dayzee shook her head, looked around the room, and said, "Hey, all of you. We'll never figure this out here in this mansion. I think this place is still possessed. We need to get to the Prism."

"What happened to your plan?" said Marilyn. "You know, the car in the garage?"

"Dead guys. Lions."

"Damn lions," Kenzie said with a big grin.

Marilyn clapped her hands and said, "Yay!"

"There's no time, even if Kozy came back," Dayzee said with her head shaking. "We need to go. Actually, I think we need that hearse, but how can we pull it up to the front door?"

"It's already pretty close," said Kenzie. "We just need to get to it without dead guys—"

"Trying to dance with us!" said Marilyn.

"That's funny, Sis."

"—and without the dead guys—"

"Bugging us for head," Sophia said with an eye roll.

"That's funny, Sissy, but true too."

"Girls! Try to take this seriously, alright? We need to find some way to—"

At the sound of footsteps plodding down the stairs into the kitchen, Dayzee stopped, shrugged, and said, "Kildare Killers, here comes your handiwork."

"We did kill them, Dayzee," Marilyn said with a pleasant smile.

"Funny," Sophia said with a grin, "that they're not from Earth, and still, they were so easy."

"I kind of like Earth, Sissy."

"Pay attention! We need to move. Now!"

"Why can't we just burn their hearts, Dayzee?" said Marilyn.

"Sis has a point. We should at least try."

"No, too much of a mess. I like keeping my house clean. Which reminds me: I still need to hire a new yard crew."

"I know," said Marilyn. "Bruno flies out, pecks at the last of Cliff's crew up on the light post, he falls, the lions rush to take a bite, the dead guys all stop to watch, and—"

"Even the ones without heads, Sis?"

"Especially them. And while all that is going on, we run for the hearse."

"What about those two?" Dayzee said as she hooked a thumb in the direction of dead Abbott and dead Hardy.

"Let's bring them to the Prism," said Kenzie.

"Oh, Kenzie, not you too," Dayzee said with a noisy sigh.

"Well," Kenzie said with a shrug, "do we even know that they want to kill us?"

"She has a point, Dayzee."

"She does, Fia. Go ask them."

"What . . . me?"

"Sissy, keep your hand warm just in case. Go on. Give Abbott a kiss."

"I kind of like Hardy better. He had a sense of humor, and he—"

"Fia! Mare! I swear, you two. Fine. I'll do it."

Dayzee turned and strutted toward the two approaching dead clones, and she stopped in their path with her hands on her hips. They closed the distance and stood directly in front of her. Each broke out a huge smile, and their dead eyes stared.

"Will you look at that?" said Marilyn. "Like a lion tamer."

"Damn lions. Oh, I need to stop saying that."

"Yes, you do, Kenzie," said Sophia.

"No, you don't," said Marilyn.

Dayzee turned her back to the dead inoculators, reached behind to grab a braid in each hand, and led them back.

"Fine, we'll take them to the Prism," said Dayzee. "They're part of what we need to figure out anyway."

"Can't we just kill them? Again, somehow?" said Marilyn.

"Let's teach them how to cut grass," Sophia said with a chuckle.

"Maybe they have to go back in that portal?" said Dayzee. "Girls, we need to figure this out. For that, we need drinks at the Prism."

"I'll serve them up," said Kenzie. "Me and Mack."

"Wow, I forgot all about him," said Sophia.

"Me too, Sissy. You know who else? Remember Jiff?"

"I do now. We need to call him to—"

"We'll figure all of that out at the Prism, girls. We need to go."

"I like Miss Marilyn's plan," Bruno said while ruffling his feathers and blinking, looking at each of them in turn.

"Really? You want to peck at that poor sucker on the pole, and throw him to the lions?"

"Damn lions."

Dayzee ignored Kenzie and waited for Bruno's response.

"Sure. Why not?"

"Fine with me, then. Go to work, birdman."

"That's funny, Dayzee."

"Thanks, Mare."

Dayzee let go of Abbott's and Hardy's braids and strutted to the front door. On the way, Bruno flitted around, squawking, and landed on her shoulder. She turned to him while pulling it open.

"Take a look, Bruno. See him up there? We need him down there," she said and pointed at lions circling around the base of the light tower.

"Um, I've been thinking, Dayzee, and I'm not so sure . . . I mean, just to kill him like that . . . I'm not sure—"

A single gunshot rang out, freezing the lions and dead guys, and Dayzee raised her fist with a big grin before the body hit the ground.

"Perfect! Let's go, everyone. Kenzie, you're at the wheel. Fia and Mare, you get the backseat. Bruno, you're up front with me. You dead guys? You're in the back, of course, where dead guys belong!"

*   *   *

Kenzie let go of the steering wheel with her right hand, exhaled sharply several times, sending feathers toward the windshield, and brushed at Bruno as he sat on her shoulder.

"A little room here, alright?"

"I just want to see where we're going. Are we there yet? Are we there yet?"

131

"Oh, boy," said Dayzee. "Next, you'll be chasing down lady pigeons, and—"

"Parrots! Lady parrots!"

"Right. You need to sit on the seat. You could change back anytime, right? We can't have you crushing our driver."

"She's right," Kenzie said, shoving the bird to the side. "Sit. Bad bird."

"She's pretty funny, Sissy. Bruno's a bad bird."

"He would be if he could get his hands—"

"Claws, Sissy."

"Yeah, if he could get his claws on some lady pigeons."

Bruno sighed and said, "I give up. I know I'm not a pigeon."

The screaming near the light post stopped abruptly.

"That lion just took his head clean off," said Dayzee.

"Oh, my," said Marilyn. "Not another one."

"Kildare Killers, Sis."

"Kenzie, maybe we should just go, huh?"

"Sure, Dayzee. There's just enough room to get around all these new cars."

She started the hearse's motor and put it in drive. She gave it some gas, nudging lions and walking corpses aside, and rolled slowly toward the exit gate.

"Uh-oh," said Marilyn.

"What, Sis?"

"We forgot the squid."

"We should have put him in the pool."

"I know, Sissy. He could have squidded all around in there."

"Should we go back for him?"

"No, Kenzie," said Dayzee. "He's on his own. Let's all get liquored up, and he can just—"

"Squid around in the pool?" Sophia said with a smirk.

"Yes, Sissy. Our show is shot to hell anyway."

"Maybe not," said Dayzee. "Let's go do some planning. Kenzie? Think you can make this thing scream?"

"Better than any headless, dead, burnt, blind, diamond-toothed cowboy from Colombia!"

"Huh," said Dayzee. "I think he still has his head."

*　*　*

"Mack, we all need drinks like you can't imagine."

Mack stood behind the bar, wiping his hands with a washcloth, and he didn't take the time to answer Dayzee. To his left, he saw Sophia, who was looking him up and down and whistling silently, then next to her, Marilyn, who smiled and gave him a quick wave. Next in line was Dayzee, shaking her head and grinning with parrot Bruno on her shoulder, and to her left were two strangers that stared blankly ahead and said nothing, their chests bare and muscular and with thick, black braids hanging down in front.

"I'm not even going to ask, Dayzee. The usual?"

Kenzie had walked around behind the bar, and she rubbed Mack's shoulders while peeking around him.

"For me and the gorgeous twins, yeah. These guys?" Dayzee hitched a thumb to her left but didn't look at them. "I doubt it matters. Anything."

He let out a deep breath, looked at the two, and said, "Definitely bottom shelf, alright?"

"Trust me, Mack, they won't know the difference."

He fixed his eyes on Bruno and said, "Hey, you look kind of familiar."

"Yep. Used to be a snake."

Mack nodded and said, "Rum?"

"Of course. Seems about right."

He turned and with Kenzie's help, began mixing up their drinks.

"Are you sure that portal by the big statue guy is gone, Dayzee?" said Marilyn. "I feel like playing around that pool table again."

"No one plays pool like my Sis," said Sophia. "If that portal is still there, she'd definitely get someone through."

"I wish we would have had time to pack our short robes, Sissy."

"Oh yeah, they were short. We could easily set up our next fountains wearing those."

"Why don't we get those fountains here anyway, Sissy? Maybe even Mack?"

"Mack would do. Hey, could we both use the same human guy?"

"We should try. I bet if we—"

"Girls. Stop, alright? You're already too worked up. We're here to think up a plan, remember?"

"Yes, Dayzee, we remember. Just how many problems do we have all at once?"

"A yard full of dead guys and—"

"Dancing and looking for head!"

"That's funny, Sis."

"—dead guys and lions. I'm glad we remembered to close the gate."

"Oh, yes, Dayzee. What would the neighbors think?"

Dayzee leaned over to grin at Sophia and said, "Such a sweet kid." She looked at Marilyn and said, "Mare, it's Beverly Hills, remember? No one cares."

"Then, why did we have to cage them all up by closing the gates?"

"Well, so we can drink in peace. You know that they'd all follow us here, and we need to concentrate."

"Oh, you're right, Dayzee. Okay, what else?"

"We need to cure not just the squid boy but me too. Remember that? Moe was going to fix me up since you killed the other two. Now, they're all dead."

"I think Kenzie's right about the squid," said Sophia. "We'll drown it in alcohol."

"Oh, Sissy, maybe that'll kill the Cliff person too."

"Let's take that chance."

"Hey, what about me? I might have a squid too."

"Oh, sorry, Dayzee," said Sophia. "We can drown that one too."

Dayzee shook her head and said, "No, Fia, we need a more reliable plan than that."

"What else is going on?" said Marilyn.

"Bruno's a bird. A pigeon, and we need to—"

Bruno squawked.

"Oh, alright—a parrot. We need him to change back or find some lady parrots."

"That's not much of a problem," said Sophia. "We'll scatter some bird seed out front. What else?"

"These two dead guys we're drinking with. I kind of like them."

"And they don't burn up completely," said Marilyn. "They're special."

"Right, so we probably shouldn't just toss them in the trash."

"No, Dayzee, probably not. Maybe they really could tend to your bushes and things?"

"That's funny, Sis."

"Well, that's another problem: finding a yard crew."

"Remember that Rake guy, Dayzee?" said Marilyn. "I still don't think that was his real name. That was just silly."

"It doesn't matter anymore, Mare. He's long gone."

"Our reality show isn't happening either," said Sophia. "Not happy about that."

"Sissy's right, Dayzee. All of Cliff's crew are dead, even that last one that—"

"Oh, that reminds me," said Dayzee. "That sniper is still out there too."

"Why did he shoot that guy up on the pole?" said Sophia.

"It's the Hills, right?" said Dayzee. "Maybe just for the fun of it?"

"You do have a point. Target practice."

"Oh, and the obvious thing that I'm trying to forget: some kind of assassin is back, and it's keeping all the dead bodies moving around."

"Nothing good about that," said Marilyn.

"One last thing," said Dayzee. "There's a portal in my basement. We need to—"

Bruno squawked and said, "It's not in the basement. It's a whole different place. There's a stairway, and a door, and a tunnel, and a—"

"Alright, fine," said Dayzee. "It's a whole extra part of the house that I never even knew about."

"Your house really is too big, Dayzee," said Marilyn.

"You might be right, Mare."

"That reminds me of one more thing we need to do. Let's draw a map!"

Chapter 16 – That Will Be the Show

"Thanks, Kenzie," said Sophia. "You still look hot working the bar."

Kenzie and Mack set drinks down in front of Dayzee, the twins, and the two dead inoculators, Abbott and Hardy.

"Thanks, Fifi. You still look hot. Period."

Marilyn elbowed her sister and said, "Aw, things are getting back to normal."

"No, Mare," said Dayzee before Sophia could respond. "Not even close." She held up her cocktail and said, "Cheers to Beverly Hills."

The parrot sitting on Dayzee's shoulder squawked and said, "West Hollywood! West Hollywood!"

Dayzee lowered her drink and glared at Bruno's beady eye close on her shoulder.

"You really need to change back soon, alright? Besides being such an annoying buzzard, we're going to need some brute force to clear out the yard."

"Clear them out where, where, where?"

Dayzee scoffed and looked away from Bruno.

"I still say they can all be trained to take care of your yard," said Marilyn. "They'll work cheap too."

"Sis, dead guys don't really work. Most living guys don't either."

"What else are either of them good for?"

"Most of the dead ones can't even see the lawn, Sis. No heads."

Mack had retreated to wait on other Prism patrons, but Kenzie remained and watched them all with a grin.

"Girls, we need to get rid of them, then we can hire a living lawn crew."

"How long do you expect that to last?" Sophia said with a grin and a nod.

"Fia, can you two stop killing the hired help, at least for a while? Here's what I'm thinking: when turkey boy turns back to that giant piece of beef, he can herd all the dead guys, even these two,"—she waved a thumb to her left—"down into the basement. They can do whatever dead guys do, and we—"

"Will we toss the heads down there, too, Dayzee?"

"Yeah, Mare. Of course. Let's bounce them down the steps. We can lock the dead guys down there first, then get on with the other problems."

"Like our next fountains of youth."

"Fia, you two have already had too many."

"I'm just so itchy, Dayzee," said Marilyn. "I'm going to drag Mack over to the pool table. Watch and see."

"No, Mare, there's no time. After the dead guys are locked up, we can—"

"What about the lions?" said Kenzie. "They're just going to stand around and watch you dragging living dead bodies around?"

"She makes a good point," said Sophia. "Oh, those lions."

"I want to say it, but I'm not going to," Kenzie said and held her lips together tightly.

"Damn lions!" said Marilyn.

Kenzie closed her eyes and shook for a second, then looked at Dayzee and said, "I feel funny every time I hear that. I'm getting back to work."

She turned and left for the kitchen, with Dayzee and the twins watching her in silence.

"She's hot," said Sophia, "but we have too much to do to keep her around, don't we?"

"Especially since there's no show anymore, Sissy. Even though she's an actress."

"Yep," Dayzee said with a big sigh. "We all are. She's right about the lions, though. We'll need to lure them out through a gate and lock them out. How can we do that?"

"Bait."

"Right, Fia, but what kind?"

"Oh, they don't like dead guys. We can't use them."

"No, Mare, they sure don't. Hey, maybe we can use Cliff."

"Lions eat squids?" said Sophia. "Since when?"

"Fia, he's not a squid. There's just one doing the backstroke inside him. Alright, that's settled. He's our guy."

"After that, then we'll drown his pet squid?"

"Yeah, Mare. If he survives. Now, about the assassin. If anyone else happens to get killed, that thing—"

"Oh, that's funny, Dayzee. 'If.' Sissy and I aren't about to stop. You know that."

"She's right. When your next grass guys get there, Sis and I—"

Dayzee clunked her glass down on the bar, then turned to stare at each of the Kildare Killers in turn, who only grinned back at her. After a few seconds, she turned to her left to study Abbott and Hardy, who were still sitting with their hands around their glasses and staring over the bar into the mirror. She turned back to the twins.

"Girls, I love you both, you know that. But with you back in the Hills, we—"

Bruno squawked. "West Hollywood!"

Dayzee exhaled loudly, closed her eyes for a few seconds, then continued.

"We've had maybe too many thrills."

"And kills," said Sophia. "Don't forget the kills."

"I can barely remember all of them, Sissy."

"You do like being bare, don't you, Sis?"

"Oh, yes. You like me being bare too."

"I sure do. Like right now, you could—"

"Girls! Stop!"

They both quieted down and began sipping their drinks, and even Bruno hung his parrot head. Abbott and Hardy had no reaction.

"It's not just that Cliff is a squid, and I have one growing in me with no way to get inoculated because those guys are all dead. It's not just because the mansion and yard are full of dead bodies, some headless,"—she paused to grin at Sophia—"and some dancing,"—she shook her head and smiled at Marilyn, "it's also—"

"Told you they were dancing," Marilyn said with an elbow to her sister's side.

"—that Bruno is still a vulture, there's an assassin after us again,"—the twins lost their smiles—"there's still a sniper out there taking cheap shots at us, and there's a portal in my basement!"

"Not a basement," Bruno said before fluffing his feathers. "Steps, door, tunnel, then portal, then portal, then portal."

Dayzee pushed her drink to one side on the bar, let out a deep sigh, and laid herself down on her folded arms. In a muffled voice, she said, "I think that's everything."

Kenzie had returned, and she'd placed both hands on the bar so that she could lean down close to Dayzee.

"And lions," she whispered, causing the twins and the parrot to laugh and chirp. The dead inoculators remained silent.

Dayzee sat back up, found her drink, finished it, and said, "Right. Damn lions too."

"Yard guys," Sophia said with a grin. "Young, healthy yard guys. Sis and I volunteer to interview them."

"In our white robes, Dayzee."

Dayzee shrugged and looked across the bar at Kenzie.

Kenzie reached out for Dayzee's empty glass and said, "No offense, Dayzee, but I'm not sure I want to help with all that. It's a lot safer here, serving drinks."

"What about the show?" said Sophia. "Cliffie said you'd be a big star, remember?"

"Oh, Sissy, I'm not sure we even have a show anymore."

Sophia smirked and said, "Dayzee will figure something out."

She looked up at Kenzie with a smile and said, "When we straighten things out, you're back in, right?"

"Well," Kenzie said with a smile, "I *am* an actress, so, yeah!"

The twins turned to look at each other. Sophia grinned and Marilyn turned her eyes toward the ceiling.

Dayzee said, "Yes, Kenzie, of course. Just hang loose at the Prism until we get things cleaned up. But you know, girls, it's not just about tossing bodies into the basement and chasing away lions. We're going to need some real focus to get through all of this."

"What do you mean?" said Marilyn.

Dayzee took a deep breath, stretching her tight blouse and threatening to pop a few buttons, and said, "Let's get another round for us,"—she paused and pointed at the parrot on her shoulder—"rum for the stork, and I'll tell you the plan."

*　　*　　*

Mack gave Kenzie a hand at delivering drinks to Dayzee, Sophia, Marilyn, and Bruno. Even the dead guys had fresh cocktails in front of them. Mack grinned at the twins and strode along behind the bar to tend to other patrons. Kenzie stood watching them, wiping her hands with a washcloth, and waiting to hear Dayzee's plan.

"Alright. Here's what I'm thinking: the show must go on. You gorgeous twins already know that, and Kenzie, you probably know that too."

"Well, sure, because I'm an—"

"Actress," said Sophia with a big grin. "And a damn good bartender too."

"Thanks, Fifi."

Marilyn giggled and elbowed her sister.

"Alright, like I was saying," said Dayzee, "we can't be sure Cliff will ever get the squid out of his guts, so we'll have to—"

"What about your little squid, too, Dayzee?"

"Well, Mare, I'm just going to hope that we figure something out before it grows up."

"And out."

"Thanks, Fia. That's a pleasant thought."

Sophia chuckled and took another drink.

"Alright, no matter what happens with Cliff, we're doing the show. You want to know how?"

Everyone stared and waited except for Abbott and Hardy.

"*We* are going to take Cliff's place. *We* are going to do everything that he and his crew—"

"Which are all dead," said Sophia.

"And dancing."

"Yes, girls, they're all dead. So, we're going to do it all. We'll set up the scenes, do the lighting, the filming, the—"

"Let's get Jiffy boy for the camera work," said Sophia.

"Oh, Fia, that's a great idea. Yep, we'll get Jiff for that."

"He'll need a new camera, Dayzee," said Sophia. "Remember how the sniper shot the old one out of his hands up in your attic?"

"I remember, Fia. Yeah, we'll buy him whatever he needs."

"I still don't understand what happened up in your attic, Dayzee," said Kenzie. "But if another scene like that's going to be part of the show, count me in."

"You want to be strapped to the wood floor, stripped naked," said Dayzee while shaking her head, "while some wooden guy—"

"She said 'guy' again!" said Marilyn.

"Well, maybe not that possessed door thing," Kenzie said with a smile at Sophia.

"Uh-oh, Sissy. Big trouble in Dayzee's attic!"

"Sis, no, she's just—"

"Hey, I'm just messing around," said Kenzie. "Whatever you all decide, count me in."

She turned and went off to join Mack.

"Girls, I don't know about another rodeo in the attic."

"That headless blind Columbian guy would have been good for a rodeo."

"Yes, he sure would have, Sissy. But he's somewhere behind the shrubs—hey, Dayzee, I just thought of something: maybe 'Kildare in the Hills' could be a musical too?"

"Right, Sis. Because the dead guys are dancing. That's brilliant."

Dayzee turned to her left, looked past Bruno the parrot, and said to the two dead guys, "Only in Beverly Hills, huh?"

She waited, but they didn't respond.

Bruno squawked, and Dayzee immediately flicked him off of her shoulder and onto the bar. She pointed at him, and he stared back without correcting her.

"Yes. I know, Bruno. Just drink your rum."

The bird began pecking into his tumbler, splashing a few drops onto the bar. Dayzee shook her head, blew out a deep breath, and turned back to Sophia and Marilyn.

Before she could speak, Marilyn said, "I don't get it, Dayzee. How could we film a reality show with all the dead guys and squids and things still around?"

"Mare, *that* will be the show. Each problem we fix will be an episode. One week, people will watch how we use Cliff for bait and lure the mountain lions out of the yard."

"Oh," said Sophia, "I get it. The next show will be Sis and I interviewing, and probably barbing and burning, a new crew that will—"

"How about if we mostly film the interviewing and them getting the yard work done, Fia? How about that?"

"Not as much fun, Dayzee. And besides, Sis and I—"

"Can't help ourselves. You know that, Dayzee."

"Look, we'll figure out the details later. The first step,"—she reached out, pushed Bruno's glass away from him, and scooped him up and back onto her shoulder—"is to turn Bruno the pigeon back into Bruno the side of beef."

"Why am I first?" Bruno said before flapping his wings twice. "Why? Why? Why?"

"Because we need you to help with everything else. Can you imagine Fia, in that tiny skirt, trying to wrestle a headless dead guy into the basement?"

Bruno pointed his head to the bar's ceiling and let out a series of chirps.

"Is he laughing at me? I swear, Bruno, you better—"

"No, Lady Sophia. Never, never, never."

"Alright, then."

"Or," said Dayzee, "how could Marilyn, wearing such a short dress and such high heels, dance a dead guy into—"

"Dance!" said Marilyn.

"He'd love it, Sis. Just remember that the headless ones will be looking for head. Don't be surprised when—"

"I'd like to see it!" said Bruno.

"The dancing or the head?" Marilyn said with a big smile.

"Both! Both, Miss Marilyn!"

"Maybe later, Bruno. You're first," said Dayzee.

"I understand, Dayzee. I can't just change myself back, though."

"I haven't quite figured that out yet," said Dayzee. "Any ideas, girls?"

"Yep," said Sophia. "For one thing, we need to make sure he doesn't run off with a bunch of lady pigeons."

"Lady parrots! Yeah, yeah, yeah . . . lady parrots!"

"Sissy is so right, Dayzee. He needs reasons to stop being birdy and get back to being beefy."

Dayzee shook her head with a grin and said, "You two, I just love you. Yes, that's exactly how we do it."

She turned to the parrot on the bar and said, "Have another drink, chicken man. You're just about done flying."

Chapter 17 – Kildare Kuestick Girls

"You want me to do what?" said Marilyn.

"Ditto that, Dayzee. Are you serious?"

A loud thump rang out from the Prism's door which led to the sidewalk along Sunset Boulevard.

Bruno said, "Lady parrot."

"How can you know that?"

"Oh, Dayzee, I—"

Three more thumps.

"I can smell lady parrots like nobody's business."

"What do they smell like?"

"Like heaven wrapped in feathers, Miss Marilyn."

"What do Sis and I and Dayzee smell like?"

"Ugh . . . nothing good, Lady Sophia. Not right now."

"Alright, enough. All of you."

"Pick me up, Dayzee, and carry me to the door. Open the door, and—"

"No, Bruno, there's no time for you to flap out onto Sunset to go make a bunch of Bruno birds."

"That's just silly, Dayzee," said Marilyn. "They wouldn't all be named Bruno."

Dayzee looked at Sophia and said, "She's a sweet kid, but sometimes, I wonder if—"

"I'll help," said Kenzie, who had, for some unknown reason, unbuttoned her blouse quite low, drawing three sets of girl eyes and one pair from a parrot.

"Wow, that's a sight," said Sophia.

"Just practicing for the cameras, Fifi," she said with a big smile.

Dayzee looked up from Kenzie's display and said, "Good. For what I have planned, we'll need your help. Your debut starts today, and for this shoot, you're the big star."

"Me? Why me?"

"Well, because you and Bruno had a little something going on, and—"

Kenzie grinned, shook her head, and said, "Oh, Dayzee, there was nothing little about it."

"No, I mean you had that short—"

"His head is up by the ceiling."

"Kenzie, I mean, you two had that hot inter—"

"Course!"

"No, Mare . . . interlude."

"It sure was lewd," Kenzie said with a grin. "I've always wanted to do it on a barstool like that."

"This conversation isn't working out," Dayzee said while shaking her head. "Look, Kenzie, whatever happened, you need to be the star of this scene."

"Huh? What do you mean, 'scene?'"

"I mean, I'm calling Jiff. 'Kildare in the Hills' begins right now, right here."

"But, Dayzee, we're still in West—"

"God, Bruno, give it a rest! We'll act like we're somewhere else!"

Dayzee took out her phone and tapped a few numbers.

*   *   *

"I hear them, Dayzee. I still hear them. They want me."

The feathery thumps against the Prism's wooden door hadn't stopped.

"Well, they can't have you. Drink your rum."

The front door swung in, spilling the Southern California light into the bar, and Jiff Roberts stepped inside. He had parrots on his head and each of his shoulders, pecking at and getting tangled in his long, wavy brown hair.

Bruno tried to lift off, but Dayzee held him to the bar and said, "Jiff, quick, close the door!"

Jiff slammed the door shut, and Dayzee yelled, "Outside with the birds, Jiff! Hurry!"

Jiff snapped the door open and tossed the flapping and squawking birds back out into the daylight before he closed the heavy door again.

"What the hell, Dayzee?"

"It's the hell of pigeons," Sophia said with a smirk.

"What do the people outside think, Dayzee?"

"Oh, Mare. Fia, you have such a sweet sister."

She turned to Jiff.

"You brought your camera, right?"

He tapped the black case under his left arm, held there by a leather strap up over his shoulder.

"Yeah, Dayzee, just like you said. What's the big rush? What's going on?"

"How would you like to be the Director of Photography, the Camera Operator, the First Assistant Camera Operator, the Second—"

"Okay, I get it. You want me to do everything but for what?"

"'Kildare in the Hills,' our new reality show."

"But, Dayzee, aren't we in—"

"Oh, not you, too, Jiff. Look, everything else will be shot at my house in the Flats. We just need a quick shoot here for what's about to happen."

"And what exactly is that?"

"Ever see a pigeon turn back to—"

"I'm *not* a pigeon, Dayzee! I'm not, I'm not, I'm—"

"Not for long, anyway," Sophia said before gesturing to Mack to bring another drink.

Dayzee waved a hand at all of them, then said, "Just check the lighting, Mr. Director of Photography. Get your camera ready. Oh, and after this shoot, we'll get you all the equipment you need."

"Sounds good. I know just what to buy. Maybe a bullet-proof vest, too, Dayzee?"

Dayzee grinned and said, "Yeah, Jiff. Maybe. Now, let's get started. Bruno, you big hunk of beef, see you on the other side!"

*   *   *

"Alright," Dayzee said to the twins and Kenzie, "you have the general idea. I don't care how you get there, but you need to end up like I told you."

"A pool cue, huh?" said Kenzie. "Actually, that sounds kind of hot."

"I'll make sure it is," Sophia said with a grin. "This is one supporting role I'm sure going to enjoy."

"Me too, Sissy. Dayzee, you're a genius director. Maybe you should be directing, too, and not just acting?"

"You might be right, Mare. All I really did, though, was think about how to lure the beef back out of the pigeon. That made me think that—"

Three more thumps on the door.

"Oh, boy. Alright, we better get going. Kenzie, you need to get in position. Jiff, I'd say start with a straight-on shot, alright?"

Kenzie smiled and left for the pool table.

"Sure, Dayzee. The lighting is actually pretty good for this too."

He turned and left after Kenzie.

"Girls, I promise you that Kenzie won't steal any more scenes."

"Well," said Sophia, "she can't barb and burn the yard guys like Sis and I."

"Sissy's right. She's probably afraid to dance with dead guys too."

"Oh, you two. I give up. Alright, it looks like Kenzie and Jiff are ready. I'm going to help Jiff stay focused. Go to work, you gorgeous Kildare Killers!"

*   *   *

Jiff stood about ten steps from the end of the pool table, his camera pointed at Kenzie, who leaned back against the table's edge. Her jeans were tight and ended well above her spiky red heels. Her t-shirt was even tighter, and it didn't quite make it down to her belt, leaving some smooth skin visible. She leaned back and looked into the camera with a smile.

Dayzee dragged a barstool over next to Jiff and sat, facing the action. Her skirt was tight, but she managed to spread her legs enough that she could hold Bruno, who was still a parrot, between her thighs. Her hands wrapped over his wings, and his wiry claws hung loose, unable to grasp anything. He stared at the unfolding scene too.

Kenzie looked to the left of Jiff and smiled, then to the right. She gestured with a finger to each side, calling unseen cast from behind the camera.

On the right side, Marilyn approached the pool table. Her white dress appeared shorter than normal, and just below its hem, her long, shapely legs ended in high white heels. Her wavy blond mane caressed her shoulders and back as she walked.

On the left side, Sophia strutted toward Kenzie, who was still smiling in her direction. Her black skirt barely covered the important details, only outlining them but not hiding the obvious curves. Her bare legs stretched down to her tall black heels with tight straps around her ankles. Her silky black hair hung far down her back, swaying side to side as she walked, teasing a view of her tight red blouse.

The brunette on the left and the blonde on the right both walked up until their thighs were against the pool table, and Kenzie gave a little hop to sit right on the table edge. Each of the twins reached for her waist, going for the belt buckle, but Kenzie stopped them.

"Oh no, girls. Not like that. Get a bit more comfortable for me, okay?"

"I'd love to," said Sophia. "Come on, Sis. We know what she needs from us."

"You are so right, Sissy."

Sophia turned toward her sister, and Marilyn reached out with both hands to unbutton her blouse. With Sophia shifting side to side, they both managed to work her shirt back over her shoulders, and it fell to the floor, revealing a lacy black bra that barely contained her.

While Marilyn brushed her sister's hair back, Sophia stretched her skirt over her hips and let it drop, causing Kenzie to stare and Marilyn to giggle softly at the sight of nothing underneath.

"That's a good start, Fifi," said Kenzie. "Now, your sister."

Sophia helped Marilyn slip the straps of her white dress down over her shoulders, and when it tumbled to her waist, her breasts were bare and out in the open.

"Just magnificent," Kenzie said, staring down at her.

Marilyn giggled and wiggled her way out of the dress, and after it had dropped, she kicked it to one side and stood there in only her heels and white panties, which she lost quickly.

Kenzie turned back to Sophia and said, "Oh, just one more thing, Fifi."

"Don't have to tell my Sissy twice," said Marilyn.

Sophia unhooked it between her breasts, pulled it open, freed her arms, and tossed it behind her. She, too, stood naked except for her very high heels.

All three looked over at Bruno, who was squirming and chirping but unable to free himself.

"Oh, you haven't seen anything yet," said Dayzee.

They both continued to watch the show while Jiff breathed heavily and kept filming.

The twins turned back toward Kenzie, and when they reached for her belt again, Kenzie said, "Oh no, girls. This shirt is too tight and uncomfortable. Maybe you could help me out?"

"Well, if you insist," said Sophia.

"Even if she doesn't," Marilyn said in a whisper, also staring intently at Kenzie's breasts behind the thin cloth, then smiling for the camera.

While Kenzie held her long brown hair up with both hands, the twins took the t-shirt's bottom hem and began to lift it up. When they'd bunched the material just beneath Kenzie's breasts, they both stopped to look at Bruno.

He continued to squirm in Dayzee's hands, and she said, "Shh, big pigeon. Just keep watching."

"I'm a—"

Dayzee gently pinched his beak closed, and he could do nothing but watch.

The girls chuckled softly and turned their attention back to undressing the barmaid seated on the pool table.

"Here we go, Sissy."

"Uh-huh. Oh yeah, Sis."

They stretched the material up, raising Kenzie's breasts, then it cleared the obstacles, and she bounced back down. The twins finished by pulling the shirt up and off of her, and they dropped it behind her on the table. They turned only long enough to give Bruno smiles.

Sophia looked Bruno in the eye and licked her lips, and Dayzee almost lost the struggling parrot in her hands.

Kenzie smiled at Bruno and said, "Such a shame you're just a bird. We never finished what we started, did we?"

She looked up at each of the twins with a smile and said, "You know, these jeans are awfully tight and making me squirm. I think I'd feel a lot better without them."

"Sissy would too," Marilyn said with a soft giggle.

"Like you wouldn't, Sis?"

"I'm getting itchier every second. I say we forget about Bruno."

"I'm at least as itchy as you, Sis. Those jeans have to go."

"Oh, look, Sissy. We're attracting a crowd."

They looked around at a few of the bar patrons, including Mack, still wiping his hands with a washcloth, standing around nearby and watching intently.

"Earth," said Marilyn with a giggle.

"What about Earth?" said Kenzie.

"It's just so easy," Sophia said with a smile. "Come on. Let's keep going. The camera's rolling."

Kenzie reached up to place a hand on a shoulder of each naked girl standing close. Sophia and Marilyn conspired to toss the belt aside, unzip the jeans, and slip them down to her ankles. Kenzie wiggled around to help, and they left her pants bunched up around her red heels.

"Oh, that's really hot," Sophia said while looking at the pink frilly lace, very tiny and stretched tight.

"Oh my God, Sissy."

They both looked up, but Kenzie was looking past them at Bruno, who fidgeted around in Dayzee's tight grip.

"Too bad you're just a bird, Bruno," said Dayzee. "Look at that. Look at what she's offering you."

She waited and watched him, then said, "Still a bird, huh? Alright, then we keep rolling."

She nodded to the twins, they looked at each other with a grin, then they both looked at the crowd gathering around them.

"Only in Beverly Hills, huh?" said Sophia.

A voice from the crowd said, "Well, actually, it's—"

"Stop!" said Dayzee. "Look, this can't be part of the show, but we'll add it to an extended version. You can all get your own copy, alright? But no ad-libs from the audience!"

There was hushed agreement and sighs of relief, and the filming continued.

Sophia put her left arm around the almost-naked Kenzie's waist, and with her other hand, she held her bare thigh. Marilyn stepped to one side and returned with a pool stick.

"It's a shame, Sis, that Bruno's just some kind of bird."

"I know, Sissy. Otherwise, if he was his usual beefy self, we wouldn't need this, would we?"

Kenzie took a deep breath, arched her back to thrust her chest out farther, then let out a deep sigh, saying, "I'd sure rather have a real man."

Marilyn whispered to her sister, "She doesn't mean an *Earth* man, Sissy."

"Shh, Sis. Hand me that stick."

Sophia took the long stick in her right hand, flipped it around, and wiggled the thick end between Kenzie's thighs.

"Ooh, that's kind of nice," she said.

"Open up, Kenzie. Let the big stick in there," Marilyn said with a giggle.

Kenzie shifted around, from side to side and up and down, until Sophia had slid the stick under her and past her, and when she let it go, about an arm's length of it stuck straight out from between Kenzie's legs.

"Mm . . ." said Kenzie, "good place for a stick."

"It's a long one too," said Marilyn, who'd placed her arm around Kenzie's waist and played with her hair, keeping it brushed back over her shoulders.

"Oh, wait," Kenzie said and sucked in a deep breath.

She wiggled herself around, grinding side to side on the pool stick until she settled in with a smile.

"Mm . . . perfect now."

The sisters turned to look at Bruno, who was trying to free his beak to say something, but all he could do was wiggle, breathe, and blink his eyes.

"Still a bird, Sissy."

"Yep. Geez, what does it take?"

"I know," Dayzee said as she stood up, Bruno still in her hands.

She walked over, careful to not block Jiff's view, and she gently placed Bruno on the very end of the stick, farthest from where it disappeared between Kenzie's thighs. He held on with his claws and stared. Dayzee let go of his beak.

"Hey," said Sophia, "this is something I want to do anyway, no matter what's going on with the bird boy."

Sophia got a hold of the cue stick, and she began to rotate it back and forth, over and over, while looking into Kenzie's eyes. Kenzie closed hers for a second and said, "Mm . . . wow, Fifi," then she opened them to watch an agitated bird beginning to flap around and shuffle his claws as his perch was shifting and spinning.

Kenzie started moaning and taking deep breaths, angling her breasts out. The crowd stared silently while Sophia and Marilyn, who had placed her hand over her sister's to help with the stick, smiled and watched Kenzie. Dayzee stood close by, ready to grab Bruno if he tried to fly off.

"Oh my God," Marilyn said with a giggle, "you really are a good actress, Kenzie. I'd swear you just had yourself a nice little climax."

Kenzie looked toward the ceiling, closed her eyes, and said, "Who's acting?"

The twins looked at each other with grins, and Sophia said, "I really know how to handle a cue stick, Sis."

"Maybe it's me doing it, Sissy."

"Hmm . . . it's both of you."

"We're the Kildare Kuestick girls, Sissy?"

"Oh, good one, Sis."

They both glanced at Bruno and Dayzee beyond him. Jiff kept his camera rolling.

"And I'm supposed to just stand here and control myself?" Dayzee said before beginning to unbutton her blouse.

She snapped it open, pulled it off quickly, and cast it aside. She wiggled her way out of her skirt, showing her barely-there, frilly purple undies.

"I'm next, girls."

"Oh, Dayzee," Marilyn said with a giggle. "That's quite a sight."

"Thanks, Mare, but I'm serious."

Sophia grinned, checking out Dayzee's panties, and said, "If I ever decide to wear any, I'm copying that style."

"Good girl, Fia."

Bruno had begun flapping nonstop, squawking mixed in with the words, saying, "I'm a man! I'm a man!"

"Oh, here we go!" said Dayzee, and she reached back to pull her barstool closer.

She grabbed the fluttering parrot and pulled him onto the smooth skin of her bare thighs.

"Don't stop, girls. We're almost there!"

Sophia grinned while looking at Kenzie and said, "This girl's already there."

"Oh, I think she's *been* there, Sissy."

"Fifi . . . I'm *still* there . . ."

The Kildare Kuestick girls kept twisting the pool stick around, hand over hand, while Kenzie looked up and began a soft squealing.

In a silent explosion of beefy flesh, a gigantic, very tall Bruno sat on Dayzee's lap, staring and too stunned to speak.

"Now, that's what I'd call naked," Sophia said with a grin while looking down at Bruno's non-parrot pool cue.

"I forgot that he'd be naked," said Marilyn.

"Ugh . . ." said Dayzee. "He's heavy too!"

She gave him a shove, and he stood, both twins still twisting but grinning at his competition for the pool stick's job.

Dayzee quickly tossed his shirt over it, said, "Stay, Bruno," and Sophia grinned and Marilyn giggled at the added weight having no effect.

Dayzee shook her head and added his trousers, and still, Bruno imitated the pool cue. He stared at where the cue stick vanished between Kenzie's thighs and shook in quiet spasms.

"We could really use him in Dayzee's closet, Sissy."

"On yeah, Sis. Hey, Dayzee, keep going."

Bruno still stared and remained frozen, seemingly not sure yet that he appeared to be something like an earthman again, giving Dayzee time to tie together the laces of his boots.

"Oh, that's not even possible!" Marilyn said with a giggle.

"Hey, keep twisting, Sis. Remember Kenzie?"

Marilyn refocused, Kenzie continued to moan, and Sophia said, "I believe he can do it. Go for it, Dayzee."

Dayzee took a step around Bruno, wearing nothing but her frilly purple underwear and her high-heeled short black boots. She shook her head and grinned while laying the laces over their new clothes rack, one big, heavy boot on each side.

No change.

"Yay!" Marilyn said and clapped her hands.

"Sis! Kenzie!"

"Oh, I'm sorry, Kenzie."

She resumed her Kuestick work, one hand over her sister's, and the pool stick continued its slow, steady, gentle spinning back and forth, over and over and . . .

"I can do it!" Bruno screamed. "Thank God, I'm not a parrot anymore. Get that stick out of the way."

Dayzee stepped in front of him, and since he was so tall, looked down with a smile at what waited breast high.

"Bruno, no." She looked him in the eye. "You can play with Kenzie later. We have too much work to do."

"But, Dayzee, I—"

"No! Later! Besides, it weakens you, remember?"

She turned her head toward Jiff and said, "That's a wrap," and slid a manicured finger across her throat.

"No, wait," said Kenzie in a very soft voice. "I'm . . . I think I'm . . . about to—"

The twins kept spinning, but they began to also lift and lower the stick. They smiled once at each other, then looked at Kenzie.

"Oh, please, Dayzee," Bruno said in a whine that didn't sound likely to come from someone so large.

Dayzee couldn't answer. She only held onto Bruno with one hand to watch the big finale.

He said to her, "That's good, too, Sweetie."

"It's still Dayzee."

"Right. Dayzee."

Jiff's camera never stopped.

Kenzie stared at the ceiling and screamed.

The twins held the cue stick up high, angling it almost straight up, with Sophia shaking her head and Marilyn letting out a soft giggle.

Everyone, including the audience, let out a deep sigh at the same time. Except for Bruno.

Dayzee turned to Jiff and said, "Alright, really, that's it. That's the scene."

She looked around the room at the hypnotized men and women, some slowly shaking their heads, others grinning like kids.

"Well," Dayzee said as she began to get dressed, and the rest did, too, "obviously, that won't be part of the broadcast. Leave your names and numbers, and who knows? Maybe you'll get a special offer soon."

Chapter 18 – Dayzee, that's Crazy

"No reason you had to get dressed again so quick, Fifi."

"Sissy didn't want to, I bet," Marilyn said with a grin after the three of them had climbed into the backseat of the hearse. Sophia sat behind the driver, with Kenzie in the middle. Marilyn had squeezed in on the passenger side. Dayzee rode up front, with Jiff driving, and Bruno had crawled into the back and lay alongside the empty coffin.

"Sis, no matter what, we had to get our clothes on. We sure do have a lot of stuff to do."

"Kuestick stuff, Sissy?"

"I just love my Kildare Kuestick girls!" Kenzie said with a big sigh.

"Well," said Bruno, "it's flat-out wonderful that *one* of us is satisfied. I'm—"

"You're probably not back to being flat-out yet, right?" Dayzee said and turned around with a big grin.

"I'll go back and help him with that," said Marilyn, and she started turning to climb over the seat.

"Nope," Dayzee said and reached over the seat to hold her down with one hand on her thigh. "Let's get back to the mansion, alright?"

"Besides," Kenzie said, looking into Marilyn's eyes, "he's my side of beef, isn't he?"

"Sis, you should probably let them finish what they started back at Dayzee's, don't you think?"

"Oh, fine. Go ahead, Kenzie. You two can go wild next to the dead guy in the box."

"Girls, there's no dead guy in the box, remember? He's wandering around in the bushes, looking for his head."

"That will always be funny," Sophia said with a chuckle.

"That was some wild scene back there," said Jiff. "Maybe even more than that crazy stuff up in your attic."

"Oh yeah, for sure, Jiff. I actually liked how that wooden guy winked at you while—"

"'Guy!'" Marilyn said with a snort.

"Well, Mare, we all know guys around the Hills even less real than him."

"'Him!'"

"Anyway, Jiff, yeah, and we have a lot more wild stuff coming up. You think you can handle it?"

"Sure, but don't I deserve something extra for the hazard, Dayzee?"

"Seriously, Jiff? It's not enough just to see us all naked, playing with pool sticks, seducing wooden guys,"—Sophia pointed at Marilyn, who giggled but stayed quiet—" . . . fun stuff like that?"

"Yeah, since you put it that way, sure. I'm in for free."

"As for hazards," Dayzee said while pointing out the windshield, "better get driving so we can start clearing them out, alright?"

"Sure, Dayzee. Why the hell not?"

He started the hearse's engine, put it in drive, and pulled out into traffic on Sunset Boulevard. Seconds later, he took the gentle curve to the left and approached Dayzee's street, where he took a left. He slowed and pulled to the side across the street from her mansion and between the entrance and exit gates.

He pointed out his window and said, *"That's* why not."

Lined up and looking through the fence, not easy to see because of the thick, dark, overgrown backdrop of shrubs behind them, mountain lions padded back and forth, and dead guys, some without heads, stood gazing at the idling car.

Dayzee let out a deep breath and said, "It's never easy, Jiff."

"Too bad the lions won't eat the dead guys," Sophia said.

"Damn lions, Fifi."

"Aw, she still calls you Fifi, Sissy."

"Don't you feel anything funny anymore when you say that?"

"No, and I wonder why? Oh, maybe that pool stick did it."

"You did look kind of cozy up on the table," Marilyn said and stared and waited.

"Oh, really? I mostly felt all squirmy."

Marilyn tipped forward to look at her sister and shrugged.

"So much for that, Sissy. The One-Eighty is gone for good."

"Alright," Jiff said, still gazing out his window, "the lions are a problem, and then, you have those dead guys that are—"

"Dancing," Marilyn whispered.

"—that are waiting for us to go in there. That's two big problems I see already."

"What you don't see is the third problem," said Dayzee, pointing past Jiff. "How do you suppose dead guys are still having a party? Even without their heads?"

"Um . . . I'm supposed to know?"

"No, of course not, Jiff. What you don't see is the assassin that came through the portal back at the Prism. That thing is what's keeping them stumbling around, trying to get us."

"There's a portal at the Prism?"

"Used to be. Right by the big statue guy. Bruno said that it—"

"Oh. About that, Dayzee."

She turned to look at him, and so did the three girls in the backseat.

"Damn, these trousers are tighter than before that game of pool," he said with a big grin.

"Funny, Bruno. Alright, you have our attention. What about the portal?"

"Um, Dayzee, I think it might still be open, but like, running on a different frequency or something."

"Why would you think that?"

"Uh, when I was watching Kenzie riding that stick, I—"

"Oh, she sure was riding it," Sophia said with a laugh.

"We helped, Sissy!"

"Like I was saying, I was watching all that, then I felt like, I don't know, someone from my past was behind me, watching me while I was watching Kenzie."

"Someone like who?" said Kenzie.

"Um, like an old girlfriend. But it's been over with us since—"

"You were thinking about someone else while the Killer Kuestick girls were pool sticking it to me? How could you?"

"'Pool sticking it,'" Marilyn said with a short giggle.

"Kenzie, no, it isn't like that. She—"

"All of you, just stop!" said Dayzee. "Now, Bruno, two questions: are you sure that portal still works, and is your old flame still on Earth?"

"Yes, portal. No, flame."

"Good to both. We might need that portal, but we sure don't need some sneaky little—"

"Oh, Sweetie, she isn't—"

"It's Dayzee, remember?"

"Right. Dayzee. She isn't little. She's bigger than me."

All three in the backseat took turns looking at each other and at Dayzee. Finally, they all started laughing.

"What a cute gal: a female side of beef," Sophia said with a sneer.

"That's a big girl," said Marilyn, slowly shaking her head. "Maybe we should order a jumbo portal?"

"Good one, Sis."

"You like that?" said Kenzie. "That's your kind of thing?"

"Well, yeah. But only before I met you. I swear that—"

"Look, everyone," Dayzee said with a hand raised, "we'll figure that all out later. Right now, we have these three problems to—"

A gunshot rang out, shattering the hearse's windshield but not striking any of the passengers. Jiff hit the gas, the tires squealed, and he raced them all to Elevado Avenue, where he slammed on the brakes. They sat a moment and watched the passing traffic.

"I hate that sniper," said Jiff, clutching the steering wheel with both hands. "Four problems before we even get inside. The worst might be the lions."

Dayzee turned and stared at Kenzie.

"I kind of like the dead guys, especially the ones looking for head."

"That's funny, Sissy. I like how they dance all the time."

"Would the headless ones still want to lead, Sis?"

"Girls, wait."

Everyone except Jiff turned to see what Kenzie would say. Marilyn held her breath.

"Damn lions!" Kenzie said with a laugh but no change.

"Just wonderful," Dayzee said with an eye roll. "Home, James."

"It's Jiff."

"Oh, boy. Fine. Home, Jiff. Turn this heap around and get close enough that we can see what's going on. And watch out for that sniper."

"Just how the hell am I supposed to do that?"

"He does have a point, Dayzee," said Marilyn.

"Yep. Sis is right."

"Alright, then, just cruise along the curb real slow, and let's see what happens."

"You mean, let's see who gets shot? I'm guessing I'm the most expendable one here. It's always the extra guy that gets killed. I've seen that in all kinds of shows."

"Oh, Jiff, you're brilliant!"

Sophia leaned forward and said to her sister, "It had to happen eventually, Sis. We've lost her."

Marilyn shrugged and shook her head, and they both sat back.

With Jiff idling along, the hearse barely moving, Dayzee said, "There. Pull up right there."

"Next to that bum? Why?"

"You'll see."

Jiff rolled up quietly and stayed back a car length, and Dayzee turned to say to Bruno, "Alright, Bruno, we need you to grab that guy, put him on the roof of this thing, and hold onto him through the back window."

"Dayzee, that's crazy. Hey," he said with a big grin, "I think I just came up with a nickname for you when—"

"Don't even think about it."

"Sorry. Okay, but then, what? He takes the bullets for us?"

"Yes, exactly. And then, he's the lion bait too. You see how simple things can be if you just think about them?"

"Doesn't sound simple to me," Sophia said with a smirk.

"Fia, these are desperate times."

"Dayzee's right, Sissy. We still have 'Kildare in the Hills' to shoot."

"Exactly. Oh, look. He's walking back toward my house. Jiff, just follow him, but don't tip him off."

"He's staggering, Dayzee. He wouldn't know if we ran him down."

Dayzee whistled once softly and said, "You know, that might be an even better idea."

"Oh, no way, Dayzee. I can't do that."

"Alright. Just follow him, then."

$*$ $*$ $*$

"Dayzee," said Kenzie, after they'd cruised along almost the entire block and were near Dayzee's mansion, "these Kuestick Kuties and I—"

"Wait, how many names do those gorgeous twins have?"

Kenzie paused and said, "Oh, I still like the name 'Fifi' the best."

"She really does, Sissy. She'll get over that carcass of beef soon."

"Hey," said Bruno. "I have feelings, too, you know."

"Sure you do," Kenzie said with a scowl. "You and that Godzilla girlfriend of yours."

"See, Sissy? She's almost done with him already."

"Alright, all of you, settle down back there. That dead guy is almost—"

"What? He's already dead?" said Jiff.

"Well, no, but he will be soon. Alright, slow down. He's almost there. Okay, stop!"

The hearse jerked to a stop, and Jiff put it in park.

"Now, what?"

"Now, this."

Dayzee tapped her phone a couple of times, and her entrance gate swung in, chasing aside two lions, just as the stumbling stranger passed by. Both lions pounced, there was a short, gurgling scream, mostly drowned out by growls and roars, and they dragged him back through the gate.

Everyone in the car sat and stared. Finally, Sophia spoke up.

"Was that the plan, Dayzee? Feed the cats?"

"No, Fia, I kind of hoped they'd all come out, stay out, and have a nice meal."

"That didn't really work, Dayzee. Might as well close the gate."

"Sure, Mare. Might as well."

Dayzee tapped, and the gate swung shut.

"Hey, I think I saw The Kid," said Marilyn.

"There's a kid in there?" said Jiff. "Shouldn't we try to—"

"No, silly," said Dayzee. "Not 'a kid' . . . '*The* Kid.'"

Jiff turned to look at her, scratched his chin, let out a deep breath, and said, "Okay. Still, what's the plan?"

"God, I'm out of ideas," said Dayzee. "Bruno, is there any way you could—"

"Nope. I'm not wrestling lions while I'm fighting with the dead guys."

"One or the other, right?"

"Yep."

Dayzee sighed.

"Well, we're in a bit of a—oh, wait a second. That car coming our way. I recognize that custom grill—it's the agent that sold me this house. Jiff, pull out and block the road. Hurry!"

"Dayzee, you probably shouldn't keep feeding people to the lions," said Marilyn. "It's not very polite."

"Sis is right, Dayzee. Maybe we should—"

"No, girls, we're only going to use him as bait. Remember how we were going to use that squid fella? Well, this guy's even better for that."

"Why? What do you have against him?"

"Oh, Mare, until I found out about the portal in the basement, I—"

"Not in the basement," said Bruno. "Stairs. Door. Tunnel. Then, portal."

"Alright, I get it. Anyway, he should have told me about it. He deserves to be lion bait."

"Maybe he didn't know about it?" said Sophia.

"Well, Fia, if he survives the cat pack, I'm tossing him right into that portal anyway. Pull across the road, Jiff, we're catching some bait!"

Chapter 19 – He's Still Helping

Before the agent's car had come to a stop, Dayzee was out leaning against the hearse's hood, showing a lot of leg. He stopped, got out, and began walking up to her before he recognized her. His black silk shirt flapped in the light breezes, and he lowered his mirrored sunglasses.

"Oh, wow, it's Dayzee Dazzle! I shouldn't be surprised that I ran into you—well, almost!—on your street. You're looking great!"

"So are you, Silvio. Boy, am I glad to see you. Perfect timing!"

"It's wonderful to see you too. How are you liking that house? It sure is big, isn't it?"

"Oh, it's big, alright. Full of surprises too."

"Good, glad you like it. It's perfect for you. It has *more* than everything you need."

"Oh, you mean, like that damn por—"

"A pool, two guesthouses, a big fence, and,"—he turned to glance at Dayzee's fence and froze.

Lions and dead guys stared back. One was holding his own head, which stared too.

"Say hello to my friend," Dayzee said as she waved for Bruno.

He hustled out and towered over Silvio, who finally broke his gaze of the lions and dead guys and looked up at Bruno high above him.

"He, um, he's not a 'little friend,' is he?"

"No, he sure as hell isn't. Grab him, Bruno!"

"Sure thing," Bruno said, and he gripped Silvio by his back collar and lifted him high into the air, where he whimpered and kicked his legs around.

"Back to the car, Bruno."

"Dayzee, what are you doing? What's this all about?"

"Oh, Silvio, I'd rather you be surprised."

"Can you at least give me a hint?"

"Oh, alright: cats."

"Huh? How about another hint?"

"Sure: dinner time!"

He kept complaining and asking questions while Bruno carried him back to the hearse, let himself in the back door, and held him through the open window.

"This is just silly, Dayzee," Marilyn said with a head shake. "But it *is* kind of thrilling."

"Thrills first, Sis. Kills later. That's what I always say."

"You've never said that, Sissy."

"I'm starting now."

"You two are so cute!"

"They really are, Kenzie. Alright, Jiff, give me a slow roll past the gate. We're trawling for lions."

"Hungry lions!"

"Kenzie, you really don't remember the right way to say it?"

"Oh, sure I do, Fifi. Damn lions!"

*　　*　　*

"God, Dayzee, tell this monster to put me down!"

Dayzee tapped her phone, and the entrance gate began to creak open. One lion peeked out through the opening, and two more stood ready behind her.

"Are you sure about that, Silvio? I bet you're not much of a runner."

"No, no, no! Tell the giant *not* to put me down!"

"That's better. I'm glad you're cooperating. Jiff, I don't know exactly what your new job title is, but here's the deal: cruise slow enough to keep the lions interested but fast enough that they don't eat his legs."

"My legs? Dayzee, let me in the car!"

"Sure, Dayzee. I'll do my best. But hey, wouldn't it be better if I was filming this?"

"Oh, Jiff, that's a fantastic idea! Grab your camera and crawl up on the roof. Kenzie,"—Dayzee snapped around to look over the seat, sending her mane whipping over her shoulder—"you're our driver now. Come on. Get up here. Quick!"

Jiff had mostly shimmied his way out the window, and his legs were still inside, trying to push him off of the seat.

"Okay, but only if we get some good shots of me driving."

"You're negotiating? Even now?"

"Yeah, Dayzee, and I want another game of pool with these Kool Killer Kuties."

"The who? This is getting ridiculous!"

"It really is getting silly, Dayzee," said Marilyn.

"Hey, maybe you have a pool table in your mansion, Dayzee. We should look."

"You're probably right about that, Fia. Who knows what's all in that place? Okay, fine to all of that, Kenzie. Now, get up here and drive."

"Deal."

Kenzie began the climb into the driver's seat, and when she needed some help, Sophia grinned, and Marilyn giggled while each gave her a hand. Then, both hands.

Kenzie paused to say to Dayzee, "This should be on film, too, because I'm more of an actress than I am—"

"Just get up here and drive!"

Finally, Kenzie sat at the wheel, gave it some light gas, and the hearse began to roll with three cautious lions standing outside the gate and sniffing the air.

"Dayzee, this is nuts! Let me in there!"

"Nope. We all have our jobs to do, Silvio."

"I did mine! I found you that amazing house!"

"Yeah, and now you're lion bait. Life can be funny sometimes. My house is funny sometimes too."

"*This* isn't funny, Dayzee! Alright, I'm sorry about the house—I should have told you. Please, just let me in!"

The three lions had begun a steady trot, following the hearse, and at least a dozen more began filing through the gate.

"What should you have told me, Silvio?"

"About the house! I'm sorry. Just bring me in before they eat my feet, and I'll tell you!"

"Sissy, what would a footless dead guy be looking for?"

"Not shoes, and he wouldn't be dancing."

"Good one, Sissy."

"Dayzee! Let me in!"

Kenzie sped up the hearse, and they all heard Jiff on the roof yell, "Hey, easy on the pedal, alright? You almost dumped me on the road!"

"Sorry!"

"Are you getting some good shots up there?" Dayzee said out her window.

"Yeah, I'm getting all of it. Dayzee, that's a lot of lions."

"Get some shots of our driver, too, alright?"

"Sure thing."

He leaned over the windshield and focused on Kenzie.

Kenzie looked into Jiff's lens with her best smile and said, "Damn lions!"

"I think you better just tell me now, Silvio, or that big hunk of beef will drop you on the road like a lump of lion chow."

"Okay! Fine! I should have told you that there was a portal in the basement!"

"Not in the basement," Bruno said as he lowered Silvio enough that his expensive shoes were skidding along the pavement.

"No, I didn't mean that! Stairs, then door, then tunnel, then portal!"

Dayzee turned to see Bruno looking at her with a big grin.

"Ha, ha ha, Bruno. *Not* in the basement."

Marilyn had been watching behind them and said, "Dayzee, I think that's all the lions. No more are coming out."

"Good," Dayzee said and tapped her phone, closing the gate.

"Oh, that's not good, though," Marilyn said while shaking her head.

One of the dead guys had just started exiting the estate, and the closing wrought iron gate crushed him right up and down in the middle, one arm and leg dropping on each side.

"Sheesh," said Sophia. "We're leaving that for the yard guys, I hope."

"What yard guys, Sissy?"

"Girls, we'll get a new crew. One thing at a time, alright? Bruno, you can bring Silvio back in."

Bruno pulled him inside just as the first lion jumped for him. With the window shut and hungry lions throwing themselves at the back door, Kenzie brought the hearse to a stop.

"You knew about the portal?" Dayzee said. "And you didn't tell me?"

"Some guy that said he was your boss told me not to tell you, and then I never saw him again. Is he still around?"

"Um, not like he used to be."

Marilyn giggled, and Sophia rolled her eyes and said, "Kildare Killers."

"Well, the Boss probably had a reason, but I'm still not very happy with you, Silvio."

"Fine. Let me go, and you'll never—"

"Nope. You're not going anywhere. Bruno, in the box with him."

"You got it, Dayzee."

Seconds later, Jiff had crawled back inside, the windows were all up, and everyone grinned and pointed at the lions all around them while listening to Silvio's muffled howls and scratching from inside the coffin.

* * *

"That's two scenes in the can," said Dayzee. "It's not exactly the 'Kildare in the Hills' we thought we'd shoot, but I'd say it's pretty good."

"Maybe not for prime time, though," said Marilyn.

"Sis might be right about that. Even Beverly Hills might not be ready for what we're filming."

"One thing we know for sure," Kenzie said while turned toward Dayzee, "is that you're a damn good director."

"Why, thank you, Kenzie. You're a very good actress too."

"She sure was up on that pool table," Marilyn said with a soft giggle.

"No, she wasn't acting, Sis, remember?"

"No, I sure wasn't," Kenzie said, again looking through the windshield at a lion that had jumped up there and was staring in at her. "I wonder if I could, though? Maybe we should try that again, and Jiff could—"

"Girls, we don't have time. We need to move on to the second problem: all the dead guys."

"Some without heads," Sophia said with a nod and a grin.

"It's good that they all have their feet, Sissy. You know why."

Sophia gave her sister a big smile. Silvio began a soft thumping inside his casket.

Still looking at her sister, Sophia tipped a thumb over her back and said, "The one in the box still has his feet."

"And his head, Sissy."

"Maybe not for long," Dayzee said while shaking her own head. "That clown knew about that portal under—hey, speaking of clowns, I forgot all about those two dead guys we left at the bar. What do you suppose is going on?"

"I bet they're not going to drink and drive," Marilyn said with a chuckle.

"That's funny, Mare. I bet they're not big tippers either," said Dayzee.

"They kind of were up in that bedroom," Sophia said with a big grin. "Know what I mean?"

"I know I do, Sissy. Not anymore, though."

"Nope, Sis, we burned them down to nothing."

"Just that part of them, though, which I still don't understand because—"

"That's one more thing to figure out later, Mare," said Dayzee. "We'll go back for them when we're done with everything else. Right now, we need to clear out the dead guys, including Moe. Headless Moe. Remember him?"

"I will when I see his head," Sophia said. "How do we even open that gate to get back to your mansion without the lions—"

Kenzie raised a hand when the big cat eyeballing her jumped from the hood and began a leisurely trot down Dayzee's street.

"Huh. That's a good sign," said Dayzee. She turned to look out her window and said, "Look at that—my cat is following Kenzie's. They probably got wind of the poodles one of the neighbors lets run in the yard down the street."

"Same with the lions on my side," said Sophia. "Hey, Bruno, what's going on in back?"

"Um, Silvio still isn't very happy, and he's—"

"No, who cares about him? What about the cats?"

"Oh, Lady Sophia, there's only one really big one that's—"

"And we know how you like really big animals," Kenzie said with a scoff.

"No, Kutie Kenzie, that's not—"

"I think I'm back to being just Kenzie, alright?"

Marilyn whispered, "Told you she'd be back, Sissy."

Sophia grinned and nodded.

"Fine. Kenzie. I was saying that I don't like big cats, and this one sure is—oh wait, there she goes. She's joining the rest of them."

"That's a welcome sight," Dayzee said with a deep sigh as they all watched the pack of lionesses trot away down her street. "Adios, poodles."

"So," said Sophia, "once we get inside, how do we get rid of the dead guys? Hey, do we even know how many there are? Weren't we keeping count for a while?"

"Oh, Fia, I sure lost track. There's a bunch of them, that's all I know."

"There's approximately a lot of them, Sissy," Marilyn said calmly.

"Oh, she brings up a good point," said Dayzee. "We need to find all the heads too."

"They're probably in a bush somewhere," Sophia said with a smirk.

"You want me to get some stills of them, Dayzee?"

"Maybe, Jiff. But if they're biting and snarling, maybe video would be better."

Bruno pounded on the box, causing Silvio to fall silent, and said, "I can drag them and their heads down to the basement, Dayzee. That's no problem. But how can we be sure we have them all? Do you even know how big your property is?"

"God no, Bruno. It's like a park."

"Weren't we planning to bounce those heads into the basement?" said Sophia. "That sounds kind of fun."

"We have to find them first, Sissy. If those guys can't find head, maybe we'll have a hard time too."

"Such a sweet kid," Dayzee said with a chuckle while looking at Sophia. "Fia, I bet you have a good joke for that, don't you?"

But Sophia was looking past her with her mouth hanging open, and she said, "I can't concentrate on that now. Look. The Kid is staring at us."

They all looked toward the fence and saw The Kid gazing at them from the sidewalk with lifeless eyes. He'd found his hat, and he held someone else's head by the hair. A thin wisp of smoke rose up from the hole in his chest.

"He's still helping!" Marilyn said and clapped.

"I bet we can get him to cut the grass too," said Sophia. "Because, you know, he still has his own head."

"I don't know, Fia. That might be asking a lot. It's still going to be a problem to find every last dead guy and head, though."

"But, Dayzee," Marilyn said, still watching The Kid, "I'm sure he'd want to—"

With a loud roar, one of the lions pounced on The Kid, who offered no resistance. He lay there until she got a good grip on his neck and began dragging him down the walk.

"Oh. So much for that," said Marilyn.

"Geez, how many times has he been dragged away?" said her sister.

"It doesn't matter, girls. I like how he keeps coming back, though. I'd give him a good reference. Anyway, we still have to figure out what to do."

"Oh, I know," said Marilyn. "Same plan."

"Sis, the dead guys and dead heads won't want to chase after Silvio. The assassin is making them come after us, remember?"

"Yeah, what are you talking about, Mare?"

"Sissy and I can be the bait!"

"Count me in," said Kenzie.

"I'll film it, Dayzee."

"Hey, I'm pretty good bait, too, right?"

"You're the sweetest bait of all, Dayzee!"

"Thanks, Mare."

She shook her head with a grin, then looked around at the group.

"Alright, it's settled, then. All four of us will get naked and—"

"We're getting naked?" said Kenzie.

"I know I am," said Marilyn.

"You always want to get naked, Sis."

"You always want me to, Sissy."

"Yeah," said Dayzee. "We're all getting naked."

"The dead guys and the heads want that?"

"They're still earthmen, dead or alive," Sophia said with a smirk.

Chapter 20 – Dead Guy Roundup

The heavy gate squealed open, dragging a kicking and waving half of a dead guy, the half with the head, across the drive and into the landscaping.

"We really need a yard guy," said Dayzee. "Someone like Carlos, who didn't ask too many questions. Remember how he cleaned up all those body parts?"

"Yes, then Sissy and I burned up him and his brother."

"He's never coming out of the can," Sophia said with a chuckle.

"Just pull in far enough that I can close the gate, Kenzie."

"Sure, Dayzee."

The hearse rolled through the gate and onto the driveway, Dayzee tapped her phone a few times, and the tall black gate swung shut, dragging the same frantic, gesturing body parts with it.

"That driveway's going to need a power wash," Dayzee said with a sigh. "Those bricks, too, where he's all smeared in the grooves. Alright, we're in. We need to hurry, girls, and get out there with our clothes off."

"Why do we have to hurry?" said Kenzie.

"Well, before all the dead guys come after us."

"So, why do we need to get naked, then?"

Dayzee turned to look at the twins, grinned, and said, "She's still kind of new."

She turned back to Kenzie and said, "Because the show must go on."

*   *   *

Jiff, seated to the right of Dayzee, swung open his door, Kenzie did the same, and all three began stepping out onto the driveway. Marilyn reached for the handle, but her sister grabbed her knee, held up one finger to delay her question, and they both waited until the front doors had been slammed shut.

Bruno was next, and he exited through the back, leaving the smothered sobbing of Silvio to keep them company in the otherwise quiet vehicle.

"What's wrong, Sissy?"

"Kenzie's wrong, that's what."

"Oh, Fifi, I know you still like her."

"Yeah, Sis, who wouldn't? She's a good bartender too. That's not the problem."

"What, then?"

"Sis, she's stealing all the starring roles!"

"We haven't even really started the reality show, yet, Sissy. This is just—"

"Oh, you're wrong. These are the best scenes. Think about it: she starred in that pool table scene, right? And just a minute ago, Jiff was leaning over, filming her driving the dead human car with lions chasing us."

"Damn lions."

"Always, Sis. But still, we need to put her back in her place."

"Back at the Prism? Behind the bar?"

"I think so. Maybe if Squid Guts gets better and we get going on a real show, we can let her have a bit part but nothing more."

"You're right, Sissy. If we do another scene at the pool—"

"That's it, Sis! Let's talk Dayzee into doing this dead guy roundup by the pool, and somehow, someway, that conniving barmaid will get bumped right in."

"She'll look like a drowned rat, Sissy!"

"And we'll still be our glamorous, Kildare Killer selves!"

*　　*　　*

Outside the car, Sophia saw Dayzee and Kenzie just beginning to undress themselves, with Jiff and his camera catching every one of Kenzie's gyrations. Dayzee was smiling into the camera as she unbuttoned her blouse.

"Hold up. Stop," Sophia said, and no more clothing was stripped aside. "Dayzee, let's run this operation by the pool, alright?"

"I like the pool," said Bruno.

"We did too," said Marilyn, "especially when you were just the right size."

"I'd be happy underwater on my hands and knees, Miss Marilyn."

"Sounds like you've been doing just about everybody," Kenzie said with a loud huff.

"It was way before I ever met you, and I—"

"All of you, listen: yes, let's get around the house to the pool. Bruno, you just watch out for The Dead Kid, in case he comes back again, and all the rest."

"That's what we're calling him now?" Sophia said while grinning and shaking her head.

"Well, Sissy, he's still The Kid even though he's dead, isn't he?"

"Girls, yes, he's The Dead Kid, and he's taking a high dive into the basement, too, if we can find him."

"I bet eventually, a lion will drag him back to us."

"That's funny, Sissy."

They began the hike around the mansion just as two dead guys, one with a head and one without and not carrying one, broke loose from the long row of shrubs near the gate.

"Only one's looking for head, Sissy."

"I know you don't believe that, Sis."

The girls kept walking, with a long pointy heel occasionally sticking into the soft lawn and having to be pulled out, and Kenzie said, "Just how many are there?"

Sophia pointed at their shuffling pursuers and said, "At least approximately two."

"That's still funny, Sissy. Counting Earth people as approximate."

"We did try to keep track, didn't we, girls?" said Dayzee. "I have no idea."

"Is Broom Bark still wandering around somewhere?"

"No, Sis, he's burned up. And his name was Rake."

"I still say that's just silly. How about the yard guys? Any of them left?"

"Nope, Mare. All gone. I think all we have now are the fresh ones."

"Sheesh, that one carved up and drying on the gate isn't so fresh."

"No, Fia, he sure isn't," said Dayzee. "Maybe we can ask the fire truck guys to hose him out into the street later."

"He's still trying to dance, Sissy. Did you see him?"

"Alright, everyone, we're at the pool, and we have at least two of them—oh, look! Here they come! Quick, girls, get closer to the pool. Let's get these clothes off!"

*   *   *

"Jiff, set up right about there. Perfect. Make sure you get shots of all of us, alright?"

"You're all drop-dead gorgeous, Dayzee, and—"

"That's funny," Marilyn said with a giggle.

"—and I will. You're first? Maybe I'll chop out a still or two and paint you again."

"I'd love that, Jiff. You still haven't delivered the other one, though, from that hotel room. Remember?"

"Oh, it's done, I just, um, I kind of like it, so I, um, it's still, I like looking at it, and—"

"I want that painting. That's not for your twisted pleasure."

"Well, I wouldn't say 'twisted,' just—"

"Hey. You two," said Sophia. "Dead guys, remember?"

"You're the director, Dayzee," said Marilyn. "What's the scene?"

"You and Fia on that side of the steps,"—she pointed to the right—"and Kenzie, you and I will stand over there,"—she pointed to the left side of the steps into the pool.

Sophia whispered to her sister, "See? She's got a little thing for that barmaid too."

"'Too?' Oh, Sissy, you know that Bruno's thing isn't all that little. Remember how his boots were—"

"Not the point, Sis. Okay, the camera's on us—help me unbutton."

"I'd love to, Sissy."

Marilyn reached out and began unbuttoning her sister's blouse, but Sophia stopped her with both hands.

"No, wait, Sis."

She walked to the other side, saying, "Oh, Dayzee, as director, I was wondering what you thought of—"

She faked a stumble on one of her tall heels, leaning her shoulder into Kenzie and toppling her into the water.

"Oh, I'm so sorry! Oh, Kenzie, so much for this scene, huh?"

"She's all wet now," Marilyn said, laughing and pointing. "Don't worry, Kenzie, the three of us will catch all those dead guys."

"And their heads," Sophia said with a snort.

Kenzie had already stripped off her jeans, put back on her shiny red heels, and had been standing by the pool's edge with only thin panties and a tight t-shirt. She stood in the water and glared at Sophia, holding her dripping hair back with both hands.

"It's quite alright, Sophia."

Marilyn whispered again, saying "No more Fifi for you."

"You might as well just enjoy a nice swim," Sophia said as she grinned down at her with her hands on her hips.

"Fia's right, Kenzie," said Dayzee. "We can handle this."

She turned to see how many dead men were being attracted.

"That's only about half of them, so just—"

Kenzie let her wet hair fall behind her and said, "No, Dayzee, the show must go on."

Jiff had been rotating his camera to catch all of the action, but at the sight of Kenzie grinning and peeling up her sopping wet t-shirt, his lens lost sight of the rest of them.

She'd moved to the bottom of the steps and stood there to finish pulling her shirt up and over her breasts. She flashed a big smile at the camera, brought it up over her head, let her soaked hair drop back down, and whipped the wet cloth in a couple of tight circles before letting it fly.

Dayzee and Sophia and Marilyn stood and stared. Bruno had fallen to his knees in the grass and groaned.

Kenzie splashed more water on her chest, and it all trickled down over her breasts, lingering in two places before dripping off completely. She took another step up, tilted her head, and winked at the camera.

Then, she took a deep breath, showing off what she'd just bared, and said in her best sultry voice, "Hey, dead guys. Got some flesh for you."

They all looked around at the sounds of shrubs rustling, branches breaking, and heads being kicked along by the advancing horde.

"Sis, this didn't exactly work out," Sophia whispered to her sister.

Kenzie climbed up all of the steps and let out a loud whistle. She shook her breasts from side to side, flicking drops everywhere, and said, "Hey, The Dead Kid! Want to lasso some of this?" She grinned and held them with both hands.

"Sissy, she's stealing the show!" Marilyn whispered to her sister.

"I, um, I don't think I like giant women so much anymore," said Bruno from his knees.

"Geez, she's even winning him back," said Sophia.

"At least she hasn't—oh, look, Sissy . . . even Dayzee looks hypnotized! What are we going to do?"

"Well, if Bruno wasn't here to catch those dead guys, I'd say we feed Kenzie to them."

"Bad Bruno," Marilyn said with a pout.

Bruno still stared up at a mostly naked, wet, and dripping Kenzie and said, "Damn, you sure are—"

She looked down at him and said, "Kind of sorry now, aren't you? You and your sweaty mammoth women."

"No, I kind of . . . I, um . . ."

He started to shake.

"Uh-oh," said Marilyn. "Big trouble."

"I feel like maybe I, um, I . . ."

"Make it a snake again," Dayzee said with a grin. "A big snake with a gigantic rattle!"

Bruno quickly stripped himself before he swelled up like a giant balloon, his arms and legs and head protruding out in odd locations, waving and kicking, while he laughed hysterically.

"Sheesh. That's not good."

"What the hell is going on?" Kenzie said as she clawed at her t-shirt floating in the pool.

"Oh, that," said Dayzee. "Sorsciencery. It really is nasty stuff."

*   *   *

"Really, Sis? You're still getting undressed?"

"Of course. I try to not let anything stop me."

"At least, keep your heels on in case we need to run."

Marilyn shook her head with a pleasant smile.

"That's just silly, Sissy. You know I can't run in these."

"I know that. I just like watching you try."

"You too, Sissy. Leave yours on."

"What about me?" said Dayzee.

"Oh, Dayzee," Marilyn said with a chuckle, "we always want you naked. Keep those sexy little boots on, though, okay?"

"Gladly."

By the time the balloonish Bruno had quit twitching and expanding and shrinking, Dayzee and both twins were naked except for their heels. Kenzie had given up on her t-shirt and stood dripping in only her panties and heels. They all watched as Bruno sprouted fur, shrank some

181

more, then grew big ears, then became even smaller, then popped out a puffy white tail.

"He's a bunny again!" Marilyn said and clapped her hands, causing her breasts to jiggle around.

"Uh . . . what's going on?" said Jiff.

"Film now," said Dayzee, "explanations later."

"He is kind of cute," said Sophia.

"Mare, Fia, him being a bunny isn't good! He was supposed to corral the dead guys!"

"And their heads. I'm not touching those," Sophia said with a frown.

Dayzee looked around and said, "Alright, I don't remember there being this many. Girls, have you been killing a whole lot more earthmen in your spare time?"

"Nope, not us, Dayzee," said Sophia.

"Look," Marilyn said as she pointed toward one of the guesthouses. "I think that used to be a mailman. There's even a trail of envelopes behind him."

"Two cops over there by the exit gate," said bunny Bruno. "Hey, the one on the left . . . who took his head?"

"Not you, you fluffy little bunny," said Marilyn, and she leaned over to rub his ears and back.

"Ah, thanks, Miss Marilyn. That feels good."

"Bruno, the yard was full of lions, remember?"

"Why are they always ripping people's heads off?" said Kenzie, still dripping. "Damn lions."

Marilyn held her breath and waited.

She glanced at her sister and said, "If ever there was a time, Sissy."

They both watched and waited, the dead drew nearer, and Dayzee finally broke the silence.

"You know what, girls? We need to run. To the house!"

"Should I film you from the front or back?" said Jiff.

Dayzee hesitated, and Sophia said, "You're the director, Dayzee. Your call."

She shrugged and said, "Both. We'll have to do it twice. We'll edit it all up later."

"Wait," said Marilyn. "We're going to run for our lives, then come back to the pool, then run for our lives again?"

"That's showbiz, Mare. Jiff, get us from the front first, because Kenzie's boobs are still all wet. That'll be a good sight."

"Right," said Sophia, "because she's the star."

"Oh, Fia, it isn't like that. Jiff, make sure you get all of our boobs while we're running."

"Okay. Sure. Should I film the rabbit too?"

"Why not?"

Jiff ran ahead and set up near Dayzee's back door. He zoomed in, focused, then whistled.

Just as the first wave of dead guys stepped onto the patio around the pool, Dayzee yelled, "Run!"

All four ran as well as they could in their heels, only Kenzie wearing panties, with a grinning bunny hopping along behind them, and Jiff shot the whole scene as they bounced their way to him.

"And . . . cut!"

"Dayzee, look," said Sophia. "Those corpses are right behind us. Shouldn't we just get in the house?"

"Oh, Fia, no. All we need is a distraction to draw them off somewhere, and we can do it all again."

"Send the rabbit out," Sophia said with a chuckle.

"No, not the sweet little bunny, Sissy!"

"Yep, Mr. Bunny, you're up," said Dayzee. "Cue the rabbit!"

She nudged him out into the yard with the pointy toe of her black boot, and Bruno said, "Are you crazy, Dayzee? Hey, that's still kind of a good—"

She lifted him up on her toe, and with a flick from her toned leg and a quick, "Fly, little rabbit," sent him tumbling into the staggering crowd. When he hit the grass, all of them leaned over to look, even the headless ones. Bruno shrieked and ran toward the guesthouses, with all of them in a slow, awkward pursuit.

"See? Easy. Back to the pool for us."

A gunshot rang out, and Bruno jumped to one side with a scream when the bullet thumped into the ground near his tail.

"I didn't know rabbits could scream," said Sophia.

"Hey!" yelled Dayzee with a fist in the air and scanning all around. "We're coming for you next!"

"And don't you dare hurt the bunny!" said Marilyn.

"Good one, Sis. That'll sure change his mind. Is that sniper really next, Dayzee?"

"No, I don't think so, Fia. I was hoping to get rid of the assassin next, once we dump the bodies in the basement."

Another shot echoed through the Flats, this time tumbling a loose head into the crowd, where it got kicked aside.

"That would be funnier if we had a yard crew to clean it up," said Marilyn.

"It's still pretty funny, Sis."

"Who is that sniper, Dayzee?"

"Oh, Kenzie, there's no time for that now. I haven't exactly been a saint here in the Hills. Come on. Back to the pool."

Beside the pool again, they watched as Bruno screamed, "I just want lady bunnies!" and dove under a large rock in the landscaping. The dead men stopped, turned, and began their migration back toward the pool.

"Uh-oh. Here they come."

"Do you really think they could, Sis?"

"Why else would they be looking for head, Sissy?"

"You two. Alright, everyone in the pool, then we—"

"Do we really have time for a swim?" said Kenzie, her voice rising as she watched even the heads eyeing her and licking their lips.

"No, Kenzie, no swimming today. But we're sure going to shake our wet asses for the camera!"

*　　*　　*

They'd just gotten out of the pool when the gang was almost upon them.

"Run, girls! And shake for the camera!"

"I love my job!" said Jiff as he followed after them, a mob of the dead right behind him.

"Quick," said Dayzee, "close that door, Jiff. We'll be safe in here for a while. At least until we figure something out."

"Wait," said Sophia, wiping water down off of her breasts and bouncing them lightly, "we should—"

"Oh, Sissy. That's a sight. You sure are wet."

"So are you, Sis."

Marilyn smiled at her sister and shook off some of the water.

Sophia turned to Kenzie, glanced down, and said, "You're a little bit wet still yourself."

"Maybe you should dry me off, Fifi?"

"She's done with the bunny guy!" said Marilyn, clapping and causing a steady bounce.

"Hell, I'll get the towel," said Dayzee, and she turned to walk toward the closet.

"Jiff," said Marilyn, "check out her strut. It's the sweetest. Get it on film, okay?"

"Wouldn't miss it."

He aimed and began filming, and Dayzee turned, blew him a kiss, and kept taking long strides to the closet, swiveling her hips around. She found a fluffy towel, turned, and strutted back, stepping hard to cause noticeable bouncing.

Kenzie had put her hands on her hips, and just when Dayzee handed it to a grinning Sophia, while Marilyn stood by silently clapping, the pounding on the doors and windows began.

Sophia jammed the towel into Kenzie and said, "Um, maybe we should run upstairs? And I never finished what I was going to say before."

"Because Kenzie's boobies are too distracting."

"Yeah, Sis. No, I was wondering about this new assassin. Does it play with knives too?"

"Oh, Fia, I have no idea. You might be right about running upstairs, though."

"The safest place is in your closet," Marilyn said with a giggle.

"We could use Bruno as a clothes hook too," said Sophia. "If he wasn't a rabbit."

"Yes, girls, that's all true. Why don't we—"

"Hey," said Sophia, "didn't we leave the squid Cliff somewhere around here?"

"Oh, where has he gotten off to?" said Dayzee.

"It's a big house, Dayzee. No way do we have time to look for him. He could have squidded his way anywhere."

"Good one, Sis."

The front door got kicked in, and Bruno, the one shaped like an earthman, stood holding two dead guys by their necks. They kicked and flapped but couldn't get away.

"Can't hold them like that unless they have heads," Sophia said with a grin.

"No, Lady Sophia, I sure couldn't. Dayzee, you said you wanted them in the basement?"

"Yeah, but, Bruno, what happened to the bunny? That didn't last long."

He still held them high above the ground, and more were stumbling around behind him.

"Oh, that. As soon as I thought of lady bunnies, I thought of all you ladies instead, and I peeked out from under that rock at you all dripping wet, and poof, I was back."

"That's all it takes? No pool table?" said Kenzie

"I think there's probably one somewhere in this mansion," said Dayzee.

"I want to play that game some more," said Marilyn.

"Yep, we don't need Bruno for that," said Sophia.

"I could use some attention from the Kuestick Killers again," said Kenzie.

"Oh, it's all of you, isn't it? Bruno, yeah, down the stairs with them. The heads too. I don't want them lying around the grounds snarling and snapping."

"Hey," said Sophia, "what about that Silvio character?"

"He can snarl and snap all he wants in that dead human box."

Chapter 21 – One of the Dead Guys

Bruno slammed the door to the basement and locked it. He leaned back against it and wiped his brow, then he walked the short hallway to find Dayzee, the twins, and Kenzie seated and standing around the bar.

"Well, that was easy enough," said Dayzee, and she finished her whiskey and poured some more. "You even found that headless Moe fellow. What a disappointment he turned out to be."

"Well, the body's in your basement, but the head is still out there somewhere."

"The new yard crew will find it," Dayzee said and took a drink.

"We're really checking things off of that list of problems, aren't we?"

"We really are, Sissy. And we got some good filming in too."

They glanced at Jiff, who was slumped into a couch, snoring.

"Too much excitement for the camera boy," said Kenzie. "That's okay, let him sleep. We sure did take care of things."

Bruno coughed, and the girls all turned to look.

"We're just messing with you, Bruno," said Dayzee. "We know you did all the sloppy work. We thank you."

They all held up their glasses, gave him their best smiles, and downed their drinks.

"Happy to help. I see you all got dressed again. You know, if anyone wants to take a swim, I'd be happy to—"

"Oh, we will definitely do that," said Dayzee, "you beefy pool boy, you. First, though, we need to get rid of the assassin."

"Hey," said Marilyn, "if you somehow killed that thing, what would happen to the guys and heads in your basement?"

"They'd start to rot," Sophia said with a grin.

"I think maybe they already did," Kenzie said and took another sip.

"Well, if they haven't started yet, they sure will. But really, girls, that won't be such a big problem because—"

"Because you'll have that new yard crew by then," said Marilyn.

"Yeah, Mare, and I hope they live long enough to clean out the bodies."

Sophia scoffed and poured another drink.

"Fia, you can at least try, alright?"

"Oh, Dayzee," Marilyn said with a gentle smile. "You know that's just silly."

Dayzee sighed, looked at Kenzie and shrugged, then turned back to Bruno.

"Alright, if you're done changing into funny things, we still have work to do."

"Right, Dayzee. The assassin."

"You have any ideas? I really don't want to go through what I did last time."

"I thought that was kind of fun," said Marilyn.

Jiff woke up and said, "I had some really sexy photos, too, before that maniac shot up my camera."

Dayzee turned and said, "That is a shame, but we're not playing with wooden door guys anymore." She pointed at Marilyn, who stifled a giggle. "We need to find another way. Bruno, any ideas?"

Bruno grabbed a bottle of beer, walked to an easy chair, sat, and let out a deep sigh. He tipped it back and finished it before looking at all of the staring eyes.

"Let's think this through. He wanted to have sex with Dayzee the last time he was here."

"Who wouldn't?" said Marilyn.

"That closet's just waiting up there," Sophia said with a grin.

"Count me in," said Kenzie. "Dayzee, you're the hottest."

"I'd blush if I still could, but I've lived in the Hills too long. Thanks, girls. Alright, Bruno, what's your point?"

"I'm just thinking out loud here, so nobody laugh, alright?"

"Oh, Bruno," Marilyn said with a smile, "you know we can't promise that."

"Sis is right. I already feel like laughing."

"Why, Fia?"

"Just thinking about all those heads in your basement, Dayzee. What are they doing down there? Should we leave a light on for them?"

"Maybe they're happy just sitting around?" said Kenzie. "Maybe they just want to relax, too, like anyone else."

"Kenzie, I think that might be it!" Bruno said with a big smile.

"No idea what you're talking about, beefy guy," said Dayzee.

"Having sex with you is fun, and—"

"Wait," said Sophia, "you know that? You've had sex with Dayzee?"

"No, I mean, I was just saying. It's got to be fantastic, though, right?"

"I'd agree with that," Marilyn said with a nod and a smile.

"Yep, got to be true," Sophia said while looking Dayzee up and down.

"Alright, girls, we do have to get some work done. Bruno's right, though," said Dayzee. "Everyone gets a smile when I'm done with them."

"If they're still alive," Sophia said with an eye roll.

"Oh, Sissy, I bet they're still smiling anyway. Ours always do."

"Keep going, Bruno. What are you talking about?"

"Did any of those dead guys actually try to hurt any of you?"

"Well, no, but they—"

"Dayzee, sex with you is fun, but so is just hanging out. Like just sitting and watching TV or something. Having a drink. Talking about stuff like we're doing now. This is really good too."

"It really is, Dayzee," Sophia said before she walked behind the bar to freshen up everyone's drinks. "Really, Kenzie, shouldn't you be offering to do this?"

"No way, Fifi. I've wasted too much time behind a bar. I'm just an actress now."

Sophia stared back for a second, then looked at her sister, who only shrugged and looked down at her drink.

"Alright, so maybe I'm good company," said Dayzee. "How would that work? We go up to the attic, get one of those closet doors, make a guy out of it, and what . . . watch a movie together?"

Bruno nodded while Marilyn giggled.

"Yep, except maybe not the furniture guy this time."

"Furniture guy," Marilyn said with a sigh. "Oh, my . . ."

"Huh?"

"I think maybe one of the dead guys will work."

"I knew they could do yard work, Sissy."

"No, Sis, he doesn't mean yard work. He—"

"Girls, hang on a sec. Bruno, you think that assassin would want to take over one of the dead guys, sit on the couch with me, maybe have a stiff drink, and—"

Marilyn giggled and said, "I'm sorry, Dayzee, but that's just too funny, with all the rigor whatever going on down in your basement."

"She's right this time," said her sister. "I wonder if they're putting all that rigor to good use?"

"You know, Sissy, we should really try to throw some dead earthgirls in with the next batch."

"What next batch?" said Dayzee, shaking her head and looking from one twin to the other before turning back to Bruno.

"Alright, Bruno. So, the dead guy will be drinking, watching TV, and what . . . we start making out or something?"

"No, I really don't think so. Just the TV. I think that might be enough."

"That'll kill the assassin?"

"No, Dayzee, I think it's just a matter of giving him some satisfaction. He'll be happy and move on to a graveyard, or a slaughterhouse, or a battlefield, or a train wreck, or—"

"Alright, I get it. Fine. There are a lot of bodies down there. How do we know which one?"

"Oh, Dayzee, it has to be The Dead Kid. He was a sweetheart."

"Mare, you burned clean through his heart after the assassin took him, remember?"

"Oh, yes, I do now. I really am losing count, Dayzee."

"Besides, Sis, we just watched him get dragged away again by a lion, remember? They're probably ripping him apart in a neighbor's yard already."

"Maybe they just want to nibble on him a little, Sissy. I sure would have."

Dayzee paused to tap her toe on the wood floor, glanced up at the ceiling, then said to the twins, "Girls, wait a sec. Do you think he was still possessed when that she-lion snagged him?"

"Well, he sure looked like it, Dayzee. He was cleaning up extra heads, remember?"

"That's funny, Sis. Even dead, The Kid was cleaning the yard for us."

"And he wouldn't be scooping up heads unless he's possessed, right?"

The twins gave each other a look, then Sophia said, "Yeah, probably, Dayzee. What's your point anyway?"

"My point is that the lions probably didn't eat him. Again. They probably left him leaning against a lamppost down the street."

"With that hole in his chest still smoking?"

"Yep, that's right, Fia."

"Is he still wearing that cute hat?"

"I hope so, Mare, wherever he is. He had it on while they scraped him along the concrete. He's the one I want."

"He really was cute. Blind as a bat, though."

"Yes, he sure was, Sissy. Remember his sparkly tooth, though?"

"Oh, that's it," said Sophia. "Lions go after the shiny things."

"Sissy, we only made that up to tell Carlos, remember?"

"Still, it might be true. I liked his hat, Sis. He was built pretty good, too, so maybe—"

"Fine, girls. I'm going on a date with a dead, blind, incinerated Colombian cowboy."

"Aw," said Marilyn, "it sounds kind of romantic when she says it that way."

Her sister only shook her head and grinned at her.

"Bruno," said Dayzee, "have you been listening? Guess what your next assignment is."

*   *   *

After Bruno had exited through the front door and slammed it shut, Dayzee let out a deep sigh and said, "Girls, I don't mind going on a date with The Dead Kid, but it's just TV, right?"

"I think that's what Bruno said. Still, he's pretty hot, and—"

"Mostly because you burned him, Sis."

"Yes, Sissy, but besides that. So, Dayzee, maybe you two will end up making out?"

"Oh, Mare, I know you don't mean that. I'd rather have another door guy, I think."

"Mm-hmm. Me too."

"Whatever happens," said Jiff, "we're getting it all on film. It's just one more wild scene."

"No, really? We have to film it?"

"Oh, Dayzee, it's just a TV date. He's not your next fountain."

"That's funny, Sissy."

"I know, Fia, but—"

A light tapping at the front door quieted them all down.

"Doesn't sound like Bruno," Sophia said with a head shake.

"It sure isn't a bunny either," said Marilyn. "They're too soft and cuddly."

"I'll get it," Kenzie said and quickly jumped up from her seat. "I can't wait to get this party started."

She opened the door, and The Dead Kid was slumped into a heap on the porch, a thin trail of smoke rising from his scorched chest and still wearing his hat. With one hoof holding down the grinning head, a small lamb still held up its other front hoof, ready to tap more on the door.

"Bruno, is that you?" said Dayzee.

"Who else?"

"I love lambs. They're fun to pet."

"How would you know that, Miss Marilyn?"

"When I was in Ireland, walking around the small towns, I petted them along the road all the time. Fed them too. They're so cute!"

"Sis is right. There were lambs everywhere. She seemed to attract them."

"I guess there's going to be a lamb in this mansion too," said Dayzee, shaking her head with a grin. "Looks like you found The Dead Kid."

"It was easy," said the lamb. "He was just down the street, standing by—"

"He was standing? How did that happen?"

"Who knows, Dayzee? It's West Hollywood, and anything can—"

"Oh, you're a funny little lamb, aren't you?" Dayzee said while grinning and pointing at Bruno. "It really is Beverly Hills this time. Well, I guess *you* can't drag him in, can you?"

"No, but . . . um, Dayzee, I . . . lambs usually don't eat odd stuff, and I—"

"No, Bruno, don't eat The Dead Kid!" said Marilyn.

"I already did, Miss Marilyn. Just a little, though, because—"

"Sheesh. We don't want to know. I thought you were a vegan anyway?"

"I am, or I was, Lady Sophia. Who knows with sorsciencery?"

"Just come in, then," said Dayzee. "Jiff, can you prop my date up on the couch?"

"Sure. Um, should we start filming now, or what?"

"Why not? Hand me your camera. I'll do my best."

With Dayzee capturing the action, Jiff stooped down, grabbed The Dead Kid's collar, and started dragging him into the house. Through the foyer, into the great room, and onto the couch he went. Jiff took his camera back and pointed it at Dayzee.

Everyone watched her and waited.

"What? How is this supposed to work?"

The lamb said, "It's a date, Dayzee. Sit next to him."

"Fia, can you at least throw a paper towel over that burnt hole through his heart?"

"That's it? That's enough to make it all okay?" she said, shaking her head and grinning.

"Not even close, Fia. It's a start, though."

All eyes were on The Dead Kid as Sophia laid a paper towel over his chest, and seconds later, it began curling up in flames.

"He's so hot."

"That's funny, Sis."

"Alright, somebody grab the fire extinguisher out of the closet. We should have doused him before he ever came inside."

Marilyn found it, pointed it, squeezed the trigger, and let just enough out to cause some sizzles and pops, then there was no more smoke.

"Cooled him right down, Dayzee."

"Thanks, Mare. Bruno, it's got to take more than me just sitting next to a corpse to make the assassin happy enough to get the hell out of our lives."

"Yes. Yes, Dayzee, of course. Just sit, get close, and I think The Dead Kid will get back to being just The Kid."

"Not with a hole in his chest," Sophia said with a sneer.

"Oh, and those teeth marks too," Marilyn said with a frown. "He's kind of chewed up."

"Fine."

Dayzee sat but left some space between them.

"Oh, come on, Dayzee," Sophia said with a grin. "Cuddle up."

"Fia . . ."

"It's for the best," said the lamb, and Marilyn began to rub its back.

"Oh, that's nice, Miss Marilyn. You sure know how to treat a lamb."

"Sis, while you were hiking around, did you ever roast a lamb for a picnic?"

"Oh, Sissy, I'd never do that. That's what earthmen are for."

Jiff sat in a chair, facing the couch, camera rolling, and Sophia sat next to Dayzee. The lamb stood nearby, with Marilyn crouched down to pet it. Kenzie stood to one side, watching.

"This might be the weirdest thing we've done yet," said Dayzee, shaking her head with a grin. "And that's saying a lot."

"Closer, Dayzee," said Bruno the lamb.

"Bruno . . ."

"The sooner we get this date going," Sophia said as she gave Dayzee a shove, "the sooner we can get back to 'Kildare in the Hills.'"

Chapter 22 – Kinda Surprised Me Too

Dayzee's shoulder was squished into The Dead Kid's, and she turned her head and winced while checking him out. His blank eyes stared straight ahead.

She looked down at the lamb, who'd closed his eyes at the playful rubbing and scratching from Marilyn.

"Bruno. Pay attention."

He looked up, and Marilyn continued.

"He's just dead. Shouldn't something . . . I don't know . . . happen?"

"He needs to warm up to you. He—"

"I'm sorry, but he's only warm where Mare burned him. He's mostly room temperature. Are you sure this is going to work?"

"Maybe you need to loosen up some, Dayzee. Stop expecting so much from him. Next, you'll be nagging—"

"Bruno, that's not even funny. Seriously, what can I do?"

"Oh, I know," Sophia said as she stood up. "Let's get a drink in your hand, and that'll get the party started."

"Couldn't hurt, Fia."

*   *   *

Sophia gestured for her sister to follow her to the bar, and when they were out of earshot, she said, "Sis, now's a good time."

"For what? For us all to have sex with Dayzee? I think we should wait until after—"

"No, to get rid of Kenzie! Even now, she's hogging up the scene."

"Okay, Sissy, but how?"

"I say we throw her down the stairs, lock the door, and since it's far enough away, and who knows what kind of screaming the dead guys are going to do, no one will even know."

"Won't they wonder where she went?"

"Um . . . let's say she ran to the Prism to pick up some booze."

"This could work, Sissy. We don't really need her. I can even call you Fifi if it'll help."

"Thanks, Sis."

"You're very welcome, Fifi," she said with a giggle.

*　　*　　*

"Hey, Kenzie," Sophia called out from behind the bar, "got a minute?"

"Sure, what's up?"

"Oh," said Marilyn, "just some advice about mixing drinks."

"Alright, but that's not really my thing anymore."

She got up, and when Sophia looked at her sister, all she got was a shrug.

"He's coming around, Dayzee," she said before leaving for the bar.

"Yep, can't wait for that," Dayzee said with a scoff.

"What about drinks?" Kenzie said from the drinking side of the bar.

"Well, not drinks so much as just booze. Sis and I need a hand getting more out of the pantry down the hall. Come on."

"Just how much booze do you two need to move?"

"Maybe we just like your company," Marilyn said with a smile and waited.

"Alright. Sure. Let's go. But let's make it quick. I believe this is going to be a fantastic scene, and somehow, I'm working my way into it."

*　　*　　*

"Hey," Jiff said, lowering his camera, "I think he just blinked."

198

Dayzee studied the dead guy's face, then turned back to Jiff.

"I doubt it, Jiff. He's about as dead as dead can—"

The Dead Kid slapped his right hand onto Dayzee's bare left knee and squeezed. His head rotated slowly, and when he'd turned it enough to face her, he tipped his head back. A smile revealed the shiny diamond still embedded in one of his teeth.

"He's alive!" said Bruno, hopping up and down on all four hooves. "Yay, he's just The Kid again!"

"First of all, Bruno, no, he's not alive—that's just the assassin messing with him. And second, do I really have to get felt up on our first date?"

"Oh, it's just some harmless date-night fun, Dayzee. Who wouldn't grab your leg if they had a chance?"

"Bruno, if you think I'm going to make out with him, you're the dumbest lamb ever."

"Hey, no need to be abusive to a lamb. Why don't you put on the TV?"

"Sure, I could do that."

She grabbed up the remote, clicked it, and started flipping through channels.

"Maybe a Western, Dayzee."

"That makes sense."

*　　*　　*

"She stockpiles booze in the pantry?"

"Yes, Kenzie. Way down the hall," said Marilyn. "Come on."

She took her sister's hand and led the way, Kenzie following and occasionally looking back at Dayzee on the couch as long as she could. Farther down the hall, they couldn't hear the date conversation anymore.

"In here?" Kenzie said and reached for the doorknob.

Sophia grabbed her hand and said, "Yep, in there, but first, let's do something fun."

199

"Oh, I like the sound of that, Fifi."

She turned, leaned her back into the door, and smiled at Sophia.

"Aw, too little too late."

Sophia glared at her sister and said, "Sis, that's—"

"What does she mean by that, Fifi?"

"Oh, um,"—she turned back to Kenzie—"she just means that—"

A soft thumping began from the basement side of the door near where they were standing.

"Sissy, what do you suppose is going on down there?"

"I have no idea, Sis. Maybe it's some kind of party?"

"Headless dead guys are partying in Dayzee's basement. Right. You two . . ."

"Oh," Marilyn said with two quick claps. "Didn't Dayzee want a report on how things are going down there?"

"You're right, Sis. I almost forgot. Kenzie, we told Dayzee we'd check on her guests—"

"Guests!"

"Yeah, all those guys in the basement."

"And their heads!"

"Doesn't Dayzee have enough on her mind?" said Kenzie. "I mean, she's got a date with a dead cowboy, Bruno's a goat, and—"

"He's a lamb. A cute little lamb."

"Okay, Marilyn, but still . . . she's worried about the dead guys too?"

"Eh, she's funny like that. We just need to take a peek, that's all."

"Don't let me stop you. Either one of you."

"Oh, you know what?" said Marilyn. "It's only safe to be around them if you can act as dead as them. Isn't that right, Sissy?"

"Yep, I read that too."

"Where did you read something like that?"

"Oh, um, it was some article about being a good actress. I think. Anyway, it takes a really, really good actress to pull it off."

"You know what? I think I can do it. In fact, I'm sure of it. I'll do it!"

Marilyn clapped while grinning at her sister, who shrugged and said, "Have at it, Kenzie."

*　　*　　*

After Dayzee had found a classic Western film and turned up the volume, The Kid's head turned to watch.

"Hey, this is kind of insulting. The dead Colombian would rather—"

"Shh," said Bruno. "Just act natural. Insulting your date won't help."

"God, what next?"

"I think you know. Give him a kiss."

Jiff zoomed in to capture Dayzee's eyes bugging out as she stared at Bruno the lamb, then over at The Kid.

"Um, his hat's in the way. We'll just have to—"

Bruno jumped onto the couch, took the brim of The Kid's hat in his mouth, and gave it a tug. That tipped The Kid's head to one side, making a soft cracking sound, and when Bruno had dragged the hat away, The Kid's head lay mostly on his shoulder.

"Sheesh, as Fia would say. The Kid isn't doing so good."

"Pry his mouth open, somebody," said Jiff. "Let's see that diamond."

"Just wonderful . . ."

Dayzee fingered around with the cold lips while The Kid's lazy eyes watched the TV, and she managed to stick them open.

"Perfect. Okay, keep going."

"You're getting very annoying, Jiff."

"It's an art. Trust me."

"Oh, boy. Alright, now what?"

"Just keep having fun," Bruno said after he'd spat out The Kid's hat. "Oh, and a kiss. Pucker up, Dayzee."

"He doesn't seem interested in me, just the TV."

"Show us some skin," Jiff said from behind his camera. "Pop some buttons."

"For him or for you?"

"For all of us," said the lamb.

"What? Don't you want lady lambs?"

"I should, shouldn't I? Maybe this nasty sorcery stuff is wearing off."

*　*　*

With her hand on the knob of the door to Dayzee's basement, Kenzie paused and looked over her shoulder at Sophia.

"Okay, Fifi, but this might be dangerous, so you're going to owe me."

"Owe you what, exactly?" Sophia said with a grin.

"Blank check."

"Uh-oh," said Marilyn.

"What, Sis?"

"Danger, that's what. I forgot about that."

"You don't think—"

"It'll be fine," Kenzie said and twisted the knob. "Blank check, Fifi. And all I need to do is take a peek and report back to Dayzee. Here I go."

She pulled the door in, and when she leaned in to see just what everyone was doing down there, Marilyn said, "Oops!" and bumped her hip into Kenzie's, sending her stumbling down the stairs.

"Hey, this wasn't part of the deal!"

Sophia slammed the door, and her sister quickly locked it. The pounding from Kenzie began immediately, but the doors were so heavy in Dayzee's mansion that it still sounded like only an unmotivated dead guy pounding.

"Well, that's that," said Sophia.

"You've changed your mind, haven't you, Sissy? You want to cash that Kenzie check, don't you?"

Sophia shrugged and said, "Like that deal is still good anyway. That's one pissed barmaid in there."

"Oh no, Sissy. She's an actress," Marilyn said with a giggle. "Let's see if she can act her way out of the basement."

The pounding grew louder.

"Uh-oh, Sissy, she's really getting angry!"

*   *   *

"Well," Dayzee said as she began to unbutton her blouse, "we do need to get rid of the assassin, and if this is what it takes . . ."

Jiff dropped to one knee so that his camera was level with Dayzee's chest, and he said, "Oh yeah, this is a good shot."

"Should the camera guy really be talking during a reality show?"

"No, Dayzee, I guess not. I guess I'm not used to this. I'll shut up."

"No, that's fine, Jiff. We can't leave shots like this,"—she held her uncovered breasts up with both hands—"as part of the show, which we'll start shooting for real as soon as we fix all these problems."

"Oh, look at that," said Bruno.

The Kid's whole body started to turn toward Dayzee, and his head, mostly still lying on his shoulder, broke out a bigger smile, and his eyes opened wide.

"Now, we're getting somewhere," said Bruno. "Keep holding them, Dayzee."

"You think he likes that?"

"Who cares?" said Jiff. "I like it. They're magnificent."

In slow motion, The Kid's left arm started reaching across, moving so slowly that Dayzee had time to object.

"Oh, no way. You see that? See what he's going for?"

"Who wouldn't?" said the lamb.

"I'm about to put down this stupid camera and grab them," said Jiff.

"You two, you're almost as bad as those gorgeous twins. Hey, where are they anyway?"

The Kid's hand found her left breast.

"Oh, this is weird. Are you sure about this, Bruno?"

"I have no idea, Dayzee. It's all guesswork."

"Oh, boy. That's just wonderful. At least, The Kid is being gentle."

203

*　　*　　*

"Wait a second, Sis. That's more danger than Kenzie has had to face so far. What if—"

"Kozy's coming back! That's him pounding on the door!"

"You think?"

"Oh, we better step back, Sissy, because that door's about to—"

Although the door was built to swing into the hallway, amid splintering and cracking, the twins watched it get yanked inward. It broke into several pieces, which Kozy tossed behind him and down the stairs, striking the dead guys that had begun the climb up.

"Kenzie sensed great danger in the basement. She had to relinquish control so that I could return and assess the situation."

"Welcome back!" Marilyn said and stepped in real close to give him a hug. She pulled herself tight up against him.

"Oh my, Kozy. Tsk, tsk, tsk. You wear that danger well!"

"That part of my anatomy must react to the danger. The larger the danger, the larger—"

"Yay!"

"Well, this is just terrific," Sophia said with a scowl. "With the door shattered, we can't trap them down there anymore, can we?"

"It's okay, Sissy. Kozy will protect us."

"No, I don't believe I will. I can assist in other ways, though. I could—"

"What do you mean, you won't protect us?" said Sophia. "Isn't that your job?"

"That contract has expired. I don't work for free."

"This is crazy. Sis, we need to get away from the basement. Those dead guys will be up here any second."

Marilyn continued to hug Kozy with her head lying on his muscular chest.

"At least, the heads can't get back up here," Sophia said with a smirk.

"Oh, Sissy, I bet the dead guys will carry them up."

"That's just great, Sis. Kozy, if you won't fight dead guys, just what kind of help can you give us?"

"I could call a carpenter."

Sophia only stared at him, and her sister said, "That last one never finished, the slacker."

*   *   *

Dayzee had one dead hand going from one breast to the other while she gazed up at the ceiling. The Kid only stared at what his date had delivered for him and so did Bruno and Jiff.

She looked down and said, "What was all that commotion? What are those girls getting into?"

"Don't break the mood, Dayzee," said Bruno, still gazing at her breasts even though he was still a lamb.

"That's right," Jiff said and kept filming. "Hey, how about if we hurry this along? Pull your skirt up just enough that he can take a peek."

"Oh, Jiff, that's sick!"

"Well, it's kind of for us too. Me and the lamb."

"Oh, Fine. I've never been ogled by a lamb before."

"First time for everything?"

"Sure, Jiff."

She wiggled around until she'd pulled the tight skirt up around her waist, revealing the frilly purple panties beneath it.

"That's a damn sight," said the lamb.

"Whew . . ." said Jiff. "Time for a close-up."

"Oh, no," said Dayzee as The Kid's hand dropped to her thigh, and he started to lean over.

"Next level of foreplay," said the lamb.

"That's not funny, Bruno."

"I've never seen anyone tip so slowly," said Jiff.

"Rigor mortis?" said Dayzee.

"I bet he'll put that to good use soon. How much you want to bet?"

"Bruno! I'm not going all the way on a first date!"

205

The Kid finally stopped when his face landed high up between Dayzee's thighs. He stopped moving.

"What did you do to him, Dayzee?" said Bruno. "You killed him?"

"He's already dead. And no, his,"—she paused to hold her mouth, looking like she was about to retch—"mouth is still alive."

"Okay, this just stopped being sexy," said Jiff. "I'll keep filming, but—"

"This was sexy? Seriously?"

"Kinda surprised me too."

*　*　*

"Sis, we really need to get going. All of them are coming up here, and you're right about them carrying the heads. Sheesh, what a sight."

"Kozy, pick me up," Marilyn said with a grin. "Carry me."

He reached down and easily lifted her up, and she wrapped her legs around his waist, causing her white dress to stretch up high around her waist.

"I should have been doing this the whole time."

"You do look really good like that, Sis. And with the danger coming up the steps, and Kozy being Kozy again, maybe you should—"

"Mm, I wish there was time, Sissy. Right here in the hallway."

"Oh, remember what Bruno said? How those dead guys really haven't tried to hurt us?"

"Yes? So?"

"So, I bet they'll just walk right past."

Marilyn grinned and held Kozy's head with both hands, and he looked into her eyes with a smile.

"Aw, this is sweet," said Sophia. "I can turn so you two can—"

"Oh, no, Sissy. I want you to watch."

Kozy spun Marilyn around and pressed her into the pantry door. With one hand, he began to loosen his trousers just as the first dead guy, carrying two heads and still connected to his own, had reached the top of the stairs.

"I sure hope I'm right," Sophia said and watched the single file of corpses heading their way.

Kozy stopped undoing his pants and turned to watch. That first dead man walked right past him and Marilyn, and by the time the second had reached them and Kozy saw that there really wasn't any danger, he said, "I'm out," and he left.

"Ugh . . . I don't even remember picking you up," said Kenzie. "Weren't we supposed to get some more bottles or something?"

Marilyn's heels hit the floor hard, and she pulled her dress down over her thighs while all three watched the quiet procession passing them with no interest.

"We were, um, just making sure you were strong enough."

"Yep, Sis is right. But now, we're out of time. Those dead guys—"

"Really don't care about us?" said Kenzie before looking down and adding, "How did my pants get opened up?"

"It's this house," Sophia said while pointing all around. "Strange things happen, that's all. Come on, let's see how Dayzee's date is going."

Sophia took Kenzie's hand and led the way back toward the great room, with Marilyn still tidying up her dress and brushing back her wavy blond mane behind them.

*　*　*

"You know what?" Dayzee said to Jiff.

"Yeah, I should have told you to lose those panties too," he said with a big grin obvious beneath his camera.

"No. No, that's not it. I was only going to say that I'm relieved he's more interested in me than the TV. That's all."

"I bet he's still listening to it," said the lamb.

"You're really not very funny, Bruno. He can't anyway because he's—"

She snapped her head around to look over the back of the couch and saw the approaching gang of bodies.

"That one found some head," she said and pointed a thumb at him. "Twice."

"Um, should we wrap this up?"

"No, Jiff, I think they just want to watch. Just like you and the lamb."

"It *is* quite a sight, Dayzee."

She turned around again and saw the silent crowd standing and watching, even the heads.

*   *   *

When they'd rounded the corner, Sophia said, "Oh, Dayzee, maybe you should try a dating service or something."

"That's funny, Sissy."

"No, he's not like a real date. Come on, this is bad enough without—girls, why did you let these dead guys and heads out?"

"We went to check on them," said Kenzie, "then I must have blacked out or something."

"She sure did," said Marilyn. "Right after she wanted to show me how strong she was."

"I did?"

"Then," said Sophia, "your basement door kind of got broken, and—"

"Wonderful. Whatever happened to that carpenter?"

"That slacker?" Sophia said with a scoff. "I'd say he got what he deserved."

"We'll find another one, Dayzee."

"Thanks, Mare.

"Maybe you should hurry this date along," said Bruno.

"What? How?"

"Give him a push."

"No, you can't be serious!"

"He's right," said Jiff.

"How would you know?"

"Eh, I don't. It just sounds fun."

"Oh, Jiff! Fine, here goes."

With both hands, Dayzee pushed on the back of The Kid's head, grinding his face in deeper.

"Alright, this has been fun, but how do we—"

His arms waved around for a second, then he stopped completely.

"Oh, wait . . . he stopped. He was actually doing pretty well there for a while," she said with a soft laugh, "but now? Nothing."

"Well," said the lamb, "there's a commercial on now, so—"

"You're not an amusing lamb, Bruno. You might think—"

Dayzee looked back at the twins just in time to see all of the dead guys collapse, sending grinning heads rolling in every direction. Dayzee snapped herself around to get a better look, and that nudged The Dead Kid off of her thighs. He crumpled on the floor, mostly covering her short black boots.

"It worked! The assassin is gone!"

"I never would have thought," said Bruno the lamb.

"What? You were just messing with me?"

"Kind of."

"Well, still, it did the trick. Now, someone get The Dead Kid off of me."

"Let's keep his hat to remember him by," Sophia said while standing behind the couch and surveying the scene.

"And his tooth, Sissy."

"Sheesh, Sis."

Dayzee grabbed his neck and lifted his head, revealing that his eyes had closed but his mouth was still open, showing one big, shiny diamond, and Jiff's camera moved in tight for a close-up of it.

"And . . . cut!" said Jiff.

Chapter 23 – Well, His Head Anyway

"Well, that's a relief," Dayzee said after yanking her boots out from under The Dead Kid and standing up. "That was kind of creepy, but it did chase that assassin away."

Marilyn walked around the couch and got down on one knee next to Bruno.

"Aw, you're still a cute little lamb, aren't you?"

She began stroking his back and scratching around his ears.

"For how long, though, Miss Marilyn?"

"Are you ready to get back to being a slice of cow?" said Sophia.

"Oh, that reminds me: Squiddy Cliff is still roaming around somewhere in this mansion."

"Yeah, he sure is, Dayzee," Bruno said before looking up at Sophia. "Yes, Lady Sophia, it's a whole lot of fun being a lamb, but I'm ready to come back."

"And lucky us," Sophia said as she walked around behind Kenzie, "we already have a plan that we know works."

Dayzee pointed at Jiff and said, "Roll camera."

Jiff raised his camera and focused on Kenzie, standing still, beaming a big smile, and staring right at the lamb. Sophia stood directly behind her, and she reached around to grab a lapel of Kenzie's jacket in each hand.

Sophia leaned in to smell her hair, then she turned her big blue eyes to gaze at the lamb too.

"I, um, I . . . feel kind of funny," said the lamb.

"Me too," said Jiff.

"Oh, not like that lamb, I bet," said Dayzee, then she quickly looked back up at the unfolding scene.

"What do good little lambs like?" said Marilyn. "Oh, I think Sissy knows."

"Oh, and Bruno," Kenzie said, "Fifi and I would probably be doing this anyway, even if you were nowhere around. Think about that."

"I . . . oh my, that's—"

"And Dayzee and I would be helping Sissy undress her," Marilyn said with a giggle.

The lamb shook a few times and snorted.

"Then, after Fia got Kenzie nice and naked, Mare and I would undress Fia, too, Bruno. Can you imagine that?"

The lamb looked up at the ceiling and yipped once.

"Dayzee and I would already be naked," said Marilyn. "Oh, except for our heels. We'd all keep those on. How about that, Bruno?"

"I, I, I, I . . ."

Sophia slowly pulled open Kenzie's jacket, and when her breasts were fully exposed, Kenzie reached up with both hands to hold them.

The lamb started shaking again and didn't stop.

"I'd be holding one of those for her," said Marilyn.

"And I'd hold the other," said Dayzee. "I'd use both hands too. Just my fingertips."

The lamb howled to the left then to the right before again staring at the scene and panting.

Kenzie said, "And I'd turn, just like this, and give Fifi a nice, long kiss."

In an explosion of wool and skin, Bruno stood naked and watching Kenzie holding herself. He had no clothes and appeared very interested.

"Like I said," said Sophia, "we know what works."

Bruno shook while Marilyn looked down at him, pointed, and said, "Clothes hook!"

She grabbed up one of Dayzee's big, heavy coffee table books, opened it to the middle, flipped it over, and laid it on him.

She clapped her hands and said, "That's my Bruno!"

"Don't stop, Sis. I bet Bruno's a two-booker."

"Lady Sophia. Miss Marilyn. If Dayzee won't let me use this, I should probably find my clothes and—"

He showed that he could carry another book.

"God, if we didn't have so much to do, Bruno," Dayzee said with an admiring grin. "Don't miss that lamb now, do you, Mare?"

"A little. But this is fun too. Where's your library, Dayzee? You must have a library, right?"

"Mare, let him get dressed, alright?"

Marilyn crossed her arms and pouted while Bruno quickly got himself clothed.

Kenzie still held herself through all of the book piling and turned her head to say to Sophia, "Did you really know that would work to change him back?"

"Actually, I didn't think it would."

She gave Kenzie a grin.

"Oh, Fifi, that's—"

Two quick gunshots rang out somewhere around Dayzee's estate, and there were two metallic clunks.

"Oh, boy," said Dayzee. "How's that for a reminder?"

"Damn sniper," Kenzie said with a grin while pulling her jacket closed.

"That's funny," Sophia said as she fluffed Kenzie's hair back.

"Oh yeah—the sniper," said Marilyn. "Who's he shooting at?"

"Silvio, I bet," said Jiff.

"In a dead human's box," said Bruno.

"In a dead human's car," said Dayzee. "Only in the Hills!"

*　　*　　*

"It's been a productive day so far. We've chased away the lions."

She paused, and everyone joined her in watching Kenzie, who only looked between them without saying a word.

Dayzee sighed and continued. "We tucked Silvio in that box, shoved the dead guys and some of the heads into the basement—even though they're all right here again, and we—"

"Sheesh. How are there so many?"

"Kildare Killers, Sissy."

"No, Sis, we only killed those two clowns that are still back at the Prism."

"They'd be even funnier if they lost their heads, Sissy. They'd finish drinking and start looking around for—"

"No, Sis, they're probably dead too. Right, Dayzee?"

"Yeah, Fia. For sure. Oh, and remind me to have the new yard crew scare up whatever loose heads are still out there."

"'Loose heads,'" Marilyn said with a giggle. "That's just silly."

"If they can find them," added Dayzee.

"The heads won't be happy," Marilyn said, shaking her own head slowly.

"No, Sis, even those heads are dead again, right?"

"Sissy, I bet the new yard guys will be looking for head anyway."

"Girls. And we finally got that assassin to leave us alone. Time for us to deal with that sniper, alright?"

"That's easy enough," said Bruno. "There's already bait in the box out there."

"Exactly," said Dayzee. "After the sniper, then we'll have to find squid belly and try to fix him up."

"You, too, Dayzee," said Marilyn. "You've got a little squid in the oven too."

"Oh God, that's right. With all the excitement, I kind of forgot."

"Can you feel it squirming around in there?"

"That's not even funny, Fia. Alright, and after we de-squid whoever needs it, we're getting a brand-new yard crew."

"As long as they're hot."

"They'll heat up with us around, Sissy. Remember Carlos and his little brother?"

"Yep. They're still in the can."

"Girls! After we get the lawn guys going, I'm finally getting a butler too. Anything else I'm forgetting?"

"A carpenter," said Sophia. "Don't get another slacker this time," she said while shaking her head.

"He wasn't really a slacker, Fia. He got stabbed. More than once. Remember?"

Sophia tipped her head at the pile of dead guys and said, "Never slowed these boys down. What was his excuse?"

"That's funny, Sissy."

"Alright, I'll get a carpenter. The house does need some work. Then, that ought to do it, right?"

"Um, Dayzee," Bruno said while scratching his chin. "What about that portal?"

"Oh my God! Yeah, there's always that too. What can we do about that?"

"I think I can help with that. Maybe change its frequency."

*　　*　　*

With the front door cracked open, Dayzee peered all around her estate, trying to locate the sniper. He held back his fire, and the only sound, besides the light traffic, was a soft pounding coming from the bullet-riddled hearse.

She closed the door and leaned back against it, letting out a deep sigh.

"Alright, we need an idea. Some kind of plan."

Sophia said, "Really, Sis? Undressing? That's your plan?"

Marilyn had already pulled the straps of her white dress down over her shoulders, and before she bared her breasts, Dayzee snapped her finger, pointed, and Jiff got his camera going.

"It's almost always your plan, too, Sissy," she said with a giggle, which gently shook her breasts around.

"So, you've already given up on that sniper? You just want that camera—"

"No, Sissy. I'm going out there, and I'm going to take my time and strut all the way to the dead human car."

"That's your plan, Mare? What good will that do? Aren't you afraid of getting shot?"

"Oh, Dayzee, I never slept with any married men around here," she said and started wiggling to get her dress down over her hips.

"Ireland, though," Sophia said with a scoff.

"Well, Sissy, so did you. Sometimes the same one. At the same time because we're twins, and we do everything—"

"Mare, back on topic. What's your plan?"

"Dayzee, I don't believe he'll shoot me. He's probably an earthman, and he'll forget all about shooting. The gun, at least."

"The one in his hand, Sis?"

"Only one of them, Sissy."

"Good one, Sis," her sister said with a big grin.

"Alright, say you make it to the car—then, what?"

"I can drive it at least this far, up to your porch, and we can all get in."

Dayzee and Sophia and Kenzie gazed at each other in silence, then they all turned to Marilyn.

"Alright, and then, what?"

"Back to the Prism!"

Dayzee shook her head and blinked a bunch.

"Mare, maybe we should just drink what we have right here."

"Oh, I know, Dayzee. But the sniper earthman will follow us, won't he? We'll go real slow, maybe circle around the block and come up behind him."

Dayzee grinned, pointed at Marilyn, looked at Sophia and Kenzie, and said, "She just might have something there."

"God yeah, she does," said Bruno. "Miss Marilyn, you're stunning."

"Aw, thanks, Mr. Beef."

"I'm getting a close-up."

"Be my guest, Jiffy!"

*   *   *

Dayzee cracked open the front door just as Marilyn's dress dropped to the floor, revealing only tiny white underwear.

"That's got to go too, Sis."

"You wouldn't need that extra step, would you, Sissy?" she said with a giggle.

"Never."

Marilyn soon stood naked except for her white heels. Sophia stood to one side of her and Kenzie to the other. Both fussed with her hair until they thought she was ready. Jiff circled around, capturing everything.

Bruno pried his eyes away from Marilyn long enough to glance out a window, and he said, "Hey, there's Moe!"

He pointed, and Dayzee shut the door, hurried to stand beside him, and followed his pointing finger.

"God, he's right there on that tree branch. Well, his head anyway."

"He's looking right at us. Shouldn't he be dead again?"

"Oh, you know what? He's not an earthman—maybe those assassin rules don't apply to him."

"Ah, yeah. He got brought back, and he stayed back?"

They both looked through the foyer and into the great room at the pile of bodies, none of them moving.

"Maybe just the head stayed alive?"

"That's weird," said Marilyn. "Those guys are weird no matter what."

"I'll tell you what's weird," said Sophia. "The other two, Abbott and Hardy . . . what does that mean for them?"

"Sissy, we really do have to make it to the Prism whether we get that sniper or not."

"Girls, you're saying that those two clowns have dead bodies, but their heads are still doing alright?"

Marilyn sighed deeply and said, "It would seem so, Dayzee. I'm not sure how people at the Prism will like that."

"Mare, remember that it's—"

She stopped to look at Bruno, who had a big grin. She pointed at him and began to smile.

While still looking at Bruno, she said, "Remember that it's happy hour. They'll be fine."

"So, we still need the dead guy car?"

"Yeah, Mare. You're sure about this?"

"Sis is unstoppable when she's naked, Dayzee."

"So are you, Sissy."

"Well, sure, Sis—we're twins."

"What about me?"

"You too," said Kenzie. "I know I am. Or at least, I can act like I'm unstoppable."

Sophia looked to her sister, who was already looking down and shaking her head.

Dayzee approached the front door, opened it while standing behind it, and said, "It's your scene, Mare. Be careful, alright?"

"Nothing to it, Dayzee. I'll give it my best strut."

"She does have a good strut," said Sophia. And when Dayzee gazed at her with her eyebrows up, she added, "Yours is sweet, too, Dayzee."

"Thanks, Fia."

Marilyn stepped out onto the porch, paused with her hands out as if checking for rain, then began a slow strut toward the hearse near the entrance gate.

*　　*　　*

Jiff knelt near the door opening with his camera aimed at Marilyn as she took graceful strides to the hearse. Dayzee peeked over him and said, "I hope she's going to be alright."

Sophia grabbed the door and pulled it open wider.

"No way that sniper will be looking anywhere else now."

"I believe that's right, Fia. That sister of yours sure learned a nice strut."

"Eh. She was strutting before she could walk. Besides, I kind of hope that maniac takes a shot at her."

Dayzee snapped her head around.

"Fia, why? Why would you want her to get—"

"Dayzee, don't worry. I just like watching her run in heels."

Looking back out along the driveway, Dayzee said, "Me too. Alright, let's hope for some gunfire."

Without looking back inside, Dayzee said, "Kenzie, everything okay with Moe?"

Kenzie had joined Bruno to watch out the window. They mostly studied every move Marilyn made, but they gave occasional glances at Moe, who was still grinning on the tree branch.

"He looks happy enough. Your house is weird, Dayzee. It's mostly because of this house, isn't it?"

"Probably, Kenzie. Bruno, have you seen Moe move his eyes yet? Are we sure his head is alive?"

"Not yet, but—"

"Good, maybe he's not really—"

"His smile got way bigger with Miss Marilyn strutting past him. He's got some pretty nice teeth for a weirdo."

Dayzee sighed and said, "Well, good. We just need—"

A gunshot exploded and echoed off of the guesthouses, and a chip of the driveway next to Marilyn flew up.

"Hey," Dayzee yelled out the door, "you're going to pay for that!"

Marilyn started a choppy run on her high heels, jiggling everything around.

"And there we go . . ." said Sophia.

"Ah, now that's a sight," said Dayzee.

"We're going to kill that sniper guy," said Sophia, "so, yeah, he's sure going to pay. But we kind of owe him too. Look at Sis go."

"Oh, you know what, Fia? I think that kook missed her on purpose."

"You're right—he's enjoying the show as much as us!"

"How did that head turn its head like that?" said Kenzie.

"That's funny, Kenzie," Sophia said without looking.

"I don't know," said Bruno, "but mine did too."

Sophia and Dayzee turned to grin at Kenzie, who smiled back, before they continued to watch Marilyn bouncing and teasing her way to the hearse in only her heels.

Chapter 24 – In West Hollywood

"That might have been the best scene so far, Sis."

"You have some real tone, Mare, but that was some sweet bouncing around too."

"Thanks, Sissy. Thanks, Dayzee. Except for there not really being any dialog."

"That's what you think."

Bruno had squeezed his large frame into the driver's seat, and Dayzee kept him company up front. In the backseat, Sophia sat on the driver's side, Marilyn on the other side, and Kenzie was squished in the middle.

"There's really more room than this, isn't there?"

Sophia scoffed and said, "Sure, Kenzie. So?"

"Just asking," she said with a big grin.

"Jiff," Dayzee said while turned around, "you might as well get all of this, too, don't you think?"

He sat cross-legged next to the casket, sometimes pounding on it to keep Silvio quiet. He picked up his camera, and each girl in the back took a turn smiling for him, then he focused on Dayzee up front, who blew him a kiss.

He lowered the camera and said, "Hey, was that for me? Or was it—"

"Both," she said with a smile. "Keep shooting. Bruno, let's do a slow roll around the drive and aim for the exit gate."

"You got it, Dayzee."

He started the engine, put it in drive, and struggled to turn the wheel, which was tight against his chest. He tapped the gas, and the hearse lurched to begin its crawl around Dayzee's front yard.

"Alright, back there. Everyone watch all around. If you see anything unusual, just—"

"Moe's looking at me," Marilyn said and made sure the straps of her dress were untwisted. "That's kind of unusual, isn't it?"

She pointed out the window, and Sophia and Kenzie leaned over to look.

"Sis is right. That's pretty creepy. Hey, Sis, why the big smile?"

"I try to always smile when I look up at the good things in life."

"That one kind of fits, Sis. Even a grinning head in a tree?"

"Sure, Sissy. Why not?"

"If we had time," said Kenzie, "I'd say we should put his body up in the tree with his head. He could keep himself company."

"Kenzie, do you feel alright? What a strange thing to say!"

"I do feel kind of funny, Dayzee. Nothing ever bothers you, though. Or you,"—she turned toward Sophia—"or you,"—she turned toward Marilyn. "Why is that?"

"You haven't figured it out yet?" Dayzee said with an eye roll. "We're not from around here, that's why."

"I know. You said Ireland. But people in Ireland are—"

"People? Farther away than Ireland," said Marilyn.

Kenzie turned toward her.

"A lot farther," Sophia said with a smirk. "Like, forget maps."

Next to the coffin, Jiff lowered his camera and said, "They're not from Earth, Kenzie. That's why. Damn, I'm surprised you didn't already know that."

"Oh, now I really feel funny," she said and held her belly. "I thought Bruno was only joking about that."

"After all we've been through?" said Dayzee. "Now, you feel funny?"

"Maybe she's got a baby squid, too, Sissy."

"Sis, that's not funny."

"Oh, I don't feel so good. I feel like I've been in a dream or something, and now, I'm waking up, and it's . . . I don't know what."

"Sissy," Marilyn whispered. "She just needs more heat."

Bruno watched in the rearview and piloted the hearse slowly along the circular drive, past Moe's grinning and staring head in the tree, and toward the exit gate.

"She probably just needs a drink," Sophia said with a chuckle.

"Maybe a game of pool, Sissy."

"You two, this isn't funny anymore. None of this makes sense. I need to get out of here. Hey, stop the car. Stop the—"

Two quick shots rang out, one taking out the front passenger-side tire and the other ripping through the roof and shattering part of the casket. A big chunk flew off, hit the back of Kenzie's head and continued past, spinning on the dashboard before coming to stop.

"Whew, that was close," Dayzee said and picked it up.

She turned around to see Sophia and Marilyn shaking an unconscious Kenzie lightly, getting no response.

"Beddy bye time for Kenzie," Marilyn said with a shrug. "Maybe a kiss would wake her up, Sissy?"

"I shouldn't take advantage of her, Sis."

"She would with you, I'd bet. I would, too, if I ever found you knocked out, Sissy, because—"

"Girls, settle down. Is she going to be alright?"

Sophia checked for a pulse and said, "Yeah, she's fine. A little nap is all."

Dayzee turned to Bruno and said, "Alright, the plan's the same. We lured that sicko out of hiding, and now, we just need to spot him. Everyone, keep looking around."

Out through the gate Bruno drove the hearse, and no more gunshots hit them. Just before they turned right onto Dayzee's street, Sophia turned to look one last time.

"Hey, I think Moe just said goodbye."

"Dayzee, maybe his head is enough to cure you of your squid child?"

"Mare, you might be right."

Sophia laughed once and said, "Now, Dayzee's looking for head too."

*　　*　　*

Bruno took a right on Sunset, and after traveling only a few blocks, he hit the brakes, carefully slowing the hearse, and suddenly, he locked it up, and they came to a stop. Sunset's gentle curve to the right was just ahead, and farther along, the Prism on the left.

"Did you see him?" said Dayzee. "That sniper? Where is he?"

"Nope. I have no idea where he is."

"So, what's going on? Are we out of gas or something?"

"No, Dayzee, nothing like that. It's just that this is a fun spot. Exactly right here."

"I don't get it."

"Neither do I," Sophia said with a scowl. "Come on, beef boy, we all need a drink."

"Kenzie more than anyone," Marilyn said with a shrug.

"Bruno, explain yourself."

"Dayzee," he said and pointed to the backseat with his thumb, "those lovely ladies are—"

"Hey," said Jiff, "I'm back here, too, you know."

"Right. Sorry, Jiff. Alright. Dayzee, Jiff and those lovely girls are in Beverly Hills. But you and I?"

"We're in West Hollywood!" She leaned across and punched his thick arm. "We should mark this spot somehow, don't you think? Then, we'd always know for sure."

"I always know for sure."

"Don't be a smartass just because you got the map download."

"Sorry, Dayzee. Of course not. How can we mark it?"

"Let's leave the casket up on the sidewalk over there."

"Oh, I don't know about that, Jiff. Some neighborhood kids might get trapped in there."

"To keep Silvio company?"

"No, Mare, we'll have to take him out at some point."

"We should have brought Moe's head," Sophia said with a grin. "We could have stuck it up on top of that streetlight."

"That would be pretty funny, Fia, especially how he'd grin at all the cars going by."

"Eh, he'd probably cuss at them."

"Yes, he sure would. That would teach my neighbors a thing or two."

"Oh, I know," said Marilyn. "I can hang my dress on that signpost right there. Everyone will know that Marilyn was here."

She started undressing, then Dayzee turned and said, "You really do undress for just about anything, don't you?"

"Oh, she sure does," Sophia said with a big smile. "That's my Sis."

"Well, those are all really good ideas, but maybe we—"

Kenzie awoke with a jerk, opened her eyes, and said, "Oh God, I'm going to barf. Hey, quick, drop that window!"

With the window opened, she leaned across Marilyn's lap, hacking out onto the road. Marilyn reached around and hugged her and patted her back, and Sophia helped by getting a handful and propping her up close to the window.

Kenzie finished, spit a couple of times, flopped back inside, and fell back asleep.

Sophia shook her head at Dayzee, grinned, and said, "There's your mark."

"Oh, only until it rains, Fia."

"You're right. Let's go back for Moe."

"Sissy, the lions would get him."

"They're looking for head, too, Sis?"

Kenzie, still asleep, mumbled, "Damn . . ."

Sophia and Marilyn both stared at her and waited, not daring to breathe. Dayzee turned around with big eyes too.

"Damn it . . . ." she said and began to snore with a hand on her abdomen.

The twins grinned at each other, then at Dayzee, who turned to Bruno and said, "Alright, to the Prism. Drinks are on me."

"With a flat tire?" said Marilyn. "What will people think?"

Sophia scoffed while Dayzee turned and grinned at Marilyn.

*   *   *

"How do we always get this parking place?" said Marilyn.

"We're their best customers, Mare. Jiff, keep your camera ready—fun things always happen here. Especially when we pick up those two dead clowns."

"Is that headless dead pretend producer still in there somewhere?"

"Didn't we take him back to the mansion, Fia?"

"We really are losing track of the bodies. I bet he hasn't found any head, Dayzee. Not even his own."

"Probably not, Mare. I'm not sure it ever got down into the basement."

Sophia said, "What about Kenzie?"

"She's still not awake, Fia?"

"Nope. She got clunked pretty good."

"Bruno, can you tote her back inside?"

"Sure. Maybe we should have changed her clothes, though."

"Think again," Marilyn said with a giggle, and when Bruno turned to see, she pulled one lapel of Kenzie's jacket aside, proving that she still wore no shirt beneath it.

"And again," Sophia said with a grin as she pulled aside the other lapel.

Bruno shook his head and said, "Kutie Kenzie. Well, not anymore."

"Besides, Bruno," Dayzee said, "who's to say she won't turn into Kozy again when you least expect it?"

He turned back to face the front and sighed, and Dayzee said, "Cheer up, big fella. I say we get her liquored up, and she'll forget all about that Goliath girlfriend of yours."

He grinned and said, "You think?"

225

"Nope. Not a chance. Sorry, Bruno."

He sighed again and opened his door and so did the rest of them. Right after Jiff had climbed out the back, he said, "What about the guy in the box?"

"He'll be fine if you give him some fresh air. Just crack it open, Jiff, and close it right back up, alright?"

"Yeah, why not?"

He unlatched the lid, pried it up, and Silvio said, "Hey, wait, I can tell you how to—"

Jiff slammed it shut, latched it, and swung shut the hearse's back door.

"What do you suppose he was talking about?"

"No idea, Jiff. We can ask him later. Come on, girls, let's get our favorite seats."

"Oh, Dayzee, not the one that held you down while the foot rest took advantage of you."

"No, Mare, that one's out with the trash. Let's see what else is going on in there. The assassin's gone, and—"

A gunshot took out the other front tire.

"Oh God, we forgot all about that psycho. Run!"

*   *   *

They all hurried inside and swung shut the large, heavy wooden door. Dayzee's chest heaved in her tight, largely unbuttoned blouse as she looked around the room. Sophia brushed back her long, silky hair, and Marilyn tugged at her short white dress. Bruno stood with Kenzie, limp and lying over his shoulder. Jiff held his camera ready and watched Dayzee's chest rise and fall.

"Not much of a crowd," Dayzee said over the low classic rock.

Sophia shook her head, pointed, and said, "Except for those two inoculator guys. They sure look dead."

"Maybe not their heads, though, Sissy. They might be singing, or nibbling on peanuts, or maybe just chatting with Mack sometimes."

Mack glanced over, gave them all a quick salute, then turned to the bottles to get going on their drinks.

"Where should I put her, Dayzee?"

"Oh, I know," said Marilyn. "Put her behind the bar."

"What, lay her down back there?"

"Nope," said Sophia, "give her a barstool. Prop her up somehow."

"Sure, Lady Sophia."

He set off for his task, hooked a stool on the way, and carried it and Kenzie around behind the bar.

Dayzee and the twins each began their own style of strut toward the bar, with Jiff several steps behind as Dayzee had directed him, filming the scene, which was almost entirely below waist level.

Marilyn sat to Dayzee's right and Sophia to her left. To Sophia's left lounged the two dead guys, still shirtless, still muscular, and still sporting long black braids.

Sophia glanced at them, then turned to Dayzee and said, "Even their heads are dead. They sure aren't singing, Sis."

"Maybe they'll dance for us later, Sissy?"

"Nope, Sis. We'd need that assassin to liven them up."

"So, Fia, why do you suppose Moe's head is still alive?"

Marilyn said, "You two are silly. It's only because it's off by itself up in a tree."

"Mare, you think if we had Bruno rip these guys' heads off, then they'd be drinking with us?"

Sophia said, "Well, maybe not drinking. Snarling and swearing? Yep."

Dayzee looked up at Bruno, who still stood behind the bar, keeping Kenzie from tipping off of her stool, and said, "Bruno, when you get some time, maybe—"

"Oh, I don't think so, Dayzee. I can't just go around tearing heads off of people."

"Those aren't people," said Marilyn. "Anyway, you did when you were a snake. Remember that?"

"Sis is right. Besides, they're already dead."

Dayzee shook her head and said, "Fine. Maybe back at the house. We could line up all the heads and—"

"Bruno!"

They all turned toward the giant statue guy with a hat, and next to him stood a thick, sweaty, unkempt woman even taller than Bruno. Her hair was a black mop pulled from a bucket of filthy water and dropped on her head. She was packed with muscles covered in tattoos, all bulging out in every direction from behind her black tank top and tight black shorts. Her black boots rose to her knees and were laced all the way up the front. Her bloodshot eyes stared as the pointed one meaty finger toward the bar.

"Just wonderful . . ." said Dayzee with a grin.

Bruno's woman reached with her other hand to scratch at the two-day growth on her chin and said again, "Bruno!"

Chapter 25 – I Just Met You

"Bruno, that's your little honey?" Sophia said with a scoff.

"Oh my, she's very large," said her sister.

"Is that how portals work?" said Dayzee, shaking her head. "You need a blast with a fire hose when you climb out of one? Jiff, catch some of that action over there."

Bruno ignored all of them and took a step toward his girlfriend, and when Kenzie started to tip, Sophia tried to grab her, but she found only one lapel.

"Uh-oh, Sissy. This should be fun."

"Hold up, Jiff. Get Kenzie first."

Jiff filmed while Kenzie kept falling, and somehow, she twisted around and worked her way entirely out of the jacket as she crumpled gently to the floor, still snoring.

"Sleeping beauty, Sissy."

"With boobs like those, Sis?" Sophia said as she bunched up Kenzie's jacket on her lap.

"Yes, if it were up to me. If I were the one drawing cartoons, I'd—"

"Girls, aren't you curious what's up with Bruno and that monster woman? Let's watch, alright? Jiff, back to the behemoth."

"That's a funny word," Marilyn said with a giggle.

"Kenzie looks way better," Sophia said while raised up off of her stool and peeking over the bar.

"Sissy's right, Dayzee."

"But, girls, this is important—we need Bruno to take Abbott and Hardy back to the house. We can't let that mutant woman beat him up."

"Aw, Dayzee, she's probably only going to kiss him."

Sophia looked over at the woman, scoffed, and said, "Yeah, while she's slapping him around. Bruno's strong, but I bet she could fold him up like a cardboard cutout." She looked back over the bar.

"Fine, Fia. Mare and I will watch."

At the sound of the heated conversation around the statue, even Sophia turned to see.

"You thought you could throw me out just like that? Just by changing the frequency of the portal?"

Sophia said softly, "Hey, that's why he messed with the portal?"

"I don't know, Fia. It's not looking good, though."

They continued to watch.

"No, Baby, I'd never turn my back on you."

"Yes," said Marilyn quietly. "Because she'd crush him when he wasn't looking."

"You might be right, Mare."

"Why did you do it, then, Bruno?"

"I swear, it was because the Guild was torturing me with all that sorcery stuff. Remember that junk? Honey, I had to get away from it."

"Oh, I remember. In fact, I broke into the lab and got the remote for that."

"The what?"

She forced a hefty hand into a tight pocket and retrieved a small device. She pointed it at Bruno, clicked it, and laughed.

"What's so funny?"

"It takes a few seconds. Hang on," she said, again scratching her chin.

In a blinding burst of scales and flesh, amid Bruno's howling and cussing then hissing, his body gyrated until it had spun itself into the same giant purple snake he'd been not too much earlier.

"Will you look at that?" said Dayzee. "Jiff, don't miss that."

"I'm liking the size of that tail," Sophia said with a leer.

"Wait until it starts rattling, Sissy. I want a turn."

"Yeah, you and the monster chick too."

"So, we're still getting married?" she said to Bruno, who didn't seem to care what he'd become.

"Sheesh," Sophia said with an eye roll, "can you imagine that?"

"No, Sissy, I sure can't."

"Girls, Bruno's engaged to her?"

They all turned to see.

"Um, sure," said Bruno, "but maybe not right now, alright? I think Dayzee still needs me, and so do Lady Sophia and Miss Marilyn. See them over there?"

He tipped his head toward them. She glared and said, "Oh, no. That tail's only for me now. You already bought me a ring, and—"

"God, how big must that be?" said Dayzee, shaking her head with a grin.

"—we're not waiting another day."

"Babycakes, I—"

Dayzee shook her head, Marilyn giggled, and Sophia grinned. All continued to watch.

"Enough!"

She picked up his cap, placed it on his head, and kicked his clothes into the corner.

"Yay!" said Marilyn after watching Bruno's clothes land in a pile that still allowed two frozen eyes to watch above it. "That stale old head is still here!"

"We just can't get rid of that head," Dayzee said. "Where's his body?"

"Like any of us could remember," said Sophia. "Oh, look!"

Still standing beside the statue, Bruno's woman reached out with both hands and got a good grip just below his snake head.

"Is that his throat?" said Marilyn. "It's the same as any other part of him. I think he's all throat. Oh, and a head."

"Not for long," Sophia said with a grin as they watched the woman squeeze Bruno tight.

Dayzee turned away from the bar to be sure Jiff's camera was catching it all, and she saw two police officers walking their way. She spun back around, and Jiff pointed his lens at them instead.

"Girls, it's the cops! Don't admit to anything!"

"What have we done?" said Marilyn.

"Sis, what haven't we done?"

Dayzee felt a tapping on her shoulder. She glanced quickly at the snake being strangled near the statue before turning around on her stool.

"Why, Beverly Hills' finest."

"Um, it's West Hollywood, ma'am."

"Oh, I guess I have to take that from you. What's on your mind?"

"Is that your hearse out front?"

"Of all the people you could ask, why me?"

"Well, you're Dayzee Dazzle, aren't you? I love all your films!"

"Thanks, we're working on some new stuff too. No, that's not my hearse."

"I didn't think so. We had a call-in saying there was a male driver that came inside this place. But I couldn't pass up the chance to say hi. You're even more beautiful in person."

Sophia leaned forward and said to her sister, "Earth."

"It's just so easy, Sissy."

"Well, I'm sure I don't look like any male driver, do I?"

He looked at her breasts, squeezed into her tight blouse, and said, "No, ma'am. But I do need to find him. I'll just take a look around."

"No, don't!"

Dayzee and the twins turned to look at the statue, which stood by itself in the shadows and still wore a big hat.

"Whew. That was close."

"Ma'am?"

She looked to Sophia then Marilyn.

"Girls, he didn't even say goodbye."

"Ma'am?"

She glanced again at the silent statue.

"Maybe because he was being choked."

"Ma'am?"

She looked the cop in the eye.

"Nothing. Yeah, look around. I hope you find whoever it is you're looking for."

"You do, Dayzee?"

"Of course, Fia. Mm . . . did you see the size of that rattle?"

"Ma'am?"

"Nothing."

Both cops scanned around the dimly lit confines of the Prism, and when Dayzee's cop fan saw Jiff, he said, "Hey, wait a sec. You're Jiff Roberts, aren't you?"

"Yep. I'm available for stills, videos, custom portraits, and—"

"Not for long, you are," he said and grabbed at the camera in Jiff's hands.

"Hey, what the hell!"

"You stole it, Mr. Roberts, and you can't keep it."

"Jiff, you stole that camera?"

"More than just this one, Ms. Dazzle," said the cop.

The struggle continued, the camera came out of Jiff's hands, and both cop and Jiff seemed to juggle it up into the air until it flew to one side, hit the bar hard, and fell into a bucket full of soapy water.

Sophia peeked over and said, "Yep. Again with the camera."

"It would have just been evidence anyway," said Dayzee.

Both cops pulled Jiff's arms behind him, and he got cuffed.

"Wonderful," said Dayzee. "Jiff, I'll bail you out. Don't worry."

"Thanks, Dayzee. You're the best."

"Isn't she, though?" said the officer as he began to haul Jiff away.

"I see two nice, uniformed fountains of youth," Sophia said with a grin.

"Oh, Sissy, really?"

"Girls, no. Jiff will be fine. But all those videos he shot? What about those?"

"Gone," Marilyn said with a pout.

"So is that big old rattly snake," Dayzee said with a deep sigh.

Sophia peeked over the bar again and said, "At least we still have Kenzie."

She whistled for Mack. He seemed to know to get a fresh round and not come empty-handed.

"Mack," she said, giving him a big smile, "I think Kenzie would rather join us at the bar."

He looked down at her, naked from the waist up and still snoring on the floor.

"Um, how?"

"I don't know . . . just drape her across the bar, alright?"

He squinted at her, then looked at Dayzee.

"Oh, fine by me."

He shook his head and turned to Marilyn, who only giggled and clapped her hands a few times.

He let out a deep breath before taking her up in his arms, and after the girls pushed aside all of their drink glasses, he laid her flat out on the bar, her head near Sophia, her trim waistline near Dayzee, and her red heels near Marilyn.

"My, she's a sight, Sissy."

"Abs to die for," Dayzee said, poking Kenzie's solid midsection with one manicured finger.

"She really is hot," Sophia said before turning to her left. She shook her head at the two unmoving dead inoculators and looked back at sleeping Kenzie. "Sorry, Kenzie, not hot enough to wake the dead."

"That's funny, Sissy. Maybe we should try to wake her, though?"

"Mare's right, Fia. We've lost everyone else. Bruno snaked his way back home, Jiff is in a cage somewhere, and—"

"Already, Dayzee?"

"Yeah, Mare. Even their cars have cages."

"Let's steal one of those next time," Sophia said with a grin. "We'll see how many headless guys we can cram in there."

"Oh, yes, Sissy, because we always have so many. I kind of miss that assassin already. Remember how they used to dance?"

"Sis, they never really—"

"You two! Back to Kenzie, alright? We should wake her up."

"So she can drive us home," Sophia said with a nod.

"But not to get her dressed," said Marilyn.

"Girls, how about if we wake her to see if she's alright? How about that, huh?"

"Sure, that's an idea," Sophia said before reaching out and tapping her cheeks lightly.

"No reaction. Sis, shake her legs around."

"How about if I take those sexy shoes from her instead?"

"Both of you, just hold up. Mack. Hey, Mack!"

He came over and put both hands on the bar, looking directly down at Kenzie's bare breasts.

"Only in Beverly Hills, huh, Dayzee?"

She squinted at him for a few seconds, and just when she was about to speak, Sophia said, "Maybe a wet washcloth, Mack? Let's wake her up if we can."

"Sure, Sophia. Be right back."

They all picked up their drinks, and Dayzee said, "It's really a shame we lost all that video."

"It sure is, Dayzee. It won't be easy doing all that fun stuff again."

Dayzee turned to look at Marilyn, shook her head with a smile, and turned back to her drink.

"Well, we still have plenty to do, even without a camera guy. Remember the squid beast? We still have to deal with him."

Mack had returned, and he said, "What's that about squid, Dayzee? I can check with the kitchen gal, and even if she has to get take-out for you, we can—"

Dayzee held her belly and said, "Oh, I think I've had enough for a while. Thanks, Mack. Just bring Kutie Kenzie back, alright?"

"Kutie Kenzie. I like that."

He dabbed around her forehead and temples, causing her to take a really deep breath and hold it.

"Oh my, she sure is a healthy one."

"She sure is, Mare. Fia? No comments?"

Dayzee turned to her left and saw that Sophia was only staring at Kenzie holding all the air in her lungs. She turned to her right and said, "It's not easy to get that one speechless."

"Cliff did," Marilyn said with a giggle. "Kept me nice and quiet too."

"Yeah, and then you needed inoculations. Mack, a little more effort, alright?"

Soon, Kenzie opened her eyes and looked at every pair of them looking down on her. She crossed her arms, found that she was undressed, and covered her breasts with her hands.

"What the hell is going on?"

"Welcome back," Sophia said with a laugh. "I knew you'd be alright."

"More than alright, I'd say," Dayzee said with a grin. "You're looking good, Kenzie."

"I still want those shoes," Marilyn said with a pout.

"What am I doing on the bar? Who undressed me?"

"Oh, Kenzie," said Sophia, "after all we've been through together, this shouldn't—"

"What are you talking about? I just met you!"

She rolled off behind the bar, found the jacket, and put it on. She tried to button it up and found there were no buttons.

"What is this?"

"Isn't the same without your hat, is it?" said Dayzee.

"What hat?"

She looked from face to face.

"Oh, boy. What's the last thing you remember?"

Kenzie held the jacket closed and said, "We had the Prism party out back, and I just met the three of you, and—"

"And we got in the limo with Bruno, and you were sitting—"

"What limo? Who the hell is Bruno?"

"Uh-oh, Sissy. Pieces of dead human boxes flying around aren't a good thing at all."

Kenzie stared at Marilyn, squinting and frowning.

"You don't remember anyone named Fifi either, do you?"

She turned to Sophia and said, "No. Bruno and Fifi and a limo?"

"Girls," said Dayzee, "I think maybe our work here is done."

"Yeah, work," said Kenzie. "I work here. I remember that much. After I find a real shirt somewhere. Mack, do you have an extra t-shirt laying around?"

"Sure, Kenzie. Let's check in the kitchen."

Kenzie left, and Mack waited and looked at Dayzee.

"Best if you don't say anything to her, Mack."

"I kind of thought so. I could be convinced to keep it all secret."

"Oh, boy," said Dayzee. "What's your price, Mack?"

"Ooh," said Marilyn, and he turned toward her. "Sissy likes handing out blank checks."

She giggled while Mack turned to Sophia, and she only grinned and nodded.

"At least once, I did," she said.

"That's what I want," he said, again looking at Dayzee. "A blank check."

"From Fia?"

"From all of you."

"He sure is a cutie," said Marilyn. "I'll give him a check."

"He can check me out too," said Sophia.

Dayzee held up her glass, both twins tapped hers with theirs, and she said to Mack, "Three blank checks, then."

Mack said, "Can't wait."

Marilyn whispered to her sister, behind Dayzee, "Probably won't survive either."

He left to help Kenzie find a shirt, and Marilyn said, "Oh, Sissy, I'm so sorry. She doesn't remember Fifi at all."

"Sis, she can sure meet her again. We need to get her back upstairs at Dayzee's place, and I'll give her some fresh heat, and we won't need a headless—"

"No, Fia, we're not doing any of that. I know it's sad, but maybe this is good. It's just you and me and your sister again. Easy come and easy go in Beverly Hills."

She waited and looked to each sister a couple of times. They grinned but didn't argue. She held her drink straight out in front of her.

"Finally!"

Chapter 26 – Enough Dead Guys

After instructing Mack to add their drinks to her tab and carry the two dead inoculators—which she'd claimed were only very realistic Halloween decorations—out to the hearse, Dayzee and the Kildare Killers stepped out into the bright sunshine of Southern California. She pulled the door shut behind her with a heavy sigh.

"I guess that kind of tied up some loose ends, girls."

"Um, there's still a head in the corner," said Sophia. "And that head's body is—"

"That's funny, Sissy. Which one belongs to the other?"

"Well, Sis, I'd say they both belong in the trash now."

"That's funny, too, Sissy."

"Anyway, the body is still around here somewhere."

"And I still want those heels Kenzie was wearing."

"Forget the head. Forget the head's body. Forget the heels. The main thing, girls, is to salvage 'Kildare in the Hills' if we can. That means that we have to de-squidify Cliff."

"And get rid of all those bodies," Sophia said with a scoff. "They sure have piled up."

"There's still a head in a tree, too, Sissy. That strange Moe character."

"Who knows . . . maybe a mountain lion snagged it by now."

"Damn lions, Sissy."

Marilyn turned to her sister, saw that she was looking down and kicking at the sidewalk, and said, "Sorry, Sissy. Not funny."

"She brings up a good point, though, Fia. We lost Kozy too. I bet that big Bruno-ish woman wrecked the portal, too, just out of spite."

"Probably. I bet she crushed it somehow just reaching through it. But you have your own portal, remember?"

"You're right, Mare," Dayzee said as they all got in the hearse, with Dayzee claiming the driver's seat. "I'm not sure if that's good or bad, but we need to figure out what to do with that. Oh, wait, we don't even know where it is!"

"I say, when we find it, we throw that box for dead humans into it. That'll get rid of that noisy guy in there. He's been very inconsiderate."

"Right, Mare. Oh God, I forgot all about Silvio too. We still need to deal with him."

"One more thing, Dayzee," Sophia said from the passenger side. "Yard guys."

"Lots of them," Marilyn said with several quick hand claps.

"At least two extra right from the start, Sis. Young ones, too, because we're going to—"

"Girls! Can we stop killing people for at least a little while?"

She looked at Sophia, who only grinned and nodded while looking through the shattered windshield. She turned to see Marilyn, who said softly, with a pleasant smile, "Oh, Dayzee, you really do ask too much of us."

∗　　∗　　∗

After pulling through and closing her entrance gate, Dayzee drove the wrecked hearse past all of the new reality show cars and parked it near her porch. She killed the motor and sat, holding the steering wheel with both hands.

"Gates were closed while we were gone, and I don't see any lions."

Sophia turned to gaze at her sister, and Marilyn only shook her head and grinned. She turned back around, pointed to a nearby tree, and said, "Found the head. Right where we left it."

"Now, Sissy's looking for head," Marilyn said with a giggle.

240

"That head, for sure," said Dayzee. "That's the closest living thing we—"

"It's living, Dayzee?"

"Grinning," said Marilyn, "and maybe cussing soon, but—"

"Oh, I don't know, girls. Something's going on with it. What I mean is that maybe there's something rattling around in that head that can still kill squids."

"That's good thinking," said Sophia. "But . . . one of us has to get it? Sheesh."

"What's that?" Dayzee said and pointed at the front door, where a folded piece of paper was wedged in.

"An eviction notice?" Sophia said with a scoff. "Haven't we been perfect neighbors?"

"Ooh, maybe a school for lion tamers put it there?"

"That's really helpful, the both of you. Let's go see."

They all got out, slammed the doors shut, and before they could take a step, Dayzee said, "Be sure to strut, girls. Pretend Jiff is still filming us."

"I always strut," said Sophia. "Don't need a camera."

"I might get undressed too," said Marilyn. "Just because I want to."

"I want you to, Sis."

Dayzee had reached the door, unfolded the note, and stood reading it for a few seconds.

"Oh, this can't be for real, can it?"

She handed it to Sophia, who took a moment to read through it.

"You have to call them, Dayzee. It's like fate or something."

She handed it to her sister, who read it with a big smile.

"If you don't hire them, I will!"

"But, Mare, maybe he suspects something?"

"Still, Dayzee, we'll have to take that chance," Sophia said with a big grin. "We need a yard crew—the sooner the better."

"But, Fia, I didn't even know Rake Barkus—"

"That's still silly, Dayzee."

"But I didn't even know he had a son."

"Yes, he does. And his name is Lief. Lief Bark."

"It's Barkus, Mare."

"It's silly either way."

"Talk about a family tree," Sophia said with a big grin.

"Yard work isn't going so well for them, Sissy. Maybe they should branch out into something else?"

"They sound pretty shady," Sophia said with a grin while looking at Dayzee.

"Funny, girls. Fine, I'll give him a call."

*　　*　　*

Dayzee clicked off her phone and said, "Lief said—"

Marilyn laughed once loudly.

"He said that his crew is already booked for today, but he can get some temps to come out right away if we need it."

"We do need them. Sis and I are itchy. I bet you are too."

"I don't think that's what he meant, Fia."

"I'm with Sissy on this one, Dayzee. How many is he sending?"

"Three. They should be here . . ."

Dayzee stopped at Sophia pointing first to herself, then to her sister, then to her.

"Fia, really?"

"Fountains of youth—all around."

"Mare, that might not be the best idea."

"Oh, Dayzee," said Sophia, "I know you want to. When was your last?"

"Not that long ago, but I sure am itching for another."

"It's settled, then. What do we need to do before they get here?"

"Wait a sec, girls. We're not talking the whole barbing and burning party, are we?"

"We could," said Marilyn.

"They're just temps, right?" said Sophia. "No one would miss them."

242

"Really, girls, no. They're not called temps because they're temporarily alive. So, just fountains. Now, before they pop in, we—"

"Yes, they sure will pop in!" Marilyn said with more clapping.

"Sis is pretty funny sometimes."

"Look, we need to do something about Mr. Squid Show and whatever baby squids I've got going on too."

"We'll need Moe's head, won't we?"

"Yeah, Mare. As for Silvio, we should probably hear what he has to say, don't you think?"

"We could," said Sophia. "Or we could bury him with all those cars."

"That's a lot of digging, Sissy. I think you must be joking."

"I am, Sis. We could just drive those away, like that carpenter's truck, and—"

"Oh, we need a carpenter too!" said Dayzee. "Girls, we have lots to do!"

"You seem to forget there's a mountain of dead guys in there, too, Dayzee. And some of them still have heads."

"You're right, Fia. This is complicated. What do you suggest?"

"Is your bar open?"

"For the Kildare Killers? Always."

*   *   *

Dayzee tended bar with the twins seated on stools, both with elbows on the bar and their heads in their hands. She set cocktails in front of each and took a sip of her own.

"I'll see what's going on with Silvio, and even though I'm not too happy with him, maybe the best thing is to let him go."

"Makes sense, Dayzee. Do you have any gloves?"

"Just some nice, long white ones for formal affairs. Why, Fia?"

"I'll get Moe's head, but I'm using gloves."

"That's fine. I can always buy another pair. I don't know what to do about that portal, though, and the carpenter will have to wait."

The twins downed half of their drinks and rested their chins in their hands again. Dayzee emptied hers and began mixing another.

"Girls, I have no idea how to go squid hunting. What do you think?"

Marilyn sat straight up, finished her drink, and grinned at both of them.

"You liked that drink, Sis?"

"Yes, but that's not it. Dayzee, if Moe can grin and turn his head, maybe he could talk, too, so we could just ask him, right?"

"Oh, Mare, you're a genius! All we need to do is—"

"Ask his head!"

*   *   *

"Good luck, Fia," Dayzee said on her front porch, then she handed her the gloves. "Time for you to look for head."

"You're funny, Dayzee."

"While you're picking a head out of a tree, I'll see what the deal is with Silvio. Mare, can you stand on the porch, looking beautiful, and watch both of us? You never know if there's a stray lion or—"

"A waltzing dead guy."

"Sis, they never were dancing, and they sure can't anymore. You saw the mess piled up in Dayzee's house."

"Oh, you're right, Sissy. Okay, I like to watch anyway."

Sophia grinned at Dayzee and said, "She really does. This one time, me and a couple of—"

"I'm sure that's a fun story, Fia, but we need to move. The temps will be here any minute."

"They call them temps for a reason," Sophia said with a nod and a smile.

"Don't we have enough dead guys around this place, Fia? I'll get Silvio, you get some head, and your gorgeous sister can watch us all."

She watched Sophia turn and begin her strut toward the tree with the scowling head, and Marilyn said, "I could watch her all day, Dayzee."

244

"Well, I wish I could too."

She turned and left for the hearse, and when she'd pulled open the back door, she was able to pry the lid up just enough to talk to Silvio.

"Dayzee, let me—"

"Stop. You said some guy called the Boss told you to keep quiet about the portal?"

"Yeah, Dayzee. He acted real nice, but that only scared me more. I thought for sure he'd have me killed if I told you. I wanted to tell you, I really—"

"Alright, tell me how you first met him."

"I was drinking up at the Prism. You know that place, right? With the big statue? I was at the bar, and he—"

"That's enough, Silvio. You've convinced me."

She dropped the coffin's lid and tapped all of her nails on the top of it while looking around the yard. After a few seconds, she lifted it again.

"Alright, I understand that it's not your fault. Do you know anything about it? Like how to close it up?"

"Sorry, Dayzee. No, I don't know a thing. And if you let me go, I swear, I won't say a word about anything to anybody."

"'Any. Body.' That's kind of funny."

"Huh?"

"Nothing. Things are just crazy in the Hills. Fine, you can go, but don't expect me to buy another mansion from you anytime soon."

"I won't. I promise."

She pulled the coffin all the way open, and Silvio climbed out. He swung his arms around and kicked his legs a few times.

"That's actually pretty comfortable."

"For a human, sure."

"Huh?"

"Nothing. Head for the gate, and I'll click to let you out. Go! Run!"

Silvio took off toward the exit gate, Dayzee tapped her phone to swing the massive gate in, and just as he started to run through, a mountain lion pounced from each side. There was only a short scream, then the sound of something being dragged down the street.

"I guess this really was goodbye, Silvio," she said and closed it up. "For sure you'll never tell anybody or any body."

*   *   *

Back on the porch, Dayzee said, "Mare, how's your sister doing with that head?"

"Look, she's got it. You know, Dayzee, in some creepy way, she looks really sexy wearing those gloves and holding that head."

"I like how she has Moe turned toward her, too, Mare. That's a nice touch."

"Maybe they're having a pleasant conversation. Moe seemed pretty nice. I bet he was only snarling because he was lonely in that tree."

"Yeah, I think you're right about him being nice. Kozy went berserk and ripped his head clean off, though."

"That was unfortunate."

"Yep. I think they're getting along, though."

"Why's that, Dayzee?"

"She could be holding his braid and swinging him around."

"I bet she didn't even think of that."

Chapter 27 – I'm Next!

"What'll you have, Moe?"

"Something with a straw."

"That's funny," Marilyn said with a grin.

The twins had taken their barstools, Dayzee was tending, and Moe's head sat on the bar off to Marilyn's right. Dayzee set his drink in front of him, and the straw poked his left eye.

"That's funny too," Sophia said while shaking her head.

"Here,"—Dayzee picked up the head and set it on a stack of books—"this should help."

The straw hit right between the head's lips, and Moe sucked some of it in.

Marilyn turned to her sister and whispered, "Sissy, where does it go when he swallows?"

"I think Dayzee's going to have some soggy books. We'll see."

"Alright," Dayzee said, "everyone comfortable?"

She looked at the head, whose contorted face tried to regain the straw it had lost. Dayzee gave it a push, and his eyes seemed happier.

"Moe, we need to—wait, you're still Moe, right? Just a lot less of you?"

He worked the straw to one corner of his mouth and said, "Oh yeah, it's still me. Never thought I'd end up headless, though."

"Well, you're not," Sophia said and pointed toward the pile of bodies. "One of those guys is."

"Okay, you're right. I'm not headless."

"I'm sorry, but that's funny too," Marilyn said and started to giggle. "A head saying that it's headless."

"Look," said Dayzee, "none of that matters. Here's the thing: Moe, we have a full-fledged squid infestation somewhere in this house. And I—"

"You have a low-level infection yourself."

"You can tell? Even like that?"

"Pretty cool, huh?"

The twins looked at each other, then at Dayzee, who said, "I'm not sure 'cool' is the word for any of this. Alright, so the question is: can you still help? Even all by yourself?"

"He's by himself!" Marilyn said with a sharp laugh.

"Sis, you might hurt his feelings."

"Maybe, Sissy, but I couldn't hurt his elbow, could I? Or his little toe? Or how about that other big part that we would have—"

"No, but I guess you would have burned that down to nothing anyway," said the head with a grimace.

"Oh, I'm sorry, Moe. Yes, I sure would have."

"You would have loved it, though," Sophia said with a chuckle.

"Girls, let's focus. Alright, Moe, what's the deal? How can you help if you're here, and there, and your inoculator is burned up, and—"

Marilyn laughed out loud, and Dayzee smiled at her.

"Moe, you know what I mean."

"My inoculator isn't burned up, Dayzee. That was just my teammates. Anyway, it's any of my bodily fluids. That's where the cure is. It's toxic to squids. Kills them dead."

"Wait," Sophia said with a frown. "Those other two, Abbott and whoever, they didn't need to—"

"Nope," the head said and grinned before working the straw around and dragging in a long sip. Some of the drink began to ooze down the sides of the books.

"Sheesh."

"Best I can do. Sorry."

"That's fine," said Dayzee. "Booze gets spilled in here all the time."

"Not like that, I bet!"

"Helpful, Mare. Alright, Moe, you're saying you need to spit on me? Is that it?"

"Well, saliva will sure do it. But . . ."

"But what?"

"If there was a body attached to this head, I bet you'd want some more creative treatment. Am I right?"

"Oh, you're saying—"

"Yeah, I sure am."

"But, Moe, your head isn't attached."

"And?"

Dayzee looked at Sophia, who grinned and shook her head, then at Marilyn, who shrugged and said, "We won't make any jokes about you getting head, Dayzee."

"I'm not promising," Sophia said with a nod and a smile.

"Oh, fine, Moe. When can we get this over with?"

"Dayzee, that's not a good way to talk about our date, is it?"

"He said, 'date!'" Marilyn said with a laugh.

Sophia said, "You already had a date with a fried Colombian cowboy, and now it's—"

"Alright! When, though?" Dayzee said, staring at Moe.

"First, we should work out the procedure for the other infected individual."

"Oh, that's Cliff," Marilyn said with a smile. "I'm not sure he'll want a date like Dayzee wants."

"Mare, I do not—"

"She's just messing with you, Dayzee," said Sophia. "She's right about Cliff, though."

The talking head said, "If Cliff were here, sitting at the bar with us, would he be able to take a drink? He's still functional?"

"Well, sure, he likes to drink."

"Okay," said Moe, "only one more question, then."

"Yeah?"

"Do you have a blender?"

"Sheesh again!"

*   *   *

"Does it really have to happen in my room?" Dayzee said with a scowl.

"I'll bet it's not the most outrageous thing that's happened up there," Sophia said with a smile, and she held Dayzee's gaze to wait for her response.

Seconds later, Dayzee smiled and said, "Well, alright, Fia. You do make a good point. But still, maybe we could—"

"Your room would be easier," said Moe's head as his tongue tried to hook his straw, and Marilyn giggled at the sight.

"Hey, give a head a hand," he said and grinned at her.

"You're a pretty funny head, Moe."

"Thank you, Marilyn. Um, I sure could use another drink, though."

"Oh, I'm sorry," she said and bumped the straw to where he could grab it.

"Wait," said Dayzee, "what difference does it make to you which room?"

"Because yours is probably the nicest room in this mansion. Am I right?"

"Yeah, you sure are. That matters?"

"Think of what's waiting for me after."

"He's making a lot of sense," said Sophia. "Even a head needs to live a little."

"But that's not the most important reason."

"Why, then, Moe?"

"I bet you have a well-stocked closet up there. You do, don't you?"

"Yeah, of course, I do. There's all kind of—"

"Lingerie?"

Marilyn snorted and laughed, and Sophia blew out her drink before she could swallow. Dayzee only stared at the head on a stack of books on her bar.

250

"Now, wait just a second. You expect me to get all dressed up sexy for this?"

The head grinned and said, "A babydoll would be nice. Really, really nice."

"Alright, you're taking this a little too far. You can't expect me to—"

"Sissy and I will turn down the covers for you two," said Marilyn.

"Hell, I'm going to light some candles too."

"Ooh, some romantic music, too, Sissy."

"Fia? Whose side are you on? Really, Mare?"

She looked back down at the smiling head and was about to say more when Moe spoke up.

"Dayzee, would you rather wait until after I take a squishy, crunchy ride in your blender?"

Dayzee let a big breath seep out and held her belly. She looked at the twins, and they only grinned back at her.

"Alright. Fine. A babydoll."

"A white one."

"Sure. I have a couple."

"With a lot of lace. I like lace."

"God. Alright."

"Heels. Get some that are really high too."

"You're a very particular, horny head, aren't you?"

"It really is my last chance," said the head before it found the straw and stared into Dayzee's eyes while sucking down the last of the cocktail.

*　　*　　*

The twins stood near Dayzee's closet door and studied the head sitting calmly on the soft quilt covering her four poster bed. Sophia had worn her gloves to carry him, she'd held him out as far as she could, and she gave him a treat and kept him facing her breasts the entire way. Dayzee had gone ahead, and shortly after the head had been placed, she exited her closet.

251

"Oh my God, that's hot!" Marilyn said with a few silent claps.

Dayzee wore one of her shortest babydolls, so short that nothing was left to the imagination. The top was frilly and lacy, as was the bottom edge. Her breasts were squeezed tight and threatened to break free any second. Her heels were tall, and her wild mane of thick blond hair fell all over her shoulders and back.

"If squid killer gets cold feet," said Sophia, "I'd sure—"

"She said 'feet!'"

"—I'd sure do you myself. I might anyway."

"Thanks, Fia. That helps."

"Sissy, we can after Mr. Head does his thing. It's not an either-or."

"I just might take you up on that, Mare."

"Hey," said Moe's head. "I have an idea."

They walked closer to the bed, one twin on each side of Dayzee.

"Yeah? What's on your mind?"

"I'll joke about that later," Sophia said with a quick chuckle.

"I say, you should all get busy doing that before I even step up to bat. How about it, girls? Give a head a break?"

"There's nothing left to break," Sophia said with a grin.

"Only my heart," said the head.

"Aw, he's a sweetheart," Marilyn said with a hand over her heart. "I'm in. Sissy?"

"Yeah, of course. I've never seen Dayzee looking that hot."

"Girls, you can't be serious. Are you?"

"The same thing goes for you twins," said Moe. "Lingerie. All of you."

"Oh, see? You had to push it, didn't you?" said Sophia.

"Fia, we weren't really going to, um, do that for him, and—"

"No, Dayzee. Just messing with the head."

"That's cruel, Sissy. Apologize to the head."

Sophia leaned over, pinched his nose, gave it a wiggle, and said, "Oh, I'm so sorry that I'm not going to do sexy things in lingerie with Sis and Dayzee for you to watch."

"Not much of an apology," said Moe's head.

"He's right, Sissy."

"Alright, can we just get going here?" said Dayzee. "I need to lay your head back,"—she tipped Moe's head onto its back—"so you can . . ."

"Oh, he flops right over," said Sophia.

"I'll help," Marilyn said, and she quickly slipped her dress straps over her shoulders and let it fall to the floor around her heels.

"Any excuse to strip, huh, Sis?"

"You know me, Sissy."

She picked up the head, sat on the bed, and spread her long legs just enough to wedge the Moe head between her thighs. She pulled his long braid over one of them.

"This is a damn good second choice," said the head, now looking straight up. "The view of your boobs from this angle is exquisite."

Marilyn swayed herself back and forth, and Moe stared with his mouth open, unable to speak.

"They really are magnificent, Mare."

"Thanks, Dayzee. Now, all you need to do is sort of sit on my lap. Come on up."

"Well, this should work, shouldn't it?"

Dayzee joined Marilyn on the bed, turned herself away, straddled her, and lowered herself down almost close enough for Moe to get busy.

"Wait, this is kind of awkward."

Marilyn grabbed her hips and said, "Oh, I'm happy to help."

"Fia, I still can't quite keep my balance. Come on and help your sister."

"Clothes or no clothes?"

"Oh, Sissy, you're silly. You know the answer."

Sophia practically ripped off her blouse and bra, shimmied out of her tight skirt, and soon knelt on the bed, holding both of Dayzee's hands.

"Where's Jiffy when we really need him?" said Marilyn.

"This sure would be a good scene but not for that Kildare show," said Dayzee.

"I know what we'd call this scene too," said Sophia. "'Menage-a-approximate-trois.'"

"Oh, Sissy, if we weren't all naked, and if Dayzee didn't have such nice lingerie, I'd sure be laughing. Good one."

"My God," said the head in a muffled voice beneath the crowded together naked girls. "This is the best moment of my life."

"Just as long as you do what you need to do," said Dayzee. "We're not doing all this just for the fun of it."

"We're not?" said Marilyn.

"I am," Sophia said with a grin.

"Oh, about that. I did tell you the truth about my fluids and the blender and all that. But . . ."

"Yeah?"

"You're not infected, Dayzee. You don't really have to do this."

Dayzee looked at Sophia, who grinned back at her, and she tried to turn to see Marilyn, but she could only feel her hands still holding her hips above the talking head.

Still raised up above the head, Dayzee said, "Why are you even admitting that? How would we ever know?"

"Ever hear of phantom pain? Like when a limb gets chopped off?"

"I have," said Marilyn. "Those aren't happy limbs."

"No," said Moe, "they sure aren't. Well, I've got something phantom that's just dying to do some inoculating."

"And it can't," Sophia said and kept holding Dayzee's hands. "This is just making it worse for you, isn't it?"

"It's getting more excruciating the longer you're all naked and all around me."

"Is it a big phantom?" said Dayzee.

"I bet it was, Dayzee."

"Sis is right. Bet it was a monster."

"Well, that's a sad story, girls, but I've heard quite enough. There's only one way to properly shush a talking head."

The head talked no more.

"I'm next!" Marilyn said with a giggle.

*   *   *

Sophia pulled the plug out of the wall, and the blender clattered and chipped its way to a stop. Dayzee's kitchen was once again an elegant, quiet room in her mansion. Marilyn joined them to look at the splattered, gooey mess inside the glass.

"Sheesh."

"He's sure quiet now," Marilyn said, looking down and shaking her head.

"Heavy duty kitchen appliances, girls. You never know when you'll need them."

"Good to know," said Marilyn. "But we still don't know where Cliff is, do we?"

"I do."

"Huh?" said Sophia. "Where is he?"

"Curled up like a dead squid, hugging a bunch of lingerie that he'd pulled down from their hangers. He looks pretty happy there."

"Who wouldn't be?" Sophia said with a grin.

"Why didn't you say anything upstairs?"

"Oh, Mare, I was thinking about that head doing its thing, and—"

"Funny," said Marilyn. "Sissy and I would have burned its thing along with those other two weirdos."

"Too bad Kozy snapped his head off," Sophia said with a smile.

"He really didn't have a good day, did he, girls?"

"Not until the very end," said Marilyn.

"Dayzee's end," Sophia said with a nod.

"Good one, Sissy. I mean, what you said. But Dayzee's end is very good too!"

*   *   *

"Alright, girls, should we take the squid kill cocktail up to the Squid King, or should we try to drag him down here?"

"Down here, of course," Sophia said while nodding.

"Why so sure, Fia?"

"We shouldn't be dragging equipment all over your house, Dayzee."

"Like what?"

"Well, a funnel, for one thing. Maybe a tarp too. We don't know how much he needs, so Cliff the Squid should probably drink that entire head."

"Wow, Sissy, really? All of that?"

"Even the bone chips?" Dayzee said, and they both stared at Sophia.

It took a few seconds, but she said, "Sheesh. Yeah, can't waste the bone chips. That might be what mostly kills the squidness anyway."

"Oh," said Marilyn, "there's something else too: what will happen to the squid inside Cliff? Will it dissolve?"

"Will he vomit it up?" said Sophia.

"Girls, maybe it'll slither out of him somehow."

"Which end?" Sophia said with a grin.

"Will it still be alive? Should we let it crawl out into your pool, Dayzee?"

"Mare, I think we're finally getting somewhere. Yeah, we'll pour that gunk down his throat next to the pool, then push him in."

"And hope for the best?"

"Yeah, Fia, that's what we'll do," she said, then turned toward the pile of bodies. "So far, that's working out damn well."

*　　*　　*

"That's funny that he could still walk," said Marilyn, "but he can't talk anymore."

"What would he say, Sis?"

"Lights, camera, action?"

"Squids don't know anything about that. He's almost all squid now."

"Remember when you thought he might be the one, Dayzee?"

"God, that seems so long ago, Fia."

"It turns out he was more than one the whole time," said Marilyn.

"That's funny, Sis. Kind of not funny too."

All three stood around a hunched over Cliff, who had wrapped both arms around his abdomen. He was at the edge of Dayzee's pool, and only a nudge would send him splashing.

"We should be wearing bikinis," said Dayzee. "Damn that criminal, Jiff."

"Sissy and I could have stopped those cops, Dayzee. We'd still have our photographer."

"Killing cops might not be the best plan, Mare."

"Yeah, Sis. There are already two dead ones somewhere in the pile. One without a head."

"A post office guy too," Marilyn said with a shrug.

"Girls, we need to forget about them for now. Mare, hold Mr. Squid Gut still, and Fia, tip his head back."

The twins managed to contort Cliff enough that his open mouth pointed up.

"Perfect. Down the hatch!"

She started pouring the mix slowly, and Marilyn said, "Maybe a little at a time, Dayzee? Let him take a breath?"

"Alright. That's a good idea, Mare."

Dayzee tipped the pitcher back until it was almost upright, but the blended head slop kept flowing.

"Oh my God," said Marilyn.

"It's like it's all one big glob!" said Dayzee.

"Sheesh."

The tail end of the mess wiggled its way into Cliff, and Dayzee tossed the empty container onto the lawn, saying, "The yard guys will get that later."

"Yes. Lief. Liefy Mulch."

They all let go of Cliff, and he stood straight up, with good posture, and the girls watched as his belly began to swell up.

"Oh God," said Dayzee, "maybe he'll explode!"

Sophia gave him a hard shove, and he made a big splash and sank to the bottom, leaving only a tight pattern of small bubbles.

"There was no time to think, Dayzee."

"You might be right, Fia, but he still might explode. Hurry! Back to the house!"

Chapter 28 – Keep Them in a Cage

"I might never use a blender again," Dayzee said as she poured whiskey into three large tumblers.

She set up each twin as they sat at her bar. She noticed that Marilyn studied her drink intently before taking a sip.

"What's wrong, Mare?"

"Just, um, checking for bones."

"There's a good joke there somewhere, Sis, but I'm too nauseous right now."

She tipped her drink back for a good swallow, then turned toward the pile of bodies near the couch.

"You know, Dayzee, besides all that rotting human flesh, things are kind of peaceful."

"You're right, Fia. Think of how many people have come and gone in the last few days."

"Yes, not even counting the dead ones."

"That's right, Mare. We lost the Boss, Bruno, Jiff, Kozy, and even Kenzie, sort of."

"Aw, Kenzie will be back," said Marilyn. "She just needed a timeout. We might be too much for her."

"Is Cliff gone too?"

"I'd say it's too soon to know, Fia. Yeah, we might have lost him too."

"Lost a Cliff, gained a squid," Marilyn said before she finished her drink.

"No, Sis, the Moe soup was supposed to—"

The intercom's frantic buzzing caused Dayzee to set down the whiskey bottle before she'd refilled her glass.

"Oh, maybe that's the squid now," Marilyn said with a giggle.

"Squids don't understand intercoms, Sis. Their tiny squid brains could never—"

"Girls, could it be Cliff?"

"Yep, at the front door, wearing a dead squid like a scarf."

"Funny, Sissy."

"Girls, there's an intercom thing outside the gate too. Maybe it's the yard guys?"

* * *

Standing next to the incessant buzzing near the desk in her kitchen, Dayzee smoothed down her short black skirt, checked the buttons on her tight white blouse, then looked down at her legs in wide black fishnet and ending with short black boots with high heels.

She turned to inspect Sophia and saw her wearing a short black skirt, too, and a tight red blouse, unbuttoned low. Her red heels were high, and her red lips amplified the blue of her eyes and the sheen of her long black hair.

A quick glance at Marilyn confirmed that her white dress was very short, like always, and tight. Her bare legs ended in spiky white heels, and her blue eyes sparkled as she swept back her classic, wavy blond hair.

"Why did we get dressed again?" said Dayzee. "Remind me?"

"Just for the fun of it," Sophia said with a grin. "Your clothes sure are tight. That took some effort."

"It really did take three tries before you two got my dress on me the right way," said Marilyn.

Dayzee rolled her steel blue eyes, smiled, and said, "Well, girls, we're ready for anything."

"Um, maybe not for a squid that came calling," Sophia said with a grin.

"No, Fia, let's hope not."

"Or a Cliff that's mostly exploded. That wouldn't be pleasant."

"No, Mare. Messy too. Well, here goes."

While looking from one twin to the other, Dayzee hit the button and said, "Yes?"

"Hi, I'm with a temp yard company. I'm Dale. Lief sent us. You're Dayzee?"

"Yeah, I sure am. You're alone?"

"No, ma'am."

He laughed once and said, "I got my partners, Solo and Merritt."

Dayzee's eyes stretched open as she smiled at the girls. She quickly said, "Hang on," and hit the mute button.

"What's wrong?" said Marilyn.

"Yeah, it's like you saw a head in a blender or something."

"Girls, no. Did you hear their names?"

"Yeah, but what about them?"

"Oh, Fia, we really should love Earth."

"Dayzee, what's going on?"

"Mare, their names match ours! We each get one!"

"Huh?"

"Sophia, it's like this: Dale is for Dayzee. Solo is for Sophia, and for Marilyn, we have Merritt!"

"That's sure some kind of coincidence," said Sophia, "but—"

"But nothing, Fia. You've been wanting another fountain, haven't you, girls?"

"Oh, yes, Dayzee. I'm itching for one."

"And I'm way overdue for one myself. Girls, this is perfect!"

"I thought you said that we should try not to kill any more yard guys?"

"These don't count, Fia! They're extra! Nobody will miss them!"

Marilyn turned to her sister and said, "Um, Sissy, I think maybe Dayzee's way hornier than we thought."

"Yeah, Sis. Maybe she has been for a long time. Doesn't mean she isn't right, though."

Dayzee took a few deep breaths, her chest swelling out each time, and said, "Girls, I think I'll be okay. I might not talk about it much, but I get so damn itchy sometimes."

"Aw, we understand, Dayzee."

"We really do," Sophia said with a nod. "Just the fountains for now, alright? That'll help."

Dayzee's desperate look gave way to a smile, and she said, "Yeah, girls. Fountain time."

Still grinning, she unmuted the device and said, "We'll be right out. I'll get that gate open for you."

"Thanks, ma'am."

Dayzee ended the conversation and turned back to the girls.

"Oh, wait," she said. "We can't let them inside the house. What about all those bodies?"

"You need an outside elevator up to the higher floors," said Sophia.

"That's a great idea, but there's no time."

"How about if we meet them in the dead human car, Dayzee?" said Marilyn.

"Sis, there are two burnt weirdos in it. Nope."

"By the pool?" said Dayzee. "Or maybe in one of the guesthouses?"

"Yeah, a guesthouse," said Sophia. "Sis and I have never killed anyone back there."

"You girls really are killers, aren't you?"

"From Kildare," Marilyn said while nodding. "Yes."

Dayzee sighed and said, "Look, let's focus on our long-term plan, alright? We need to get this whole place cleaned up so we can really get started on 'Kildare in the Hills,' with or without Cliff."

"Starting with the lawn, you mean?" said Marilyn.

"Yeah, Mare. First the yard. Then the pile of bodies. Then the carpentry."

"Corpses in the corpse car," Sophia said with a smirk. "Those too."

"They're not dancing in there either, Sissy."

"Nope."

"Oh, and I bet something is going on in the pool," Marilyn said, shaking her head. "That's going to need a deep clean."

"We have no choice, girls. The only way we'll have enough energy to do any work ourselves is to get going on those fountains."

"Good plan," said Sophia. "We'll get charged up and get busy."

"That does sound good," said Marilyn. "Even though I don't stop until I'm done, even if I'm tired."

"Nice, Sis. Keep them coming."

"Now, I really miss Bruno," said Dayzee. "And Kozy. It's a lot easier to give orders while sitting at the bar."

"Looking sexy as hell," Sophia said with a grin.

"Just like my gorgeous twins!"

Dayzee's smile sank into a frown as she shook her head, looking from one twin to another.

"Girls, while we've been standing around talking, those guys might already be dead."

"What? Why?"

"Mare, remember that Silvio creep? I kicked his ass out through the gate, and before he'd taken two steps, two hungry she-lions got him. There are still lions out there!"

"Well, hit some buttons on your phone, then, Dayzee. Get those boys in here. We need them alive."

"Right, Fia," Dayzee said and got out her phone.

*　　*　　*

By the time they'd opened the front door to see, they watched three clean-cut young men, wearing uniform shorts and t-shirts, walking along the drive and past the reality show cars.

"Hurry, Dayzee. Close it again."

"You're right, Mare."

They watched the gate begin to swing shut, but before it had closed completely, three lions slipped in and disappeared behind the row of bushes along the fence.

"Just wonderful."

"Damn lions," Marilyn said with a sigh.

Her sister turned to her and said, "I guess that's still pretty funny, Sis."

"Alright, well, so much for the guesthouses. Girls, we have to let them in."

"Or else, what?" Sophia said with a smirk. "They get killed?"

"Sissy just wants to add them to the pile, Dayzee."

"No, we need those fountains. We'll never get through this any other way."

She waved to the three men and called out, "Hey, you better hurry. Come on."

They looked at each other and shrugged, but they picked up their pace and were soon standing near the porch.

"Lief said you needed some work done right away, and since his crew is busy somewhere else, he sent us. Just tell us what you need."

"I like his attitude," Sophia said softly, still standing behind Dayzee.

Her sister elbowed her and whispered, "Sissy, they're cute!"

Dayzee looked past the crew for a second, then back down at them, and said, "What did you do, walk here?"

While he answered, she looked back toward the fence and saw three lions peeking out from the foliage.

"No, we got dropped. We'll just call dispatch when we're done. What exactly do you need?"

"Let's go inside, and I'll fill you in."

Sophia leaned toward her sister and whispered, "Yeah, Sis, there's a joke there, but we don't have time."

At that, Dayzee turned to the twins and said, "God, you are so right. We don't have time. Let's get going on this quick."

"You mean the lawn, lady?"

Dayzee turned back to Dale, looked past him at the advancing lions, and said, "Yeah, that's it. Inside, everybody!"

*   *   *

"I liked how they followed us so obediently into your living room, Dayzee."

While shaking her head at the three spent, sleeping yard men, Sophia said, "I liked how you gave your guy some heat and hypnotized him as soon as he walked into the foyer, Sis."

Dayzee sighed and said, "I liked how the Kildare Killers didn't kill this time."

Sophia grinned and said, "We still can. Sis and I wouldn't even have to wake them up."

"Ooh, Sissy, that's so tempting. Barbs and heat. Real heat."

"Girls, no. Don't you feel better after that? Besides, they have work to do. Dead guys don't get all that much done."

"We couldn't get one to even rake up pieces of bark," Marilyn said with a shrug.

"He never would have dug a hole for us either, Sis."

"Girls, I don't even mean yard work. I want them to drive those new cars out of here."

"Why? I like them," Marilyn said with a pout.

"Because, Mare, everyone involved with those cars is dead. If we send them back, maybe no one will come snooping around."

"That's smart," said Sophia. "So, the yard guys aren't doing any yard work?"

"Maybe trimming the bushes will have to be enough, Sissy," Marilyn said with a giggle.

"Sis, you know that can't happen with us even a little bit," her sister said with a grin.

"Oh, you girls, I just love you two!"

*　*　*

While the fountainized guys slept and regained some strength, Dayzee peeked out through a front window. The twins looked over her shoulders.

265

"Good. Those damn lions went back into the woods."

"How will those guys get out to the cars?" said Marilyn. "They'll be ripped to pieces."

"Eh," said Sophia, "we'll just toss them on the pile."

"I know you're joking, Fia. Just wait. I have a plan."

They all stared without talking for a minute, and when they saw a jogger pass the exit gate, running toward the entrance gate, Dayzee said, "Almost. Just a little bit farther . . ."

She tapped the code quickly on her phone, and the big entrance gate began to swing in just as the runner began to pass by. In a rush of short brown fur and pointy, gleaming fangs, the three lionesses raced out onto the sidewalk.

"Oh, good move, Dayzee," said Marilyn.

The screams and growls disappeared down Dayzee's street, and she tapped to close it up again.

"Well, that was easy enough," said Sophia. "Earth can be pretty cool sometimes."

"Check that off the list," said Dayzee. "Alright, time to get those boys going."

"Whoever invented that fountain business was pretty smart," said Marilyn. "I like how they don't remember anything."

"Oh, Mare, I think it just works out that way. It's too traumatic for them, so they block it out."

"We could keep them in a cage and do it every day, then," said Sophia.

"Yeah, well, not with these three. Let's get them going on the cars."

*　*　*

When the last groggy driver had piloted his expensive vehicle through the exit gate, Dayzee hit her phone to slam it shut.

"I kind of miss dead guys getting jammed up in there," said Sophia.

"Hey, whatever happened to the other one? Remember him? I mean, both of him?"

"Oh, Mare, I think the lions cleaned all that up."

"No," said Sophia. "They don't eat them after they've been possessed, remember?"

"Oh, that's right," Dayzee said with a nod. "But maybe it's okay now that the assassin's gone."

"So," Sophia said with a smirk, "maybe we shouldn't keep saying 'damn lions,' huh?"

"Who knows, Fia? They're good sometimes, bad other times."

"Like us, Dayzee?"

"You and your sister are always just gorgeous, no matter what. Alright, here's what I'm thinking: that dead guy wagon is pretty big, and I think we could get all the bodies in the back."

"It's got two flat tires, though."

"It'll just have to do, Mare."

"Will there still be room for heads?" Sophia said with a grin.

"Yeah, Fia. Maybe. They'll be easy to wedge in somewhere."

"If not," said Marilyn, "you have a remarkable blender, Dayzee."

"Sheesh, Sis."

"What about that portal, Dayzee?"

"Oh, Fia, I forgot all about that again. I say we just leave it alone, and maybe it'll leave us alone too."

"We don't even know where it is."

"No, Mare, only Bruno knew."

"When he was a mouse," Sophia said with a chuckle.

"Yes, Sissy, and then his gorilla woman choked his snake throat and poofed him away."

*   *   *

Dayzee slammed the hearse's back door shut and wiped her hands.

"Never thought I'd do that kind of work. At least we got them all in there, though."

"Even the heads!"

"Yeah, Mare, we didn't even have to grind them up. Alright, I can get a carpenter out here tomorrow, and Lief and—"

"That's even sillier than 'Rake,' Dayzee."

"Lief and his crew can clean up the outside tomorrow too. Girls, I think we've earned a drink."

"Sounds good to me," said Sophia.

"It was fun to have a talking head on the bar. We should do that all the time," said Marilyn.

Dayzee stared and shook her head, and Sophia grinned and nodded, then they all started walking back inside.

"I'm having whiskey," said Dayzee, "because with all the blood and—"

Her phone screamed inside her tight pocket. She looked at the number with a smile, tapped to answer, and said, "Lief! We were just talking about you!"

Chapter 29 – I Am the Collector

Dayzee wedged her phone back into her pocket and said, "Well, so much for that schedule. Lief and his—"

"His twig?" Marilyn said with a giggle.

"I hope he's got a branch, Sis."

"I'm sure he's very grounded, too, Sissy."

"Good roots?"

"Girls! See? Too many fountains! Look, I think we'll be alright. The bodies are out of the way, even the loose heads, and—"

"We never did count them, Dayzee."

"No, Mare, but it doesn't really matter. They're just dead. Even the heads."

"I just had a weird thought," said Sophia. "Moe, that head guy—he didn't die so easily, right? That slop that we blended up kind of all stuck together like it was—"

"Still alive, Sissy? Moe is alive, but he's just soup now?"

"Yeah, I bet he is. Maybe that's how it works: he's in there beating up the squid."

"Why didn't he talk to us after we souped him up, then?"

"Well, Sis, that would have freaked us out, don't you think? We would have dumped that creepy, yapping mess down the drain. He kept quiet to make sure we'd let him do his job."

"Girls, I think you're onto something. We'll check into that when we fish that squid monster out of the pool."

"Eh . . . he probably drowned by now," said Sophia.

"No, Fia, I looked before, and Cliff was floating on his back with his belly still real big. He can breathe. Alright, we got a little sidetracked here, talking about heads."

"Damn heads."

"That's a pretty good one, Sis. You're sometimes way more clever than I thought."

"Thanks, Sissy."

"Girls! I was trying to tell you that the Lief guys are coming this afternoon."

She turned toward Sophia and saw the big grin.

"What, Fia?"

"Lief is coming? What do you suppose his favorite piece of equipment is?"

"A leaf blower, Sissy?" Marilyn said with a giggle.

"Exactly, Sis!"

"Alright, you two, we need to focus. Is there anything else we're missing, or are we good?"

They paused to look around inside Dayzee's mansion, and all eyes turned toward the hall closet.

"Did you hear that?" said Dayzee.

"Oh, yeah," said Sophia. "Dayzee, that's where mouse Bruno squeezed his chubby mouse ass in to go find that portal."

"It's in my closet?"

"Oh, that's silly, Dayzee," said Marilyn. "Remember how Bruno described it? Stairs, then a door, then a tunnel, then the portal?"

"Oh, alright, but it's through there, right?"

"Yep. I'm guessing something just climbed through the portal. I bet that's what that was."

They all listened for another moment, and at the sound of a large, heavy door slamming shut with a grinding of metal and splintering of wood, they all looked wide-eyed at each other.

"Uh-oh," Marilyn said with a shaky voice. "You know what that was."

"Yeah, Sis. A door. A big one."

"It still got destroyed, Sissy. Wasn't big enough, I'd say."

"Wait, girls. Listen."

They heard the sound of a weighty impact at a distance.

"Um, Bruno said there was a staircase?"

"Yeah, Mare. Just listen and—"

A second pound rang out, louder than the one before.

"Uh, Dayzee. Whatever that is, it's climbing the steps."

"Fia, maybe it's just—"

Two heavy thuds rang out so close together it shocked the girls into silence. Then two more, close together.

"That's not just an it," Dayzee said, barely above a whisper. "I count two of them."

"They must be huge too," Marilyn said, with no trace of a giggle.

The pounding continued, each time with two footfalls heavy on the steps, close together each time.

The twins pressed up against Dayzee, and she put her arms around them. They all held their breath and waited, but they heard nothing more.

"Well, that was close," said Marilyn. "Maybe there are just more mice down—"

They heard two more closely spaced footfalls and the sounds of stone stairs crushing into small pieces, which tumbled back down, echoing through the closet door.

"Um, Dayzee?"

"Yeah, Fia?"

"I know we're all hot, and we have really fun barbs and stuff, but, um, maybe we should—"

"Run for our lives?"

"Uh-huh. Yep."

"I'm with Sissy on this one."

"Like, upstairs, you mean?"

"Uh, Dayzee," said Sophia, "whatever those are, they have no problem with stairs."

Two more heavy impacts crushed more rock, louder than before. Closer to Dayzee's closet.

"The Prism, Dayzee," said Marilyn. "It's our only hope."

"In the hearse? That wagon full of carcasses?"

"Yep," Sophia said with a blank face. "Let's just be really quiet, alright?"

"Sissy's right, Dayzee. Maybe they don't know we're here. Let's just get out of here."

"Fine, girls."

Still hugging each other, they all took careful steps, backing all the way to the front door and mostly keeping their pointy heels quiet. Without taking their eyes off of the threatening closet, they continued out onto the porch, and Dayzee pulled the door shut without a sound.

*   *   *

Dayzee took the driver's side, Sophia had the window seat, and Marilyn was squeezed in between them. With the engine fired up and her hands on the wheel, Dayzee paused and turned toward the twins.

"What about the squid motel?"

"Eh, he's on his own."

"That's funny, Sissy. Only if Moe the head did his job."

"He's still a head, girls?"

"We can't stick around to find out. I say, let's get this meat wagon moving."

"Fia, you're right. Let's go and just hope for the best."

Dayzee put the car in gear, let it idle to a slow start, then slammed on the brakes at the sight of Lief and his crew passing her exit gate. From the sudden stop, a bloody arm fell over Sophia's shoulder, its hand resting palm down on her left breast.

"Oh, sheesh," she said and flicked his hand aside. "Even these guys?"

"You know what they want, Sissy."

"And it isn't a dance, Sis. What they want is—"

"Girls, stop. Forget about the corpses for a sec. We can't let Lief and his twigs, I mean, his crew, come in here. Not with whatever those things are taking over the mansion."

"Maybe those things just want the house, Dayzee? If that's all, then they'll still need a yard crew because—"

"Mare, I can't let some trash from a portal take my house!"

"Hey," Sophia said with a smirk, "maybe they're carpenters? How funny would that be?"

"Oh, Sissy, maybe they are. There's so much that has to be—"

"Girls, they are not carpenters! And they can't have my house. Here's what we'll do: we'll tell the tree boy that he'll have to come back some other time. The three of us will hang at the Prism for a while and figure this out."

"With all that dead body cargo?" Sophia said with a grin.

"Approximately how many are there, Sissy?"

"I know there's at least one head missing. Moe in a blender. Other than that, I don't—"

"Alright, we'll figure that out later. Come on. Whoever or whatever is coming through my closet will never find us there."

Dayzee paused their journey only long enough to promise Lief that she'd call him soon, and she and the Kildare Killers rode their hearse full of bodies all the way to the Prism, leaving a trail of blood and an occasional head along Sunset Boulevard.

*   *   *

"That's a new look," Mack said, staring down at Sophia's left breast. "Let me guess: Halloween, still?"

"Yeah, Mack, we just never stop with that. Kenzie around?"

"Not yet. Her shift starts soon, though. You ladies sticking around long enough for a drink?"

Dazyee said, "As many as it takes, Mack. Boy, do we have some things to figure out."

"I think Sissy is trying to figure some things out too," Marilyn said with a soft chuckle.

"Sis, I was just asking."

"Mack," said Dayzee, "maybe some menus, too, alright?"

"Sure, Dayzee. Anything for you girls."

He turned and left them alone, with Sophia on the left, Dayzee in the middle, and Marilyn on the right. All three turned toward the big statue in the corner at the same time.

"Hey, Dayzee," said Sophia. "Whatever was coming up those steps—which is kind of funny because you were saying there was probably another staircase somewhere—could have just come through this portal, right?"

"Um, I guess so, Fia."

"Oh, I know," Marilyn said with a bright smile. "Different portals go to different places."

"Oh God, you might be right, Mare. The one in my basement might not—"

"It's not in your basement."

"Alright, fine, Fia. I'm just saying, maybe that one doesn't even go back to our planet. Who knows where it might go?"

"I know," said Marilyn. "Maybe it goes to the squid planet."

"Maybe Ireland, Mare?"

Sophia scoffed and said, "The best thing would be if it led to someplace where we could dump all those bodies."

"What bodies?" Mack said as he set drinks and menus in front of them.

"She's talking about Kenzie's body, I bet," Marilyn said with a giggle.

Sophia leaned forward and said, "Well, Sis, which would you prefer?"

"Oh, you make a good point, Sissy. Kenzie's way hotter than them."

"Girls," Dayzee said and held up her glass, "a toast to get our brains started."

Dayzee clinked to each side, then said, "Drink up."

They downed them, and Sophia said, "Keep them coming, Mack."

"You got it," he said and walked away, wiping his hands.

Dayzee took a deep breath, held it a moment, then let it out slowly.

"Fia. Mare. We're safe here, so we can figure out the house later. The first thing we need to do is get rid of those bodies."

A rickety voice rattled from their left, from a body perched three stools past Sophia. Air wheezed in and out between almost every word, saying, "I have an offer to offer."

Three heads turned at once to see a figure so thin that his black pin-striped suit seemed draped over a hanger. His shirt was black, as was his hat—a fedora wrapped in a black silk band and boasting one short black feather—but his tie was bright red. He had a single black rose in his breast pocket.

His pale yellow face turned toward the girls and offered a mirthless smile, which was mostly just a wide stretching of dry lips to show two rows of brown teeth. All were crowded in tight, and they chattered rapidly without a sound after he'd finished speaking.

Below his busy, silent teeth, his chin was flat across the bottom, with squared-off corners. His thin slit of a mouth appeared to have been gouged out of a block by the strike of an axe, a cavity into which the teeth had been packed. His eyes were small and close together, and they moved in their own directions before they both had focused on Dayzee.

He reached up with his right hand to tip the brim of his hat, showing that all of his fingers, which were as thin as pencils and with one extra joint, were adorned with pale white jewelry glinting in the neon light like bones baking on a beach.

With only his teeth chomping soundlessly, he froze there, sunken, dead gray eyes unblinking and staring at the girls. Seconds passed in silence as he gazed with his busy, silent choppers on display.

Beyond him, another one, dressed the same, faced forward and remained quiet. That individual's mouth was also open in a tight grimace, and when the girls leaned forward enough to see, they saw more quietly chattering teeth.

"Just wonderful . . ." Dayzee said under her breath. "What now?"

"Even for Beverly Hills," Marilyn said in a whisper while shaking her head, "that's a bit much."

"Sheesh. Somebody call a dentist."

*　*　*

"Just who the hell are you supposed to be?" said Dayzee.

"I am The Collector."

"And the other one?" said Sophia, tipping her head to look around him.

"She is the sweetest sweet sweetness of my existence."

Sophia turned back to Dayzee with a smirk and said, "Great. More clones. Looks just like him."

"Sissy, I'm not sure this is so funny. They're creepy."

"So, does that one have a name?" said Dayzee.

"She is The Collector."

"'She?'"

"She is very much a she."

Dayzee said, "Same name, huh? How does anyone tell you apart?"

His eyes never blinked, and his teeth never slowed as he raised one bony finger to point at his hat's feather. He froze again like a photo of a corpse. Dayzee looked past him at the other one, who was also completely unmoving. Both mouths showed rows of quiet, vibrating teeth.

"Oh, I see. Hers is gray. Yours is black. Black for boy, gray for girl."

"That's probably the only difference," Sophia said with a smirk and leaned back.

"Oh, Sissy, let's never find out."

Dayzee nudged Sophia to lean forward and said, "Um, what exactly do you collect?"

His teeth held still as he whistled air in and out through the gaps, and his eyes never blinked, only squinted. When the whistling had stopped, the eyes opened wider, and the teeth started again.

Sophia turned to Dayzee and her sister and said, "I think he just laughed."

"Wait, Fia. Let's hear what he has to say. So, um, what do you collect?"

The stranger to his left leaned forward and froze in place, staring at the girls and chattering with no sound. The Collector closed his eyes, tipped his head back and inhaled deeply, and his teeth never stopped.

He focused again on Dayzee, his teeth stopped, and he said, "Of course, cadavers, of course."

"Dayzee," Marilyn said in a slow and deliberate whisper, "maybe we should get out of here?"

Without turning away from the two Collectors, Sophia said, "I'm with Sis, this time. These people are messed up."

"Girls, the Prism is our hangout. No portal trash—oh, wait. Hey, funny guy," she said, staring at the closest one. "Did you come through that portal at my house?"

"Yes," he said and allowed a moment of silent chatter. "Apologies. Your carpentry will need to be carpentered by a carpenter."

"Now, that's funny," Sophia said with a snort then a laugh. "You have to admit it, Dayzee."

"Sissy is right about that."

"But you two weigh . . . what . . . like a six-pack each?" Dayzee said with her own smirk and the twins laughing. "How did you make all that noise?"

"At first, our steps stepping on the steps could not be helped."

He raised his right arm, elbow bent, with one long, spindly finger pointed toward the bottles of liquor beyond the bar. The girls looked where he pointed.

Then, with a loud crack, the elbow released, allowing the forearm and finger to drop down, where it swung like a pendulum until it settled and pointed toward the floor.

Dayzee and the twins looked down. Beneath the neat hem of his suit pants protruded heavy horse's hooves shod with thick metal shoes.

"Oh my God," Sophia said while laughing out loud. "You guys can't be for real."

She turned to her sister and said, "Hey, Sis, is the circus in town?" before turning back to The Collector with a grin.

He only froze, eyes wide and staring at her, still pointing at his hooves, with his teeth chattering like mad.

Sophia said, "Um, never mind," and looked down at her empty glass.

His eyes relaxed, and he rested his arm on his lap.

"How the hell did you sneak into our bar, then?"

"We have since adjusted the adjustments of our gravitational adjusters."

Dayzee stared, shook her head with another grin, and said, "Alright, so you're corpse collectors, and—"

"We Cadaver Collectors collect cadavers."

Dayzee sighed, rolled her eyes, and said, "Right. Got it."

She shook her head, turned, and waved to Mack for another round, then turned back to The Collector.

"So, what are you doing in the Prism?"

"We wish to offer you an offer."

"On?"

"You have cadavers. We have good goods for good bartering."

"Well . . . goodness!" Sophia said with a sneer.

"Sissy, shh. That *was* funny, though."

"What makes you think we have corpses?" said Dayzee. "I mean, cadavers?"

"We are delighted that you trailed the most delightful trail all the way here."

With his teeth still working, he closed his eyes and whistled in a long, deep breath.

"Oh, Dayzee," said Marilyn, "I bet there's a bunch of blood and guts all the way down Sunset from—"

"Not any anymore," he said and tipped his head back, air wheezing in and out between his unmoving teeth, which quickly got busy again when the wheezing had stopped.

"Already, that's getting old," Sophia said with a smirk.

She took a fresh drink from Mack, and when he looked to her left, he shook his head and said, "I've learned to not even ask."

"Smart man, Mack."

He sighed and moved along the bar to other patrons.

"That's actually pretty useful, Dayzee, if they somehow sucked up all that dead human stuff. They'd be a big help if we—"

"Wait a sec, Mare."

Still studying the staring character, and being studied by the one frozen behind him, Dayzee said, "Let me see if I have this right: you want to trade something for those bodies?"

"You have piled a tasty pile, a sample of which we have sampled, and transported them in your small transport. We will fairly pay fair payment for you adding additional cadavers."

"Alright, sure, but what do you have to trade? We already have enough money."

"Potion. We specialize in special potions blended with a blend of sorcery crystals. You have felt the feeling of fountains? You can taste the tasty taste of geysers."

Sophia snapped herself around, spilling her drink, and said, "Whoa. Just how many bodies do you want?"

"Really, Fia?"

"A geyser!" Marilyn said with a few quick hand claps. "Yes, how many?"

"You too, Mare? Girls, where would we even—"

Dayzee's phone rang, she took it out, tapped it, and said, "Cliff! How are you feeling?"

"Like I just woke up from a nightmare that I can't remember. How about you?"

"Oh, life is always interesting. You feel alright, though?"

"Better than I have in a long time. Oh, and I can't for the life of me remember why I changed my name to Cliff. It's Dirk."

"Oh, that makes sense."

"Huh?"

"Nothing, Dirk."

"Anyway, I just made a couple of calls, and I'll have a film crew here in maybe an hour."

"Hang on."

She muted her phone and told the twins, "Girls, Cliff is back to being Dirk, and he's getting another crew. The real shoot for 'Kildare in the Hills' starts in an hour."

She looked at Sophia and saw her counting her fingers.

"Fia, seriously?"

Sophia shrugged, smirked, and picked up her cocktail. She mouthed the word "geysers" and batted her big blue eyes before taking a deep drink.

"You and those beautiful eyes of yours, Fia."

"It's how we feel inside that you see in our eyes," said Sophia. "It's not about the blue, Dayzee."

"Perfect, Sissy."

Dayzee shook her head and unmuted the phone.

"How did you get a crew so fast, Dirk?"

"Oh, that was easy. These folks are all on parole for one crime or another. They're not the most savory bunch, but they do know what they're doing."

"Hold on, Dirk."

She muted her phone and said, "Girls, Dirk hired a bunch of criminals. How about that, huh?"

"Sweet," said Sophia. "No one will miss them."

"Sissy's right, Dayzee. They need to be collected."

"But, Mare, they're not cadavers, just convicts."

"Who are Sissy and I, Dayzee?"

Dayzee grinned and shook her head, but she didn't answer.

"Say it, Dayzee," Marilyn said with a giggle.

"Fine. You're the Kildare Killers."

Marilyn nodded and offered a pleasant smile.

Dayzee looked over at Sophia, who was grinning, then back at Marilyn, who was still smiling.

She unmuted the phone.

"I'm back, Dirk."

"Oh, and Dayzee? There's some yard guy here with a crew too. Name's Lief, I think? Anyway, I let him in, and he's got a big crew cleaning up the grounds. It's looking good."

Dayzee smiled and said, "Just what kind of crew? How do they look?"

"Oh, you know, they're doing good work, Dayzee. I can, um, I can tell because—"

"Dirk. Tell me."

"Um, they must be on some kind of work release, I think. Really, who wears orange jumpsuits to manicure a lawn in the Flats of Beverly Hills?"

"Hang on again."

She muted and said, "Girls, Lief is back with a big crew, and they're already working. And get this: they're all prisoners let out to work."

"I kind of like Earth sometimes," Sophia said and whistled for another drink.

Dayzee looked over at Marilyn and saw that she was counting on her fingers too.

"Mare! Really?"

"Geysers, Dayzee," she said with a shrug.

Dayzee turned to Sophia, who was only gazing at her with a big grin, raising her eyebrows in time with the jukebox.

Dayzee turned back to The Collector, and he said, "A double dose of doses is an erupting volcano eruption. With all of your belief and believing, you still might not—"

"Believe?" Dayzee said, grinning and raising her eyebrows.

He laughed again—squinting, with air whistling in and out between suddenly still teeth. Then, they began again, and he became a shabby photo. Except for his teeth.

Dayzee faced the bar and held it with both hands just as Mack brought them a fresh round, then retreated to the kitchen.

She raised her drink to her lips, tipped it back to swallow every drop, then tapped it on the bar a few times before sliding the glass away. After a quick smile for Marilyn and Sophia, she chuckled and looked again at The Collector.

"I have only one thing to say to you."

He waited quietly, a frozen corpse with soundlessly chattering teeth.

"Welcome to Beverly Hills, handsome!"

Enjoy the Story?

Thank you for reading! Please consider leaving a review and/or a rating at your favorite bookseller or with your favorite book club. Help your fellow readers meet Dayzee Dazzle!

For more about Edward Allen Karr and his books, visit:

www.LakesideLetters.com

What's Next for Dayzee Dazzle?

Dayzee Dazzle and The Cadaver Collectors
Thrills N Kills in The Hills Book Four

Life for Dayzee Dazzle and the Kildare Killers, Marilyn and Sophia, will never, ever be the same again.

The Cadaver Collectors deliver an unprecedented level of destruction to Dayzee's mansion in the Flats of Beverly Hills as they seek corpses to consume. Nearly everyone ends up in some degree of death: the on-loan prisoner yard crew, the temp film crew, all of the firemen, most of the neighbors, the producer of their "Kildare in the Hills" reality show, their photographer Jiff . . . even Mack, their bartender from the Prism on Sunset Boulevard.

As the gigantic house burns around them, they all try one last desperate ploy to lure some unknown savior through the portal hidden far under Dayzee's house. They use everything that they think will help: nakedness, sex, danger . . . even a couple of mountain lions pitch in.

And what they succeed in summoning to that dark chamber far beneath Dayzee's mansion offers a rescue that is wanton and deadly and changes lives forever.

Have You Met Lin Finity?

She's the powerful star of her own series titled the Fringes Of Infinity. In the beginning, she's forced to learn how to control the unstoppable, magical power she earned at age fifteen. After killing her abusive uncle with her deadly new ability, she locked it away inside herself. Now, she's in her forties, and it's back. She calls it *Mayhem*. And it's done waiting.

Book One and the Novella are free in e-book format. Just visit https://www.LakesideLetters.com

Lin Finity and her Mayhem Rising
Lin Finity in Holding On

About the Author

Edward Allen Karr was born, raised, and continues to reside in Ohio, USA. His adult life has followed a meandering path, ranging from working an automotive assembly line to designing space flight hardware. And through all of it, he's seen that life is a captivating and ultimately unexplainable endeavor. His writing seeks to add a splash of wonder to a world already awash in it.

*   *   *

For more information, please visit:

www.LakesideLetters.com